# Born to Be Mine

# Born To Be Mine

The Alpha God: Book 3

by
Lexa Luthor

Luthor Publishing
2020

**Born to Be Mine**



Luthor Publishing
www.LexaLuthor.com

Editors:
RJ Creamer
Julia V.

Cover Artist:
May Dawney of May Dawney Designs
www.maydawney.com

ISBN-13 (paperback):
978-1-7340426-4-1

ISBN-13 (ebook):
978-1-7340426-1-0

First Edition – April 2020 – 01 02

# Contents

# Prologue

Under the canopy of autumn leaves, Charlie followed the trail from the village to the river where she liked to fish. Across her shoulder, she carried a pole that had a rudimentary hook on it, and a basket of bait was in her left hand. She also had a heavy satchel on her back that was filled with things for her afternoon.

Five minutes later the sound of the river's rushing water stirred Charlie's excitement, and she increased her pace. The days were getting shorter with winter approaching, which left less time for fishing or anything else. Whenever Charlie finished her chores for her human foster parents, she would collect her things and rush off to find solitude and see her secret friend.

Charlie neared the riverbank and watched the racing water, knowing there had to be fish. As the temperatures dropped in the Kardos province, food would become scarce, including the river fish that Charlie brought home. She set all her items down by the large boulder, then went in search of wood and kindling. Once she had made a small fire, she prepared the fishing line with bait, sat on the boulder, and started to cast her line while waiting for her company.

An entire hour passed before Charlie spotted her friend on the other side of the river. She perked up and waved at the older girl. *Dorlon is so cute*, Charlie thought. Dorlon was an Omega from Melitt, the neighboring Kalmar village. The river separated their two villages and provided an intentional buffer between their cultures. But ever since the day Dorlon and Charlie met at the river, their friendship flowed stronger than the water's current.

Climbing off the boulder, Charlie propped her fishing pole against it, then hurried to the fallen tree that joined their worlds. She hopped onto the tree and watched Dorlon do the same, both meeting halfway across, suspended over the river. After the fateful day they first crossed paths, Charlie had taught Dorlon how to swim, but despite Dorlon's new skill, Charlie didn't like Dorlon crossing the tree alone.

Dorlon followed Charlie the rest of the way and eyed the rushing waters under them. "The ice is coming," she said, pointing at the tiny crystals clinging to the rocks in the river.

Seconding Dorlon's thoughts, Charlie didn't look forward to the deep winters in Kardos. At the end of the tree, she hopped off, then helped Dorlon down. Charlie scooped up her friend in a firm hug, laughing at Dorlon's playful snarl.

Dorlon returned the hug. "How are you?" For over a year, Dorlon had devoted their time together to teaching Charlie how to speak, read, and write Kalmarese. In return, she was learning bits and pieces of English, which had proven difficult for her. Charlie seemed to have a natural ability to learn new languages, and Dorlon admitted aloud she envied her friend's skill.

"Great now." Charlie beamed and walked her friend over to the side of the boulder where the fire was burning. "How have you been?" She hadn't been sure if Dorlon would show up, and she couldn't stop smiling now.

Dorlon shrugged and leaned against the boulder next to the fire. She wore a long fur coat, which kept away the early winter chill.

Charlie frowned and tucked her hands into the leather jacket that her mother had given her. It was still too large for her, but it made it easier to layer underneath it. "What's wrong? Did something happen at home?" Over time, she had learned about Dorlon's upbringing and her different relationships with each of her family members. Dorlon and her father were too much alike, and it caused minor explosions that ended with Dorlon hurt.

"*Joh.*" Dorlon stared at the fire, features icier than the cool air.

Charlie neared her friend and touched her shoulder. When Dorlon flinched, Charlie jerked her hand away and said, "He hurt you."

"He did." Dorlon crossed her arms, then looked at Charlie. "Because I tried wearing pants again." She indicated Charlie's own jeans. "Father warned me what would happen if I did it again."

Charlie opened and closed her mouth a few times. She failed to imagine her own father being angry with her for wearing pants or anything he deemed masculine. He had encouraged her to be herself, to dress in a way that made her comfortable. "They're just pants and…." She dropped the argument after Dorlon's glower. She hated that Alphas received an automatic pass when it came to their treatment of Omegas. The only way for Dorlon to receive protection from her father was if another Alpha sided with her, such as a mate. But Dorlon was still a few years away from being given to an Alpha mate.

"Father does have a point." Dorlon licked her lips and slouched against the boulder. "We're not humans."

"It's not about that," Charlie argued. "It's about—"

"Charlie, we're not like your people." Dorlon held her friend's gaze and reminded, "We're Omegas, not females."

Charlie shook her head and gathered Dorlon's larger hand into her own. "You're more than an Omega. You're an individual, like me or anyone else."

Dorlon sighed and squeezed their hands together. "Maybe one day it'll be like that." She gave Charlie a bitter smile. "But probably not before I die."

Charlie wished she could save Dorlon from the Kalmar lifestyle and the expectations of an Omega that went with it. One day her friend would be mated to an Alpha, who would knot and breed her like a horse. Her heart fractured at Dorlon's pending future, wanting to change it and knowing she was too small and too human to do it. In the future, their friendship would be buried under the planet's soil because the Kalmar would kill them otherwise.

Inching over, Charlie hooked her arm across Dorlon's back and pulled her in closer. "I'm so sorry, Dor." Dorlon's head rested on her shoulder, and it felt like the weight of their combined people on her. Charlie's bones shuddered under the pressure, but she didn't break. Her friend needed her. She turned her head and kissed Dorlon's crown, whispering, "*Perka gi.*"

They stood together for some time, finding comfort only in each other's company. Their friendship was special and a rarity among their people. The Kalmar loathed the Earthlings, while Charlie's people kept the "mongrels" away from their lands. Nobody was able to broker peace, and the only thing holding the stalemate was the advanced weaponry the Earthling brought with them.

Charlie stirred when a distant sound caught her ear. She lifted her head and narrowed her eyes toward the direction of the unfamiliar noise.

"What is that?" Dorlon whispered.

"I think someone is coming," Charlie replied, her voice low. "Get behind the boulder." She glared at Dorlon, who stayed at her side. "Go!" she hissed and shoved her friend to the river side of the boulder.

Dorlon caved and tucked herself around the backside of the boulder.

Charlie reached behind her back and produced a bowie knife she pointed toward the oncoming stalker. "*Come out*!" she ordered in English. She flexed her grip on the handle and continued to creep closer to the source that was hidden behind a few bushes. "*Come out or I'm going to attack you with my knife.*" She held her breath and prayed the person showed themselves before she had to make good on her threat.

"*Wait! Don't! I'm coming out.*"

"Raine?" Charlie asked, straightening up but still pointing the weapon. "*What are you doing here?*" She neared her sister and asked, "*Did you follow me?*"

Raine came around the shrubbery and tucked her hands into her coat pockets. "*I just wanted to see where you go all the time.*" She peered over Charlie's shoulder, then tilted her head as a furrow creased her brow. "*Who is that?*"

Charlie groaned at Dorlon's natural curiosity and turned around, confirming that Dorlon and Raine had seen each other.

Dorlon was standing tall next to the boulder, her features tight with interest. "Who is she, Charlie?"

Charlie sheathed her bowie knife behind her back and sighed at her human friend and Kalmar friend crossing paths. It was something that was never meant to be, and the unexpected change created a ball low in her gut. Switching back to Kalmarese, she peered over her shoulder and replied, "She's my sister."

"Sister?" Dorlon frowned and approached them. "She has darker skin, curly hair, and brown eyes. She looks nothing like you." She remained a few steps behind Charlie, but her attention locked on Raine.

"Not my sister by blood," Charlie replied in Kalmarese.

Raine placed her hands on her hips and glared at Dorlon before she turned her displeasure on Charlie. "*You can speak Kalmarese?*" She pointed at Dorlon and asked, "*How long have you been friends with an Omega?*"

Charlie bit her lip and glanced away until Raine snapped at her.

"*How long, Charlie?*"

"*About a year,*" Charlie whispered, flinching at Raine's furious gaze. "Raine, *I—*"

"*You're a total dickweed!*" Raine launched forward and shoved Charlie, who stumbled once; then Raine rammed harder and sent Charlie down. After sitting up, Charlie watched everything unravel between her two best friends from different worlds.

Somehow Dorlon managed to snatch Charlie's bowie knife, and she surged forward, swiping at Raine. But Raine jumped away and backed off, hands at the ready, as Dorlon waved the knife and continued to growl.

"*Rojoh!*" Charlie scrambled to her feet and grabbed onto Dorlon's outstretched hand, attempting to keep her at bay. As a human she was weaker than Dorlon. "Don't hurt her."

Dorlon remained still but kept the blade between her and Raine. Her long canines were on full display while she snarled and continued protecting her friend.

Raine glanced from the blade tip to Charlie, slight fear shining in her eyes. She opened her mouth but faltered and stumbled a step when Dorlon held her position.

"Stop, Dorlon." Charlie implored and latched onto her friend's arm, willing her to listen. "Raine is my sister. She's hurt that I've been lying to her." Ever since landing on Kander, her and Raine's relationship grew more strained by the war humans waged against the Kalmar. Whereas Raine had stood up against the Kalmar's mistreatment of Earthlings, Charlie hid from it and waited for it to pass. "*Krafka*," she pleaded with her friend, her voice shaking.

Dorlon lowered the knife and huffed before she held out the handle to Charlie. She leaned in and whispered in Kalmarese, "She touches you again, and I'll throw her in the river." She released the knife to Charlie, then went over to the fire. She busied herself with putting firewood into it.

Charlie sheathed the blade and looked at Raine, who remained standoffish after the escalated fight. "*I'm sorry*, Raine." She caught the shine in Raine's honey-brown eyes and cringed at how ugly things were between them.

"*It's cool. I get it.*" Raine looked over at Dorlon and nodded once. "*You got yourself a new bff.*" She focused on Charlie again and said, "*I hope she's better than me.*" She turned and started to leave, but Charlie grabbed her wrist.

"*Don't go.*" Charlie squeezed her friend's arm and shifted closer. "*I can*'t *replace you. I just miss you.*" Her voice continued to tremble, but she didn't want to lose Raine. The distance between them had grown over the noreds, and she hated it. Her friendship with Dorlon was the only solace she'd found after arriving on Kander. "*Do you have to go back right now?*" Like Charlie, Raine had been given to a foster family after they landed on Kander.

Raine shook her head and glanced away, seeming to hide her open emotions.

"*Stay with us,*" Charlie said, need heavy in her tone. "*Please.*"

Raine fidgeted and bit her lower lip, denial crossing her features.

"*Just give her a chance.*" Charlie searched her friend's eyes. "*Please*, Rae Rae."

After a sigh, Raine nodded and allowed Charlie to tow her by the arm to the tiny campsite. Once she released Raine, Charlie folded her arms and stared at the fire. Charlie smiled at Dorlon to try to ease her nerves. "Is it okay if Raine stays with us?"

Raine lifted her gaze at the mention of her name and looked between Charlie and the campfire.

Dorlon shrugged and replied, "*Ja.*"

Charlie took the opening and said, "So this is Raine." She indicated her sister, then pointed at Dorlon next. "Raine, *this is* Dorlon."

Raine eyed Dorlon, then said, "*Not like we can talk.*"

Charlie grumbled at her sister's flippant attitude. "*True, but maybe we can teach you some Kalmarese.*"

Raine narrowed her eyes. "*Why would she teach me? Most Kalmar don't—*"

"*She's not like most Kalmar.*" Charlie smiled, turned to her friend, and asked, "Will you help me teach Raine some

Kalmarese?" At Dorlon's mock glare, she smiled bigger and batted her eyes; she knew the trick would work.

Dorlon snorted and a slight grin pulled at her lips, until she looked at Raine. "I can teach her a few curse words without telling her that they are bad."

"Dorlon." Charlie shot a sour look to her friend and said, "Be nice." She chuckled at Dorlon's dramatic sigh when she agreed to help Charlie. Beaming again, Charlie turned to Raine and started with the simplest of things. "*You know how to say 'hello' in Kalmarese?*"

"*Turen,*" Raine replied.

Charlie nodded and said, "*And 'yes' in Kalmarese is…?*"

"*Ja.*" Raine shifted closer to the fire, which forced her farther into Charlie and Dorlon's space. "*And 'joh' means 'no.'*"

Charlie suspected that Raine had a few words down already, like most Earthlings, but so few had the opportunity to learn Kalmarese. The Kalmar seemed to want to keep their language a secret from the Earthlings. The only mutual language that the Kalmar and Earthlings had was what they could spell in blood. "*Okay, so do you know how to ask 'how are you?' in Kalmarese?*"

Raine shook her head.

Just as Charlie spoke the first word, Dorlon cut her off.

"You should teach her how to say 'stop' in Kalmarese," Dorlon said. "It's the most important word among our people."

Charlie hesitated and frowned at the weight in Dorlon's words. "I forgot."

Dorlon had a brooding look and held out her hands over the fire for warmth. "You shouldn't forget that lesson, Charlie. It could save your life one day."

After a sigh, Charlie agreed, then looked over at her sister. "*Dorlon wants me to teach you the word 'stop.' It's a really important word in their culture.*" She recalled what Dorlon had explained to her once they were able to hold conversations. "*It has a lot of weight and strength to it.*"

Raine's features became taut and her brow wrinkled with lines. "*Why?*"

Charlie picked up two pieces of wood and placed them in the flames. "*It's kinda hard to explain, but when you tell a Kalmar to stop, they will stop whatever they're doing or saying. They will stop and listen.*"

"*But what if they don't?*"

Charlie recalled what Dorlon had taught her about the Kalmar's culture and why the word was so powerful. "*If the Kalmar doesn't stop, it's a mark on their honor. They've broken the trust.*"

Raine gazed over at Dorlon, who held Raine's gaze for the first time since the earlier fight. Switching her attention to Charlie, she said, "*You told her to stop.*"

"*Yeah.*"

"*Does it even matter for us? We're humans.*" Raine unfolded her arms and tucked her hands into her dark, lined canvas jacket.

"*Dorlon listens to me.*" Charlie had a slight smile and shrugged at her sister.

Raine snorted and said, "*She shouldn't.*"

Dorlon surprised them both and said, "*I agree.*"

Charlie rolled her eyes, then gave Dorlon a playful punch to the shoulder.

Raine smirked at Dorlon's teasing, then asked, "*So what's the word?*"

"*Rojoh*," Charlie and Dorlon replied together.

Raine pursed her lips and said, "*Rojoh.*"

* * *

"*It's like an hour from sunset*," Raine said.

"*That's plenty of time.*" Charlie was carrying an armload of wood that she and Raine had chopped together. They returned to the camp where Dorlon was organizing a few snacks that Charlie had brought with her. "*I think we can teach her in an hour. It'll be fun.*"

Raine released an exaggerated sigh, then grinned. "*All right.*" Like Charlie, she carried wood and unloaded it by the fire.

"Raine and I were thinking we could teach you to play a game." Charlie put a few pieces of wood into the fire and returned to her earlier seat on a blanket. "I think Raine needs a break from Kalmarese." The two hours of switching between English and Kalmarese had worn on Charlie.

Dorlon chuckled and sat down on the blanket with the other two. She placed the food in the center and looked at her friend. "All right. What's the game?"

Charlie stretched, grabbed her satchel, and pulled out a worn set of cards. She shook the deck out of the box, revealing the comic book characters on the back of each card. Its vintage-looking artwork depicted popular female superheroes. The deck held special meaning to her, as it was a gift from Raine for Charlie's sixth birthday when they were on the *Liberator*. She and Raine had passed a lot of time by playing different card games, but they both had one favorite.

"I'm not sure there's a word in Kalmarese for it, but we call it *Bullshit*." Charlie tried to hold back her grin, but it grew when Dorlon eyed her. "It's fun!" She shuffled the deck several times and noticed how fascinated Dorlon seemed.

"What is that?" Dorlon asked.

"It's called a *deck* in English." Charlie held it up and said, "It's made up of…." She searched her mind for the word that was close to the English word for a card. "Like paper." She shrugged and inserted the card into the stack. She glanced at Raine, who was snacking on the food with a contented look. "Okay so here's how this works."

For ten minutes, Charlie explained both the deck of cards and how the game was played. Even with their language barrier, the game only required one word and the rest was all cemented in the players' abilities to lie about their hands. As Charlie dealt for the first game, she heard Dorlon whisper the English word.

"*Kulshet.*" Dorlon grumbled and looked at Charlie for help.

"*Bullshit,*" Charlie said.

Raine swallowed her mouthful of jerky and looked at Dorlon. "*Buuull.*" She waved at Dorlon to repeat after her.

"*The B sound is super hard for Kalmar,*" Charlie whispered to her sister.

Dorlon sighed and attempted only half of the English word. "*Kull.*"

Raine shook her head and went slower this time, dragging out the *B* sound for Dorlon.

Charlie finished dealing and allowed the two to continue their lesson. She smiled at them getting along after the ugly first encounter. She hoped all of them could form a solid friendship. But Raine could still tell others about Dorlon once they returned to New Earth. On the walk back home, they would have to talk about it.

"*Bullshit,*" Dorlon declared, pride seeping in voice.

Raine laughed and nodded. "That's good," she agreed in Kalmarese.

Charlie chuckled at them, then scooted closer to Dorlon. "I'll help you the first game. Okay?"

Dorlon nodded and mimicked Charlie's motions with the hand of cards. At first, she was confused until they played a few hands. She lost the first game, but could play without help by the second.

"You just have to be a good liar," Charlie reminded after she dealt the cards again. "Don't let your facial expressions give away anything." There were other clues or indicators when a player was hiding a card, but Charlie wasn't about to give away all the secrets of the game. Dorlon had to learn a few things on her own. "*Okay you're first,* Raine, *since you won.*"

Raine smirked, pulled a card, and called it before putting it down. She waited for anyone to call her out, but silenced passed. Dorlon went next followed by Charlie. They went a few rounds and called bullshit on each other. As the game heated up, Dorlon was the closest to winning and ahead by two cards. However, the stack of cards had built up, and as Dorlon prepared to put down her second-to-last card, Charlie noticed Dorlon's hand curling in her lap—Dorlon's tell.

She *smirked*. "*Bullshit!*"

Dorlon sucked in a breath, then her shoulders fell. "*Vuk!*"

Charlie laughed and picked up the stack for Dorlon. She heard Raine's own snicker and traded a grin with her sister.

"*I guess that's a cuss word*," Raine whispered, grinning from ear to ear.

"*Oh yeah*." Charlie chuckled at Dorlon's continued swears and was pleased with her own hunch about Dorlon's little tic when lying. Glancing toward the suns, she noted that the lesser sun was almost gone, while the primary one was inches above the horizon. "We should probably stop."

Dorlon peered over her shoulder at the suns. "*Ja*."

Together, the girls gathered up the things around the campsite and put out the fire with dirt. Without the heat, they shivered and buttoned up their coats to their necks. Charlie shared a long hug with Dorlon and promised to see her soon.

Raine stood away from the pair, watching them and waiting for Charlie. She started to turn when Charlie neared her, but hesitated at hearing Dorlon.

"Raine?" Dorlon was holding out her arm and offered a friendly smile.

Raine shifted on her boots, glanced at Charlie once, and then closed the short distance. She hooked arms with Dorlon and held it for a long moment. "*Tah*," she said, but there was more written in her features that she spoke in Dorlon's native tongue.

Dorlon dipped her head, then released her arm before heading to the fallen tree.

Charlie stood next to Raine, her gaze steady on Dorlon. She traded a final wave and waited there until Dorlon made it across the natural bridge. "*Come on, sis.*"

Raine took the fishing rod and basket, then led the way back to New Earth. "*She seems pretty cool.*"

"*Yeah, she is cool.*" Charlie followed her sister into the rusty-colored woods, using an animal trail to guide her. She noticed the slow, sly grin on Raine's face and asked, "*What?*"

"*She's so cute too!*"

# Chapter 1

"*Charlie*," Kal whispered with thunder and heat in her voice.

Charlie stood before the Alpha and searched the dark ashen eyes above her. Her skin was hot and itchy, her clothing confining. As she inhaled, she swore Kal reminded her of warm autumn spices, and it excited her blood to the point that she wanted to strip. Instead, she adjusted the heavy saddlebags on her right shoulder and hoped she didn't drop them with her shaking frame. For a moment she was unsure whether she would be invited into the cabin or rejected. She clutched the bags' leather tighter as she waited for Kal to make the final decision.

Kal remained poised in the doorway, filling it with her brawny body. She was breathing heavily and gripping the door with white knuckles, as she seemed to struggle with her inner Alpha. Although she only wore a breast wrap and loose, black bottoms, sweat was beaded along her brow.

Charlie used all her willpower to not look below Kal's waistline where she imagined there was already an erection. As a kid, she heard many tall tales about Alphas in ruts, but now she wondered if there was truth behind them. She cleared her throat, swallowed once, and did her best to remain silent, knowing Kal was in charge.

"You should *not* be here."

Charlie bit her lip and withheld a moan at how Kal's voice rumbled and called to Charlie. She struggled not to shove Kal into the cabin and tear both their clothes off. Such a strong need to have sex had never existed in Charlie's life until today. Her mind was growing fuzzier with each tick, but she took a deep breath and focused herself a bit longer. "I'm where I should be." When Kal narrowed her eyes, Charlie whispered,

"You need me." A shiver raced down her spine after Kal's deep growl, but it wasn't threatening. "And honestly—" She hesitated, feeling the truth heavy on her chest. "—I need to be with you."

Kal shifted closer, pressing their bodies together.

Charlie almost dropped the saddlebags after Kal's noticeable erection pushed against her stomach. She couldn't fight her needy moan this time. She stiffened when Kal bent over her, nose brushing near her ear, then decided this was her last chance to nudge Kal over the edge. "I won't leave. I can't leave." She closed her eyes while Kal breathed in her scent, savoring the sweet smell. "I know you're in pain. Let me help you." At the thought of Kal's misery, her chest strained and eyes stung. "*Krafka*, Sumner." Her shoulders sagged with each heartbeat; but then the weight vanished.

Kal had taken the saddlebags and stepped aside for her lover, inviting her into the cabin.

Still trembling, Charlie entered the cozy interior that wasn't much larger than Kal's quarters in the Great Tower. She noticed the lit fireplace and a long sofa with a wooden table in front of it. Her attention skipped to the oversized bed beside a window. To the right was a basic kitchen with all the necessities to be comfortable for noreds in the woodlands. Between the kitchen and bedroom space, a closed door probably led to a washroom, and Charlie suspected there was an outhouse somewhere on the property.

"Did you come here alone?"

Charlie faced her lover and replied, "*Ja.* Only Dorlon knows I'm here." She waited for any recognition in Kal's features about Dorlon knowing they were lovers. If Kal pieced it together, it didn't seem to matter. All that stood before her was a rutting Alpha who wanted to mate *her*.

Kal set the saddlebags down on a wooden bench beside the closed door. She approached Charlie again with arousal etched on her face. In their previous liaisons, Charlie had felt Kal's cravings buried under the layers, but tonight was different. Kal's face was open and raw with hunger, which made Charlie's heart jump. As Kal made a grab for her, Charlie stumbled back and held up her hands. She promised Dorlon she'd have Kal take the medicine. But Kal's only purpose was to knot and mate Charlie, for life.

"Wait, wait." Charlie clenched her teeth when Kal snarled at her. "Just listen to me for a tick." She was forced back another step as the Alpha advanced on her. "I have medicine with me that can help block some of the rut's effects on you. You'll be able to think clearer and have more control."

Kal narrowed her eyes, her lips curling to reveal her canines.

Charlie grumbled at her inability to reason with Kal, who lunged at her. She sidestepped Kal and continued holding her hands up. "Please, Sumner."

"You came to give me suppressants?"

Charlie lowered her hands, and a blade lanced her heart. "I came… for you," she whispered, crumbling at the mixed message she was sending Kal. "If you're gone for a nineth, then your people will notice." Kal paused and she sensed she was getting through on some level. "I don't want you to take the blocker, because I'm selfish and want you just for myself."

Kal straightened. "Blocker?"

"It's different from a suppressant. It's taken after a rut has started. The blocker won't stop the rut, but it'll make it bearable." Charlie held her ground, relieved Kal was listening to her. "Take some of the pain away."

Shaking her head, Kal refocused on Charlie and pursued her again. "Mating you will take the pain away."

This time Charlie didn't run and was grabbed by her lover, but she pressed a hand against Kal's heated chest. As in her earlier dream, her palm was coated in moisture from the rut's increased body temperature. She felt like she was being held by an ember, and the heat radiated through her clothes. "*Ja*, it will. But your people need you."

"They can survive a nineth without me," Kal hissed, lowering her head.

"Until they find out you've knotted and mated a human," Charlie whispered, nuzzling Kal's temple. She wanted to give in, slide her hand over muscles until she could clutch the hard penis, and allow Kal to take her to bed for as long as they pleased. Her body hummed with desire, nearly overwhelming her rational thought.

"You don't wish to be mated, at least by me." Kal's rumbling voice held accusation in it. She attempted to straighten up until Charlie cupped her flushed cheeks and pressed their foreheads together.

"I-I-I want that." Charlie squeezed her eyes shut and trembled from her confession. Being mated in the Kalmar culture was binding for life. It was more difficult to break than a legal marriage back on Earth. "I do want that with you." She swept Kal's wild, dark strands behind one ear. "But I know how important your people are to you and what you've sacrificed for them. I know what our mating would do to your people." She pulled her head back and gazed into blown pupils. "It's your choice. But if you mate me, I will take you off this planet rather than stand by and watch you be killed." She shook her head and whispered, "Screw them all."

In those dark eyes, she watched an awareness come to life, and she already knew the outcome. As Kal made her decision, Charlie held back her tears.

"Give me the blocker."

Charlie nodded and gathered her strength before breaking their contact. She went to the saddlebags to retrieve the two purple pills from a container, then glanced at the Red Cherry Ring she'd transferred from her duffle bags when she left Tarrak. Her fingers brushed over it, but she left it alone and returned to her lover.

Kal was seated on the sofa and bent forward. Her features were twisted while her trembling hand rested against her clenched stomach. All of her exposed skin glistened in the firelight, which caused Charlie to whimper. She lifted her head when Charlie offered her the pills.

After Kal swallowed the pills without any liquid, Charlie sat down and said, "It'll take several hours for the blocker to work through your system and kick in." She hoped for the planet's sake that the blocker worked. As she traced her fingertips along Kal's bicep, she said, "I can help you with your pain until then." The selfish, needy part of her wished the medication was useless with Kal's biology. She feared that the Alpha was already being pushed back by the blocker and that Kal would refuse her. But then, dark eyes stared at her, reading into her spirit. The same string from earlier become taut around Charlie, cutting and seeping pain from her bones.

Kal stood, then reached behind her back to free the black wrap from her chest.

Charlie ogled at the muscles flexing along Kal's back, until the wetness between her legs made her follow Kal's example. She whimpered after getting the leather jacket off, tossing it to the floor, then removing her boots and socks. With some control, she was careful to put the belt with the attached lectra gun onto the fur in front of the fireplace. She glanced over at Kal and faltered at seeing the nude Alpha.

Kal snarled at Charlie that prompted her to hurry up.

Throwing her underwear onto the pile of clothes, large strong hands snared Charlie and pushed her toward the sofa. She faced the furniture and dropped to her knees on the edge of the sofa. Clutching the couch's back, she peered over her shoulder to see Kal stepping up behind her ass. Kal had once told her that the rut would make her penis thicker but not longer. At the moment, though, she had no chance to see for herself, and she shivered at the thought of taking it.

*Being a human lover might catch up with me*, she thought as the head of Kal's cock kissed her opening. But Charlie convinced herself she could handle it, and she rocked her hips to encourage the Alpha to fuck her. "What are you waiting for?" she taunted, earning a growl before the pressure against her entrance spiked as the head surged into her. "Fuck!" she cried out from the sudden drive.

Kal bent over Charlie and twisted her fingers into her golden locks. She jerked Charlie's head around, growling at her. "Mine," she declared, staking her claim. Thrusting her hips forward, she drove her cock deeper into Charlie.

Clawing at the sofa, Charlie panted and prayed her heart didn't burst. From the corner of her eye, sharp teeth reminded her that the Alpha ruled tonight, but Charlie wasn't quite ready to give over everything. She loved challenging Kal's Alpha until she had no choice but to submit. "*Joh*," she said, hissing in protest. "I can still fuck who I want." She grinned like the devil and provoked the Alpha with a last whisper. "Like Magnar." Her entire body was wrenched up from the sofa back until her feet were on the sofa, and her twisted head was pressed against Kal's chest. She shook against the muscular body wrapped around her, melting into the powerful hold.

"Did you fuck her?" Kal's voice thundered through the cabin, and she dug her blunt nails into Charlie's stomach.

"Do you smell her on me?" Charlie held a proud tone and saw Kal's foot now on the sofa cushion, next to Charlie's feet.

Kal tightened her grip on Charlie's hair, making Charlie whimper. "You could have washed it away." She trailed her hand downward until her fingertips grazed Charlie's clit. "Did you fuck her?"

Stiff against Kal, Charlie bit her lip and gyrated her hips, then gasped at how Kal's cock shifted in her. She wanted her clit rubbed more, but Kal denied her.

"Tell me," Kal ordered, her breath hot against Charlie's temple. She pulled her hips away, dragging her thick shaft through clenching walls.

Charlie moaned as she sensed the difference in girth, but she tensed when there was barely anything left in her. "I won't." She grabbed the muscular arm across her chest and clawed into the skin with both hands. She was unprepared for the sharp thrust back in and cried out.

Kal bowed her head, pressing her nose into Charlie's damp temple. "Tell me now." She pulled her hardened length out of Charlie and allowed the head to press against Charlie's sensitive G-spot. "Or you can fuck yourself alone." For emphasis, she edged her cock's head out of Charlie's entrance.

Leaning into Kal's hold, Charlie whimpered and pleaded, "Please don't." She gasped when Kal nipped at her ear. "I need you inside me." Her heart ached to be close to Kal like this.

"Then tell me," Kal ordered, still firm. She rubbed her cock's tip against Charlie's G-spot, and a rumble vibrated in her chest.

"We didn't," Charlie whispered, coming undone for her lover. "She wanted to, but I told her *job*." Kal's pleased growl excited her and caused wetness to rush out of her and coat Kal's shaft. "She's not you," she confessed. "Nobody else is you." She choked on her next breath as Kal's hard length pushed into her and filled her again. "Oh fuck!"

Kal's pace was slow, and she shifted her arms until she had a strong hold on Charlie. "Spread your legs."

Knowing Kal could handle her weight, Charlie obeyed and gave Kal better access. She kept one hand on Kal's forearm while she gripped Kal's hip. Gazing down, she caught a glimpse of the enlarged cock protruding out of her. She wanted to grab it, find out firsthand its thickness. But already Kal was driving her hips, and Charlie cried out from the first thrust. The strong rhythm kept her screaming, and she tried opening her legs wider, needing all of it.

Kal moaned and growled with Charlie, pushing deeper each time. She had her head tilted back but lowered it and bit at Charlie's throat.

Like Kal, Charlie wanted the permanent mark that signaled the Alpha's claim over her. The idea that she was okay with it made her body slacken deeper into Kal's hold. But they knew the consequences if they mated, even though it pained them both to hold back. Seeming to sense Charlie's despair, Kal nuzzled her cheek and pumped her hips harder, pushing them closer to the edge.

Then the soft slaps grew louder, matching their cries. Charlie was startled and peered down at the hard length driving into her. She held her breath when nearly all of it buried into her, almost sending her into an orgasm. For the first time, Kal's full length sank into her, at last. The beautiful sound of their skin slapping excited them both. At the base of Kal's penis was a distinct, newly formed ring, and it knocked against Charlie's entrance.

Charlie arched her back and bit her lip, holding back from begging for the knot. She had no idea if it could fit in her, but even attempting to be knotted could mean the end of Kal's reign, perhaps her life. Kal's very essence would be merged with Charlie's own, and every Kalmar would smell it. Tears pricked behind her sealed eyelids, and she allowed Kal to make the final decision about their future.

Grunting and thrusting, Kal nipped at Charlie's neck but held back from a true bite. She trembled and drove her hips hard, pushing them both into an orgasm. Aftershocks rolled through their joined bodies, and Charlie relied on Kal's strength as she leaned back into her. It wasn't until she felt the gentle licks against her nape that she opened her eyes. She noticed the dull pain at her neck but knew Kal hadn't staked a final claim.

Reaching back, Charlie hooked Kal's neck from behind and whispered, "I hope that's not all you have in you." She smirked at the threatening growl in her ear but lost her bravado when Kal's hand snaked down her stomach and touched her clit. She rallied her stamina to keep up with an Alpha in rut.

Kal slid her other hand under Charlie's neck and tilted her head back onto Kal's shoulder. "It's you that needs to keep up." Her throaty chuckle shook both their bodies, and she continued massaging Charlie's clit. All of her cock was still buried in Charlie, and she didn't seem interested in pulling out.

Charlie ground her teeth and felt her gut clench in response to the teasing. Her fluttering walls were hugging the thick length in her. "Oh gods," she whispered, her body flushed with arousal already. "That feels so good." Sharp teeth nipped the top of her ear and sent shocks through her body. She rocked her hips that caused Kal to do the same. She hissed and moaned when the throbbing length stroked and teased her. But when Kal rolled her pulsing clit harder, Charlie clawed at any skin within reach. "Don't stop."

After a releasing Charlie's ear, Kal whispered, "Come on me." She pumped her hips once, encouraging Charlie to let go. Her finger applied just enough pressure and tipped Charlie into another orgasm.

"*Vuk!*" Charlie bucked against the strong hand between her legs, dug her heels into the sofa, and pushed back against the Alpha's frame. Slick wetness oozed free and coated the little bit of exposed shaft. She quivered a few times, then collapsed into the arms holding her body. Behind her, she listened to Kal's heavy, deep groans, the Alpha still within Charlie's silky insides, which were squeezing around her cock. She wondered if Kal was drained from holding them up, but they remained in the same position for several minutes.

Kal released a low chuff and breathed in deeply before lowering her leg from the sofa. With one hand between their bodies, she dragged the thick muscle out of Charlie, and they both groaned in protest. She then picked up Charlie in her arms and carried her over to the bed.

Charlie cupped her lover's hot cheek and whispered, "I'm starting to think you like doing this." She chuckled at the rich thunder in Kal's chest, then brushed the black hair away from Kal's face. Once she was lowered to the side of the bed, she scooted out of Kal's arms and expected Kal to follow her, like many times in the past.

"Get on your knees near the edge," Kal ordered, her voice heavy and dark.

Feeling her heart skip, Charlie stilled her anxiety and shifted onto her knees to face Kal. Her wrist suddenly in a firm grip, she was unsure what to expect and tensed when Kal kneeled to the floor.

"Closer," Kal ordered, placing Charlie's hand on her shoulder.

Inhaling deeply, Charlie realized what was in store for her and inched forward until she felt the warm breath between her legs. With her other hand she threaded her fingers into Kal's mane and balanced herself. Kal's two hands gripped Charlie's butt cheeks to further support her, but all her attention shifted to the heated breathing below her waistline. Peering down, she studied her lover breathing in her scent, and it aroused her. Kal had told her she tasted sweet, which baffled her, but the Kalmar had a much stronger sense of smell than humans.

Kal yanked Charlie and brought her aching clit into an eager mouth. Her long tongue snaked out and started sliding through the wetness. She moaned after tasting Charlie again.

At first, Charlie tensed from having someone licking her clit—even if they had done this just days ago. She didn't often let anyone touch her this way, the intimacy of it making her feel exposed. But as she gazed down, her fear was quelled because it was Kal, the only lover who wanted to please her more than themselves. Moaning and whimpering, Charlie started rocking her hips, and her stomach quivered each time the rough tongue brushed her swollen clit. She dragged her fingers through long strands as she admired the planet's most powerful Alpha on her knees and pleasing Charlie. She felt like a god who was being worshipped, and an overwhelming emotion rushed through her.

Each stroke of Kal's tongue said Charlie was hers. Kal moved a hand and used her fingers to open Charlie wider to expose her aching sex. Tilting her head, Kal started sucking hard against the pulsing clit. When Charlie bucked against her mouth, she tightened her grip on Charlie's ass, not letting her budge.

"Sumner!" Charlie snarled and clawed into Kal's shoulder, no longer able to restrain her jerking body. Curse words tumbled from her mouth until they turned into low, pleasurable cries. The first climax was quick, but Kal kept stroking her and building her higher. Charlie's body vibrated with passion, and she tilted her head back, letting out the screams. Her knees slid, allowing her sex to sink deeper into the Alpha's hot mouth. Arousal sliced through Charlie's belly, and made her whimper in need. "Pleas-s-se, Sumner." They'd been dancing around her next release.

But the begging worked as Kal sucked on the swollen bud, then flicked the tip of her tongue over it. She sent jolts through Charlie's body, and the pending orgasm's pressure was palpable for them both. Charlie's heated yells encouraged Kal, who moved her tongue faster until Charlie froze, stiff in Kal's embrace.

"Oh fuck," Charlie gasped as the orgasm cut through her, pleasure searing throughout her body. She fell forward and leaned against Kal for support, almost sliding off the bed. But Kal rose up, gripped Charlie's sides, and pulled them both up onto the bed. Somewhat dazed, Charlie curled against the Alpha's body that cocooned her. All around her, long, deep rumbles anchored her until the shaking faded away. Peeking out from Kal's chest, she gazed up into black eyes that shined in the last bits of sunlight streaming through the window's shutters.

Kal was resting on top of Charlie and pressed a safe amount of weight against her. She reached up, swept her hair to one side, and pushed her nose into Charlie's neck. She nipped at damp skin at the nape, licking and biting her lover.

For awhile, Charlie admired Kal, who'd pleased her moments ago as if she were the most perfect mate on the planet. In reality, there were thousands of potential, even better, mates on Kander than Charlie. There were safer mates who carried much less baggage. She wanted to tell Kal to keep searching for that right one, but when their lips brushed together, she lost her words. Nothing felt as good as when they kissed, and no one fucked her as well as Kal; Charlie was going to savor it until it was taken from her.

Breaking the slow kiss, Kal shifted on her knees and reached between their bodies. The tip of her cock pushed against Charlie's sex, but she hesitated when Charlie grabbed her wrist.

"Wait," Charlie whispered, then cringed at how it sounded to both their ears. She pressed her palm against Kal's chest, feeling the threatening growl growing deeper. "I have a toy th-that you might like." When the growl faded away, she took her opening and whispered, "I know you want to knot me." Stretching her arm, she clutched the lower half of Kal's cock and groaned at its increased thickness. "I want it too."

Kal clenched her teeth and lowered her head closer. "If I knot you…."

Charlie swallowed and slid her hand until the prominent ring at the base of Kal's shaft filled her palm. "There's no going back, I know." She wanted to squeeze the knot but withheld her urge in case it incited the Alpha. "This toy might help you feel like you're knotting me."

Kal snarled before saying, "Nothing could feel like knotting you." She pressed her hips against Charlie's thighs.

Biting her lip, Charlie contained a whimper that would further entice the Alpha. "I know, and this is the best I can do for now." She pushed their foreheads together. "Will you at least try it for me?" She brushed her fingertips along Kal's jaw line. "*Krafka*, Sumner."

After a nod, Kal pulled away from her lover and rolled back to sit on her butt in the middle of the bed. She eyed Charlie, who sat up and hurried off the bed.

Quickly, Charlie collected the Red Cherry Ring from her things and returned to the bed. She paused at the foot to appreciate the handsome Alpha.

Still seated, Kal had her left leg bent toward her body while her other leg was propped up. She leaned most of her weight against her left arm that was stretched out behind her body. While she waited for Charlie to rejoin her, she massaged the tip of her penis with her right hand.

Charlie stood there, feeling the arousal spread between her legs. She'd never imagined having such a gorgeous lover as Kal or finding herself so attracted to someone who, by humans' standards, was a blend of sexes. But each time they had sex, Charlie was drawn to Kal more deeply. It was the same line that jerked on her heart and forced her to crawl onto the bed, closer and closer to Kal. She forgot her original intent until Kal spoke to her.

"What is it?"

Sitting back on her haunches, Charlie held up the one toy she'd saved from the destruction of the *Pacifica*. "It's called a Red Cherry Ring." She trailed her fingers along the outside of it until she hit the first touch button. The ring started pulsing a soft red that indicated it was on and ready to be programmed. "It's a cock ring." At Kal's narrowed gaze, she took deep breath and steadied herself. "It looks too big right now, but we can control that. It's supposed to slide down your penis to wherever you want it, usually the base. Then we can control its size so we can make it smaller until it gets snug around you."

Kal no longer eyed it with suspicion but tilted her head before focusing on Charlie again. "How does that help?"

Charlie grinned at Kal's interest. "Well, if we apply the right amount of pressure around your penis, then it should make you stay harder for longer." She tensed when Kal growled at her, but she held out a hand. "Not that you're lacking in that department." She blew out a breath when the Alpha's ego calmed. "But I think if we do it over your knot, then it might feel like you're in me."

Kal plucked the toy from Charlie's hand, turning it through her fingers. "If it does work, then I will *fercher* inside you."

Charlie frowned at the new Kalmarese word and worked through its meaning. "You mean you'll release *quima* inside me?" She retained the new Kalmarese word for ejaculation in her mind, not expecting to have this conversation tonight.

"*Ja*." Kal lowered the ring onto her knee. "I will impregnate you." A certain glint shined in her eyes that caused Charlie to squirm.

Charlie blew out a breath and said, "You won't be able to. I take a medicine that keeps me from getting pregnant." On the ride here, she'd double-checked with her techbit; she still had fifteen days to go before taking the injection again. But Kal's bitter look made her cringe, and she said, "But if I were to go off it, I could get pregnant." Somehow, she felt the need to cool the Alpha's annoyance about the medicine. This wasn't the time to elaborate that she refused to bring a child into this universe. Delving into the topic now could send them into a tailspin, so instead she pushed it away and refocused on the ring.

Kal picked it up and held it out to her, seeming to accept its help. "Put it on me."

Scooting closer, Charlie took the toy and waited until Kal pulled her hand off her cock. For a moment, she studied the cock's very swollen head and licked her lips. Clearing her throat, she focused on her task and guided the ring over the tip then down the shaft. "I'm going to make the ring shrink. Tell me if it gets too tight." Charlie peered up and waited until Kal nodded before she put her fingers on the edge. Once she had Kal's consent, she glided her fingertips clockwise along the ring. "It's touch-sensitive, so brushing my hand this way will make it get smaller." As it shrank, she slowed her hand's movement so it didn't clamp around Kal's knot too hard. "If I twist the other way…" She demonstrated, turning her hand to the left as if it was a dial. "It'll turn brighter red to indicate it's expanding." She paused, then started trailing her touch to the right so it fit snugly around Kal's knot.

Hissing, Kal clutched Charlie's hand and said, "It's enough there."

Charlie pulled away and nodded. "You can control it later, just like I showed you." A worried look crossed her features. "We don't want to leave it on for too long, though. It's not safe after about an hour." She was glad when Kal nodded her understanding, not wanting them to take it too far. She stared down and smirked at the cock ring clamped around the base of Kal's shaft, hugging the knot. It could provide a temporary solution for them until they figured out everything else.

Kal returned to rubbing the enflamed head of her cock. When Charlie lifted her head, Kal's blown eyes burned into her. "You want to suck on me again."

"*J-ja*," Charlie admitted, bending lower until a hand under her chin halted her.

"Later." Kal narrowed her eyes and leaned in closer to Charlie. "Sit on my stomach." She lowered her leg some and leaned back on both forearms.

Not refusing the invitation, Charlie climbed onto her lover and groaned when her pulsing clit touched Kal's well-defined abs. Kal's burning skin felt so good against her sex, and she ground against her. "Oh gods," she whispered, rocking her hips and shivering at Kal's toothy smile.

"Sit on my cock," Kal ordered, remaining far too still for Charlie's liking.

Somehow it felt like a trap to Charlie, but she obeyed her lover anyway. She pressed both hands flat against Kal's stomach muscles, one hand sliding up from the sweat until a breast halted it. She peered beneath herself and aligned her entrance with the flared head that had weeped white beads. She was almost certain it was droplets of *quima*, having never seen it until now. Testing her body first, Charlie eased the head into herself and felt it stretch her wider than before. "Fuck. You feel bigger." She heard a throaty laugh and jerked her head up. "Are you?"

Kal's lips curled, and she whispered, "We're just getting started." She then indicated her lover's current position poised above of her. "Keep going." She was breathing heavily, hands twisted in the blanket.

Charlie took a deep breath to ward off panic and relaxed the rising strain in her shoulders. *She'll stop if I ask her*, she reminded herself. Her lover wouldn't break their trust that they'd agreed upon on the first night together. The rut didn't change their trust or arrangement but in fact reinforced both. Licking her lips, she bobbed on the shaft's head, letting it tease her.

Kal groaned and dropped her head back. Her entire body jolted a few times, but she never pushed her hips up, allowing Charlie to remain in control of their sexual position.

Needing more, Charlie eased her body lower and loved the fullness in her. "Oh god that feels so good." She met Kal's passionate stare when Kal lifted her head back up.

"More," Kal snarled. "All of it."

Charlie was panting and had about half the length in her. Earlier she'd managed to get most of it in that had allowed Kal's front to smack her ass. She prayed she could handle it again, though Kal's girth felt bigger now. With caution she continued inching the hard length deeper, and it made her whimper. She groaned after going as far as possible, her arms and legs straining to keep her from dropping more. "I can't."

Sitting up now, Kal gave a low, heavy rumble before saying, "You can, but you're too tense." She canted her head and whispered, "It'll only hurt." When Charlie met her stare, Kal grinned and said, "If I mount you, you'll take it all."

Leaning her forehead against Kal's shoulder, Charlie pictured the Alpha behind her, pounding into her until she ejaculated. Somehow the human taboo position had become Charlie's favorite and excited her more than anything else. She loved having the Alpha dominate her, control her, and fuck her like an animal. The level of trust she had in Kal when she was bent over was always exhilarating to her. She gulped for air, then nipped at tan, spicy-tasting skin under her lips.

"That's what you want, isn't it?" Kal asked, voice rich with desire.

Nodding, Charlie could admit to her secret. "*Ja*." Without pretense, she rose up and groaned at the loss of contact. She waited until Kal was out of the way before she recentered herself in the bed on her hands and knees. In front of her, Kal remained on her knees and seemed to consider some plan—if the wolfish smile was any indication. "Sumner," Charlie whispered, headiness in her tone.

But Kal was the Alpha between them, and her rut was at the forefront of her mind. She seemed alert about Charlie's needs and wanted to play. She grabbed near the base of her shaft and massaged the full length, giving Charlie a show. As her hand slid to the head, she slowed and displayed the bit of *quima* that trickled out; then she smeared it around the tip. She groaned and closed her eyes.

Charlie clawed at the blanket and was about to reconsider their agreement if Kal didn't give her something. Her glare must have registered with Kal, who smirked and moved around Charlie. A flutter of excitement passed through her when the Alpha positioned herself behind her. This time, there was no foreplay, and she had only a second to pray that the sex toy would help Kal.

The first drive was hard and stung, having determination behind it. Charlie shuddered and dropped her head, but she remained on her hands and knees. As her fingers curled into the blanket, her muscles tried to hold onto Kal, who was pulling out at a painstaking speed. Kal paused before she slowly pushed into Charlie, who moaned loudly. They both loved when Kal asserted her Alpha. She wanted Kal to rut into her and split her open. Their slow pace was maddening, and she had to prod Kal's Alpha.

After Kal withdrew, Charlie lowered to her elbows and raised her ass higher for the Alpha. She shivered from the growl behind her as she dropped her head to the soft bed and waited for her reward. A grin creased her lips when she felt movement behind her, then all the gentleness was gone.

Kal latched onto Charlie's hips with a strong grip that ensured Charlie wouldn't get away. Her first thrust forced a cry from Charlie, but she didn't stop or slow down. The pace was punishing, skin slapping skin. Her grunts matched Charlie's yells, and her growls grew more animalistic than before.

With an outstretched arm, Charlie held onto the bed as the Alpha rutted into her, deep and fast. She blinked away the sting in her eyes and screamed or grunted each time Kal's throbbing length drove through the wet heat between her walls. Gritting her teeth, she ground back into the Alpha's next pump and felt the cock ring hit her sex. She whimpered at being left unknotted, something so special between mates among the Kalmar. Charlie ignored the tightness in her chest, rocked her body back, and matched the Alpha's thrusts. Charlie sensed that her lover was just as close to breaking apart as she was.

"Charlie, *vu*—" Kal's snarl broke, and her last, forceful thrust split them both. She toppled over onto Charlie, just able to hold up her massive weight with her left hand. With her other arm, she hooked across Charlie's damp stomach and grunted as she nudged her cock just a bit deeper.

Gasping for air, Charlie whimpered at the cock ring's pressure against her entrance. But then the first warm shot of *quima* rushed into her, filling every void. Her inner muscles clamped around Kal's length, locking it inside her. But without the knot, the *quima* trickled out from her entrance and was lost. As more *quima* rushed through her, she fought the searing in her eyes, but the salty tears came anyway and burned down her cheeks, tainting her orgasm. She hadn't planned to be knotted or bonded to anyone in her life. As Kal withheld her knot,

Charlie fought the sharpness in her chest and swallowed her silent pleas for Kal to knot her.

Kal continued nuzzling Charlie's neck, clenched teeth pressed against flushed skin. She never bit down but growled deep and long. Her hold on Charlie was almost crushing as her hips applied a bit more pressure to Charlie's ass. The cock ring barred her from pushing the knot into Charlie and binding them for this lifetime.

As the orgasm faded, Charlie gulped for air and grabbed Kal's arm across her abdomen. Her body quaked but not with pleasure. A few sobs escaped, and she sank into the bed. Along her back she felt the stronger body cover her and shelter her from the rush of emotions. A muscular arm went under her and turned Charlie onto her side, then a powerful thigh shifted over her hip. She remained nestled and hidden in the Alpha's arms. Her lower body was filled with the swollen length buried in her. Even if she was sore, she wasn't ready to let Kal retreat and undo their connection.

A soft thrum pierced Charlie's downward spiral and soothed some of the pressure in her chest. She then noticed the massaging against her chest and remembered her lover was suffering as well. Covering Kal's hand, she squeezed a silent promise that they would figure something out. A soft touch brushed her ear, tracing the outer edge of it, and Charlie whimpered at the Alpha's tenderness.

"Mine," Kal whispered, final and unbreakable in the single word. She snaked their laced hands upward, coming to a stop over Charlie's pounding heart.

Charlie curled her fingers between Kal's bigger ones and dug her nails into a callused palm. They had no union ceremony, nor were they mated through a bite claim nor even a knot to blend their scents as a couple; but there was something unseen that bound them. Charlie squeezed Kal's hand tighter, accepting the unspoken truth between them.

# Chapter 2

Lennox raised the handgun and aimed for Charlie, who stood in the center of Kal's bedroom. They had been caught—Charlie and Kal both half dressed in front of the messy bed where they'd knotted and bit each other for the first time. Lennox had already spewed angry words at his leader, shaming her for what she'd done.

Charlie glanced at her lectra gun still holstered in her belt by her boots a few feet away. She lunged for it, praying she was fast enough. Charlie yelled as the first shot rang out, but the sound was outmatched by the roar from Kal. Jerking up with the freed gun, she watched Kal drop to her knees in front of Lennox. She hadn't seen Kal move to shield her from Lennox's shot.

Rushing to Kal's side, Charlie froze at seeing the blood seep between Kal's hands that were pressed against her stomach. "*N-n-no.*" She caught Kal from behind, balancing her after she fell to her knees. "*No no no.*" She dropped the handgun and reached for Kal's wound, but Kal's increasing weight overwhelmed her. Charlie lowered her lover to the floor and touched a pale cheek. "Sumner?" She covered Kal's hands with her own and whispered, "Can you heal it?"

Kal was panting, and her voice was weakening. "It doesn't work that way."

"*Joh,*" Charlie whispered, then a darkness surged inside of her. She snared the lectra gun, swung her arm around, and aimed for Lennox, who was rooted in shock. Curse words tumbled from her mouth as she drew her finger back on the trigger. But a strike to her elbow threw off her aim, and the shot hit the wall next to Lennox. She swore and gazed down at Kal, who'd hit her arm.

Lennox stumbled away, collapsing to the floor and dropping his weapon.

Turning back to her lover, Charlie saw the green fading from Kal's eyes and leaving a sweet amber color. "Oh gods, *joh!*" She cupped Kal's cheeks and smeared blood along unmarred skin. "Sumner." She bowed until their foreheads connected together.

"I remember everything."

Charlie raised her head, hating the honey brown in her lover's gaze. Kalatas's spirit had fled Sumner's dying body and left her with all that she'd forgotten since becoming Kal. "*Krafka, joh,*" she whimpered. "Sumner." Like a prayer, she whispered her mate's old name over and over.

"Charlie, I'm here."

Jerking back, Charlie opened her eyes and twisted her head around, reorienting herself in the cabin. The nightmare untangled itself from Charlie's groggy mind, but the tears were still fresh until Kal wiped them away. She focused on her lover's face that grounded her, then noticed the green in Kal's eyes after being masked by the rut last night.

Kal tightened her arms around Charlie, sealing their bodies together under the blanket. All around them daylight streamed through the cracks of the covered windows. The cabin was cool, but they were warm together.

"Sorry. I didn't mean to wake you." Charlie cleared her throat, warding away the roughness. Exhaustion was still heavy in her bones, as she hadn't slept well during Starr's rescue mission and then rushed off to find Kal. They'd had sex until dawn but napped on occasion until Kal's rut was sated enough that they could sleep.

"I've been awake," Kal replied.

Turning until she faced her lover, Charlie touched Kal's cheek and admired the vibrant green in front of her. "Welcome back."

"The blocker is starting to work," Kal whispered, but a wolfish smile creased her lips. "Mostly."

"I guess so." Charlie heard the displeasure in her own voice and changed the discussion. "What time do you think it is?"

Kal responded with a rumble first, then replied, "Perhaps close to suns high."

Groaning, Charlie rubbed her forehead, rolled onto her back, and stared up at the wood beams. "We should get up." She peered over at Kal, who was still holding her. "I need to eat something." She noticed that the dark coloring under Kal's eyes was fading. "You probably haven't eaten in awhile." Gossip about Alpha ruts included their ability to go days without food.

"*Joh*." Kal breathed deeply and nudged Charlie's temple. "But I did bring food, and there's a root cellar here."

Charlie reached up and played with the wavy strands that spilled over between their bodies. "Any *pizza*? I love a good *pizza* after sex." She chuckled at Kal's raised eyebrow and then sighed at the lack of pizza on Kander, or anywhere for that matter. "I can't believe a human hasn't started a good *pizzeria* in Tarrak. I could go for a *rancher pizza* with extra sauce on the side for the crust." She started laughing at Kal's eyebrow arching to a new level.

"Will *surra* do instead of…" Kal pursed her lips and said, "*Piz-za*."

Charlie smirked at Kal stumbling through the old English word, but she enjoyed Kal's attempt. "I love *surra* too. Maybe it'll be my new favorite after-sex food." She shook with silent laughter after Kal rolled her eyes.

"Then I will make it." Kal rose up and pushed the blanket off them.

"Wait. What?" Charlie twisted her head as the blanket was put back over her. "You can fuck *and* cook?"

Kal was still nude as she walked around the bed. "*Ja*. I can do many things." She went to the sitting room and pulled on a few meager pieces of clothing.

"Wow," Charlie whispered, not expecting an Alpha to cook or do anything domestic. Alphas were known for working hard outside, while Omegas took care of the home, including raising the kids. It was rather old-fashioned in Charlie's mind, making her dislike Alphas more for setting the social norms in the Kalmar culture. It was no wonder Omegas looked up to female Earthlings, who long ago struggled against such social injustice. But the injustice between the sexes didn't truly end until Earthlings left their home planet, as they needed every able body in order for their species to survive in outer space. That new mindset became more crucial after Earthlings landed on Kander and had to fight to live.

Blowing out a breath, Charlie put aside her recent memories of Earthlings' history and climbed out of bed. She neatened up the blankets and pillows before collecting her scattered attire in the sitting area. A bath was in order, but food had priority, and from the smell in the kitchen, it would be ready soon. Shrugging, she pulled on the frayed jeans without underwear and yanked her T-shirt over her torso. As she neared Kal, she tamed her wild hair with her fingers.

Kal worked fast in the kitchen, like an old pro knocking off the dust after being away too long. She had her back to Charlie while she moved around and prepared the food.

Charlie folded her arms and stood several steps back, silently commending the Alpha's skill with a chef's knife. Over time she had cooked many meals herself but didn't claim to be an expert. Anything that Charlie made was at least palatable, and a few dishes ranked in the exceptional range. Watching Kal cook was both heartwarming and sexy.

"After breakfast we can bathe," Kal said, over her shoulder.

Clearing her throat, Charlie nodded and asked, "Anything I can do to help with that? Heat up water?"

Kal hesitated after going over to the stove top and lighted it with a match. "There's a full pot of water over the fireplace in the bathroom. If you light it, that'll be a start."

"Got it." Charlie shifted closer to the sealed door to her left but paused next to it. She stared over at Kal, who only wore a breast wrap and very short bottoms that reminded her of boy short underwear back on Earth. Reaching blindly for the door handle, she kept missing it thanks to Kal's distracting body.

"Food will be ready soon… if you can get the fire started in the bathroom." Kal cracked an egg over a cast iron pan.

"Right." Charlie smiled and nudged the door open with her shoulder. "On it." She rolled her body against the door, exhaling a breath once she was alone in the chilly room. Playing with her hair, she assessed the space that had a washbasin to her left and a tub in the center. An outhouse was located outside of the cabin, as Charlie had confirmed last night. Turning to her right, she went to the large fireplace.

There was a full, gigantic pot hanging over the fireplace, where logs and kindling were already organized under it. Charlie located the matches on the short mantle and started the fire. When she returned to the main room of the cabin, she and Kal sat down to a hot breakfast, which they sorely needed after last night.

They ate in comfortable silence, other than Charlie's occasional hum of enjoyment. She was famished but tried to pace herself. After her stomach was sated, she sat back and sipped the warm *kello* from the mug in her hands. She eyed Kal, concluding that the blocker was working.

"How are you feeling?"

Kal put the dirty utensil onto the plate and leaned back in the chair. "More in control."

Charlie dipped her head, then took a sip of the herbal drink. It gave her a beat to formulate her next words, unsure how Kal would respond. "We have a lot to talk about." She lowered the mug into her lap, allowing the drink to heat her hands.

Kal tilted her head and remained quiet.

Charlie had been thinking about their situation for hours before she even arrived at the cabin. The long ride had given her plenty of opportunity to consider so many things, maybe too many. As she focused on Kal, she realized a huge issue that needed to be solved before they could talk about anything. "I seriously can't discuss any of it when you're sitting there in nothing but a damn..." She hunted for the word in her head, then it came to her in English. "*Bikini.*"

Kal's rumble was deep and a glow entered her eyes.

"And I could really stand to bathe." Charlie lifted the collar of her shirt to her nose. "Like right now."

"Finish your *kello.*" Kal stood up with the dirty plates. "I will prep the tub." She deposited the dishes on the kitchen counter, then went to the front door.

Charlie twisted around with a furrow across her brow. "Where are you going?"

"To get more water for the tub." Kal pushed the bolt back and opened the door.

"You barely have anything on," Charlie protested as she held out a hand at Kal's minimal attire. "And it's freaking cold out there."

"There is no one around for many marches." Kal stepped out but not without a grin. "I'm still hot from my rut." Then she was gone.

Rubbing her brow, Charlie shook her head and went back to the herbal drink. "Am I going to wake up from this?" she asked herself but already knew the truth. Some remote part of her expected to find herself back on the *Pacifica*, as if none of her adventures since coming to Kander had happened. But one day she would have to accept that her life's trajectory was changing from what had become comfortable and easy for her. Swallowing the rest of the *kello*, she popped out of the seat and neatened up the kitchen while Kal made a few trips with filled buckets of water.

She met Kal in the bathroom and helped get the pot of heated water poured into the tub, which was smaller than the one back in Kal's quarters. They both stripped off their clothes and climbed into the inviting herbal-infused water. A groan escaped Charlie after she slumped against the side and stretched her legs.

"How are you feeling?"

Charlie lifted her head off the tub and considered her answer, warmed by Kal's concern. "I don't know right now." She was ignoring the jumbled mess in her head until they could talk it out. "There's a lot going on and…" She held up her hands and whispered, "And here we are hanging out in a cabin in the middle of nowhere like it's a vacation."

Kal tilted her head and said, "We are in a safe place together for the first time."

Sighing and dropping her hands, Charlie nodded. "*Ja.* You're right." Maybe hiding out here was the best scenario for them right now because they had so much to work through in a short amount of time. Dorlon would be expecting Kal back sooner than a nineth.

Kal leaned forward and reached across the distance. She clasped Charlie's wrists and urged her to come to her.

Giving in, Charlie crossed the small space and followed Kal's wishes by sitting in the Alpha's lap. She melted into the comfortable position, feeling tiny compared to Kal's larger structure; but she also felt like she was meant to be a part of Kal. She relaxed into Kal's front, hard nipples brushing Charlie's shoulders. She leaned her head back and listened to the thrum rattling deep in Kal's chest.

"What was your dream?" Kal asked, her voice vibrating against Charlie's shoulders.

Charlie grumbled and closed her eyes. "Just a stupid nightmare." Kal's hand moved to Charlie's thigh, massaging the area. Somehow she sensed her answer wasn't enough for her lover, so she sighed and told Kal the dream's details, then whispered, "I tried getting you to heal yourself, with the spirit."

"It doesn't work that way."

"*Ja* that's what you told me in the dream too." Charlie lifted her head and stared across the room. "Kalatas left you because you were dying, and all your old memories came back." She pushed her wet hair aside. "I was a complete mess holding you. It was a great dream," she muttered, sarcasm dripping in every word.

"But a dream," Kal said. "Lennox is a trustworthy advisor."

"Even if he finds out you've been fucking a human behind his back?" Charlie asked, peering back at Kal's stony features.

"It is sometimes hard to calculate a person's emotional reaction," Kal admitted aloud. Then she sighed and turned her head toward Charlie. "But I would not jump in front of a gun. It is foolish and safer to jump you."

Charlie smiled and placed her damp palm against her lover's burning cheek. "My hero." She leaned in and pressed a kiss against Kal's temple. "So whose cabin is this anyway?"

"It's Dorlon's."

"Really?" Charlie frowned and shifted in Kal's lap. "I don't remember her ever having a cabin, especially so far from Kardos."

"It was given to her many years back."

"Given?"

"*Ja.* A dying relative gave it to her. He was a blacksmith, and he built this home."

Charlie gazed about the cabin, eyeing it with more respect. She imagined that Dorlon's relative had spent much of his effort and coin to build the home. Attached to the stable was a forge with a tall chimney that climbed up toward the trees. "He picked a beautiful place to build it." She considered the cabin's purpose after Dorlon took possession of it. "Do only you and Dorlon know of it?"

"*Ja.*" Kal twisted around and stretched out her arm to claim a soap and cloth from a small shelf behind them. "In the early days, Dorlon would stay here during her heats. But now she has little time to visit and doesn't go into heats anymore." She held out the soap to Charlie and said, "The water is cooling already."

Charlie agreed and grabbed the items from Kal. They bathed before the water was too chilly, then toweled off and dressed in fresh clothes. The tub remained filled so they could clean their clothes and let them dry before the return trip to Tarrak. Feeling refreshed, Charlie tried to prepare herself for the pending conversations about their future. Her heartbeat went wild, and her face became flushed. She dug out her hairbrush to distract herself with something rhythmic and noticed Kal was boiling more water.

"I didn't think Alphas could be so domestic," Charlie said, keeping her tone even in hopes that Kal's Alpha wouldn't react.

Kal organized two ceramic mugs with *kello* and kept her back to Charlie. "Dorlon taught me how to cook." She turned and leaned against the counter, her bare arms folded against her chest.

For a moment, Charlie adored her lover in a black tank top that had a few pinholes in it. She noticed that Kal's black pants were much looser than the standard ones. "I guess fighting and cooking are two life-essential skills." She dragged the brush through her wet hair a few more times, then toyed with it.

"But there are cooking skills I learned before her." Kal had a distant expression. "Especially with a knife."

"Maybe something your mother taught you," Charlie said, pointing the brush at the ruler. "There is such a thing as muscle memory if you've done something enough times." She went to the bed where she had placed her saddlebag, then stowed the hairbrush. "I'm going to use the head." She rammed her feet into the boots without tying them. While slinging on the leather jacket, she noted Kal's curious gaze. "Going to the bathroom. It's called a head on a ship."

Kal chuffed low and turned to the herbal drink.

Outside, Charlie shivered from the cold day and noticed her breath forming in the air, despite the suns having been up for awhile. "Great." She trudged around the house to the back. When she returned to the cabin, she was happy Kal had started the fire, and she gravitated to it. "I forgot how damn cold it gets here."

"The ice is coming," Kal said from her spot on the sofa.

Charlie hummed at the memory of those exact words. She remained beside the fire and warmed up. Raine wanted her to visit New Earth, which was farther north in the Kardos province. She shivered at the idea of going there, knowing they already had snow and ice by now. It was a bad time of the planet's rotation for her to have made a six-nored deal with Raine. Thinking of her promise, she peered over at Kal, who had no idea that Charlie was staying for an extended period.

*Why did I agree to stay on Kander for so many months?*

But staying grounded on Kander with Kal was a pleasant idea. Charlie smiled to herself and studied her lover, who appeared relaxed for the first time since Charlie's arrival at the cabin. It was a good sign that their conversation would go well and that the rut wouldn't taint Kal's mind. Picking up a steaming mug, Charlie sipped from it and wandered over to the sofa to sit next to her lover. Kal sat with her legs spread, mug on her thigh and her full attention on Charlie.

"I'm not really sure where to start this," Charlie whispered, sighing and rubbing her forehead.

Dipping her head, Kal said, "I assume you saved Starr."

"*Ja.* All of us survived the mission." Charlie drank more *kello*, then set the mug onto the wooden table. "Starr was a bit banged up but okay. She decided to stay with Magnar for now."

"You'll be purchasing another ship soon," Kal said.

"I think so." Charlie leaned her side against the sofa, trying to be comfortable though her chest muscles were taut. "I'm kind of, sort of staying on Kander for the next six noreds." At Kal's curious features, she said, "I made a deal with Raine that if she went on the mission I would stay." She flashed a weak smile and shrugged. "I don't have a clue where I'm staying or what I'll even be doing." Grabbing the mug, she muttered, "Polishing my gun a lot, I guess."

Kal responded with a strong rumble, then drank from the mug.

"But something serious came up on the rescue mission." Charlie felt her lover's attention sharpen, and she hated to have to give her the news. "I overheard Victor talking to another soldier. He mentioned the Sworne." She searched Kal's eyes for any hint of reaction to the new information, but Kal remained indifferent. "They were talking about getting a head start before the Sworne arrive."

Sitting forward, Kal set the mug on the table and released a throaty huff. "Did you learn anything else?"

Shaking her head, Charlie peered into her mug and pictured a Sworne's nightmarish features from her childhood, but she pushed it back. "*Joh.*" Like Kal, she set aside her drink, losing interest in it. "What's weird, too, is Serrato Corps still has their Sworne starship."

"Like the *Liberator*?"

"*Ja.* It's called the *Borba.* They kept it and still use it."

"For what?"

"I don't know." Charlie swept loose, damp strands behind her ear.

Kal was silent, then narrowed her eyes and asked, "Have you heard any news about the Sworne in the galaxy?"

"*Joh.*" Charlie took a deep breath, trying to calm her heartbeat. "That's what's so strange. I don't know where Serrato Corps is getting their information. If the Sworne were coming or are already here, there'd be chatter all over the Milky Way." She sighed and let her shoulders drop. "I did send a message to Sallarus to see if he's heard anything, but he hasn't responded." It didn't help that Charlie had shut off her techbit's comms after Dorlon instructed her to shut all tech down to ensure Kal's privacy and safety. They'd have to wait until back in the city to see if Sallarus replied.

"It could be several noreds before the Sworne arrive," Kal said, her voice distant.

"Or days." Charlie fought a tremble in her body at the idea of the Sworne coming back. "And who knows where they'll show up first. They could be all the way over in the hundred eleventh quadrant of the galaxy and not come here for awhile, if at all." She listened to Kal's low thunder and could only guess what the ruler was thinking when it came to Kander's safety.

"We don't have enough information," Kal whispered.

Agreeing, Charlie clenched her lower lip between her teeth and tensed at what other information she had to tell Kal. "There's something else."

"What?"

Charlie's skin prickled from the dark tone in her lover's voice. "Serrato Corps has a contact here on Kander."

"It would explain Fairlee's kidnapping."

Bowing her head, Charlie considered the informant that worked for Serrato Corps. "My guess is it's an Earthling." At least her gut instinct was coming to the conclusion that a human among her former people was working for Serrato Corps. "Maybe somebody from Serrato Corps slipped in." She peered up at Kal and whispered, "Or maybe one of the Earthlings in New Earth defected to Serrato Corps." Slumping against the sofa, she grumbled and folded her arms. "And we still don't know why Serrato Corps was after the darakar." As the silence drew on, she looked at Kal, who masked her features but had to be processing everything. Charlie had no idea what Kal was thinking, as she hadn't quite learned how to read the ruler.

Charlie tried to ignore the nagging sensation in her gut, knowing the situation wasn't hers to handle; yet she kept getting sucked into it. She rubbed her brow and stared into the flames jumping and falling in the fireplace. "I also got a bounty on my head," she whispered, closing her eyes when a steady growl grew louder. "Victor got my contact information somehow. We talked for a minute. He wants me to return Starr to Serrato Corps. I'm sure you can guess what I told him."

Kal grunted, then fisted a hand in her lap, her knuckles going white.

"The Grand Marshal is sending down a kill order and bounty for me." Charlie huffed and stood up, needing to stretch her tense body. "Not that it hasn't happened to me before." She leaned against the wall, near the fireplace, and looked over at Kal. "But it's never been an entire army hunting me. They'll probably broadcast the bounty across the entire galaxy." If that happened, then no place in the Milky Way would be safer for her. She crossed her arms and wished the fire's warmth could chase off the anxious jumps in her stomach. For a moment she searched Kal's face for a reaction or even indicators of her lover's feelings. There was very little in Kal's stony features, and it caused an ache in Charlie. Whatever walls the rut had torn down last night had returned, thanks to the blockers.

*Never thought I'd hate those blockers*, Charlie realized. They had been a godsend for Starr's moody ass. Some piece of her wished she had attempted talking to Kal last night while vulnerable in her rut. But even with a lack of words, Kal's reactions and feelings last night were on the surface. The experience had been special to Charlie. She couldn't ignore what happened between them. With or without the rut, their attraction for each other was mutual and growing stronger at an increasing rate. Charlie had to at least make a push.

Charlie peeled away from the stone hearth, paced, and wrang her hands as if they held the answers in them. "We need to talk about last night." Her heart drummed against her chest, trying to break free. "What's going on between us?" She circled back and went to Kal, then knelt and touched Kal's thigh. "I really need you to talk to me." She squeezed the muscle under her hand. "Please, Sumner. I can't read your mind." A wave of relief rushed through her when Kal covered her hand.

"Sit," Kal said, her tone firm but patient. Once Charlie was next to her, Kal hesitated and seemed to be searching for the right words. After a low rumble, she said, "I'm changing, Charlie."

Jarred by the echoing words, Charlie popped off the sofa and stomped over to the fireplace before spinning around. All the capped frustrations boiled over, and she snapped, "That's exactly what you told me in a dream a few days ago! We were standing out on the balcony of your room, talking about my rescue mission." She growled and said, "The dream was so real." She blew out a breath, expelling some of the fire in her. "What does that even mean?" She returned to the previous spot beside Kal. "Changing how?" She clenched her pants instead of grabbing and shaking Kal.

"Some things are being returned to me," Kal whispered as if she were confessing secrets. At Charlie's worried look, she sighed and took a deep breath before explaining herself. "When I first became Kal, I had random sex a few times with different people."

Charlie steadied herself, held her tongue, and allowed Kal to speak after having been so quiet.

"I don't know why I did it the first time. Maybe something residual from my former life." Kal frowned, a rare feature on her. "But I felt nothing during sex, not even natural pleasure. I had sex two other times, sporadically. Those times were to see if it was the same outcome, and it was."

Charlie mirrored her lover's displeasure and asked, "You felt nothing?"

"Nothing emotional and nothing physical." Kal grinned, but bitterness tainted it. "It was no different than washing my hands, tying my boots, or sharpening my sword."

Charlie knew it was the Spirit of Kalatas that had disconnected Kal from her body and mind. If a ruler was plagued by feelings, good or bad, then they were weak. At least, she was certain that was what Kalatas believed.

"But the day you entered the *alping* room, your sweet scent overwhelmed me, and I burned all over. As Kal, it was the first time anyone made me so fucking hard."

Charlie's cheeks were on fire, not quite ready for the confession.

Kal leaned in closer and whispered, "I could have let you return to your ship until the kidnappers showed up for the ransom. But I had to have you, and you wanted me. I had to know if I would feel something." She ran her thumb along Charlie's jaw, and thunder rolled in her throat. "Anything."

Now knowing the truth, Charlie whimpered and clasped Kal's hand into her own. "I know you feel what I'm feeling when we're together." She was certain of it after last night.

"*Ja*." Kal lowered her head until her lips touched Charlie's neck. "I feel so much pleasure. I have desire and passion. I feel like an Alpha again. I want to claim you, protect you, and fuck you." She trailed her lips up until they were next to Charlie's ear. "I feel close to you and alive again."

Charlie ignored the pricks behind her eyelids, not willing to cry like last night. For the first time, Kal was telling her everything, and she would hold onto it. "W-hy?" She cleared out the croak. "Why do I make you feel something when others can't?"

"I don't know," Kal whispered. "But it is changing me." She withdrew and held Charlie's gaze again. "I recall fragments from my old life."

"Like what?" Charlie was wired by both arousal and Kal's memories.

"I remember my mother's face, but not her name." Kal had a slight smile, and a thrum came from deep in her chest. "I recall climbing a tall tree just outside my village."

"What village?"

Kal shook her head.

Charlie frowned and asked, "Wouldn't it be the same one that Fairlee was returned to?"

"Perhaps." Kal tilted her head and let a sigh escape her. "I did not ask what village she was from."

Charlie suspected Kal didn't ask because it didn't matter, at least at the time. Whatever Kal's previous life had been, it was irrelevant to being a ruler now. And yet there were mixed signals such as painting a mural from a fleeting memory or telling Charlie her old name before it was taken again. Fairlee had mentioned that she could feel her twin sister for an instant, then the connection would shatter as if her sister died. "You don't want to forget," she whispered, peering up. "You don't try to remember, but you also try not to forget."

Kal remained quiet, eyes distant and her features blank. "If I remember too much, will I become a poor ruler?" She focused on Charlie and whispered, "You believe Kalatas stole my identity. But perhaps Kalatas freed me from things better forgotten."

Frowning and chewing on her lip, Charlie remained calm and considered Kal's perspective rather than react to it. "There are bad things that come along with the good." Sighing, she could understand Kal's point and even Kalatas's purpose behind erasing what might burden and hinder someone. Charlie had come to respect Kal's sacrifices so that she could rule the planet. Before she could say anything else, Kal left the sofa and went to the bedroom area.

Kal retrieved a leather book from her own saddlebags and returned to Charlie's side. The black leather book was worn, a writing instrument peeking out in the middle, and it had a tied leather string across the front. Kal undid the strap, flipped through the tan pages, and graphite images passed before Charlie's eyes.

"This is the tree outside the village." Kal turned the book and showed the drawing to her lover.

Charlie stretched out her hand but refrained from touching it. The picture depicted a grand tree with thick, outstretched branches and leaves that reminded Charlie of an oak tree back on Earth. Beside the tree was a gravel road with ruts from heavy use. Far beyond the tree were rolling hills and tiny figures that were perhaps livestock for the village.

"Did you draw this?" Charlie placed her hand against Kal's wrist, then looked up from it.

"*Ja.*" Kal flipped a few pages back and turned the book again.

Charlie sucked in a breath when a new drawing jerked her back to her recent death. This time, she touched the drawing and allowed her fingertips to trace the outline of the former *Pacifica* shuttle. But rather than a silver fuselage, it was dented and twisted metal in the woods. After the crash landing, she had never returned to the accident location, and seeing it on paper made her breathing quicken. She had died there.

Kal seemed to sense Charlie's distress and covered the image with her hand, breaking Charlie's spell. "When I found you, you were already dead. I didn't think about what I was doing, I reacted and started healing your body." She released a low breath and began closing the journal, allowing the pages to flip past. "I called your spirit back, and you came without hesitation." Meeting Charlie's distraught gaze, she whispered, "It was the first time I experienced fear and hope."

Charlie covered Kal's larger hand with her own and studied their size difference. "I'm sorry." She peered up and whispered, "I'm sorry you faced that alone."

"I had Dorlon."

Squeezing Kal's hand, Charlie suspected Kal had hidden the surge of emotions when she discovered Charlie's body at the crash site. "Maybe for moral support but not emotional support."

Kal lowered her head. "You returned to…" She paused, then said, "You returned to your body." She withdrew the journal, broke their contact, and closed the book.

"I thought it was all just a bad dream." Charlie slouched against the sofa and recalled the memories from what she assumed was the afterlife. "I was at a cabin and waiting for my parents." She released a shaky breath and asked, "Would they have shown up?"

"*Ja*, most likely." After straightening up, Kal tilted her head and added, "Certain spirits return to each other time and time again."

"Even across the galaxy?"

"Across the universe," Kal promised.

Charlie was comforted by the idea that she would one day see her parents again but not right now. Kal had beckoned her back to life, and she accepted it. Her spirit followed the line from the afterlife to the living, and now she was seated beside the Alpha, who was without a doubt a god in spirit. She blew out a breath and nodded once, accepting what she was learning from Kal. She set it aside for later thought and shifted mental gears to what really gnawed at her mind.

"So where does all this leave us?" Charlie chewed on her bottom lip, then shook her head. "Leave you and me." *Is there even an us? We did just have a fucking emotional night of sex.* She sighed at her musing and rubbed her sweaty palms on her pant legs.

"It is complicated."

Charlie huffed and replied, "You're fuckin' telling me." She toyed with her hair and pushed most of it to one side. "You wanted to knot and bite me last night." She licked her lips at the thought of their night together. "And I wanted you to do those things." Closing her eyes, she relived the memories and managed to swallow a rising moan. "What is going on with us?" She gazed up at Kal in search of help or even an explanation. "How can I make you go into a rut? I'm just a human."

"It has nothing to do with your race," Kal explained, voice lowering an octave. "It is your scent."

Shaking her head, Charlie was at a loss about their changing relationship and what it could mean for them. "If we continue down this path, it could get us both killed and probably send this planet into a civil war." She jumped and her jaw dropped open when Kal chuckled at her. "What can be funny about that?"

"Dorlon must have learned to be dramatic from you," Kal replied. After Charlie glared at her, she huffed and became stern again. "It could encourage the revolt."

Charlie recalled Dorlon's mentioning a revolt, but it appeared small so far. She suspected her assassin, Morris, was a part of it. "How is a revolt any better than a war?"

"A revolt is brief and easy to put down." Kal stretched out her legs and pulled down the pants that had bunched up between her thighs. She sighed before saying, "The Alphas are adjusting to the changes, but it takes time and pushing them."

Frowning, Charlie considered the statement and what she'd learned since returning to Kander. "Changes like the Earthlings settling on the planet and the Omegas rising up."

"Becoming equals," Kal corrected. "It will take many years for Alphas to adjust to having Omegas beside them in equal capacity. They are accustomed to protecting their Omegas, not working alongside them."

Charlie listened and smiled after understanding Kal's ultimate goal to forge equality between Alphas and Omegas. It was a huge risk that would have profound impact on the society's future. She was humbled by Kal's determination. "If men and women can do it, so can Alphas and Omegas."

Kal revealed a wolfish grin, as if she already knew the future outcome. "*Ja*."

"But that still doesn't resolve this thing." Charlie indicated the space between them. "Whatever this thing is with us." Then silence returned, and she shook her right leg, wishing Kal would open up again. She almost stood up, but Kal's firm hand stilled her jittery thigh.

"I promised you that I would keep fucking you until you told me to stop." Kal squeezed her lover and whispered, "And I will fight for you, protect you, and one day mate you."

Charlie was gasping. Her clit throbbed and heat pulsed in her veins, but she shook her head.

"If you wish it," Kal said in a voice that rolled with thunder.

Closing her eyes, Charlie covered Kal's hand with both of hers and held with all her strength. "I don't want you to die." She gazed up into the green eyes humming with life. "Not for me."

"If not for the one who makes me feel, then for whom?"

"Die for your people, not for me." Charlie had sworn she wouldn't cry again, but tears fell off her cheeks and landed on their joined hands. "I don't want to get you killed for…." She had no idea what it was between them, but it was strong and pulling them together, as if trying to bind them.

"Then tell me now to stop fucking you," Kal ordered, her tone growing fierce.

Charlie choked on the word that were too heavy and were slicing at her heart. Her tears stung the more she tried to will herself.

"Tell me," Kal snarled as she leaned down until her lips were near Charlie's ear. "Tell me to stop."

Charlie reached up and tangled her fingers in raven locks, as she whimpered in pain. The single Kalmarese word *rojoh* held a great power in each of its letters among the Kalmar. If she whispered it, she feared their entire relationship would come undone in a few ticks. "I don't want you to stop, but I don't want something to happen to you because of me." She swallowed hard and whispered, "I will take you off this planet if I have to. I swear it."

"You can always try," Kal whispered. "I would never fault you for trying." She nipped at the soft ear, earning a delightful hiss.

Charlie swiped the tears from her face and swallowed against the stiffness in her throat. She was breathing hard and wanted to melt into her lover's touch. She needed and craved Kal more each time they were together.

"Do you want me to fuck you now?"

Turning her head, Charlie captured soft lips and moaned when their tongues brushed against each other in a frantic mess. She withdrew and whispered, "*Ja.*" She didn't have to wait, as she was lifted off the sofa into strong arms and taken near the fireplace.

Kal lowered Charlie onto the soft animal fur in front of the fire, similar to their last night in the Great Tower. She watched Kal stoke the fire to ensure they would be warm enough. Just as she reached for the waistband of her jeans, Kal was already pulling off her black top. Charlie was entranced and remained motionless while she enjoyed the show of Kal's pants coming off. In those ticks, she realized the truth that took the air from her.

*I don't want her to ever stop.*

# Chapter 3

"Are you sure? It will be cold."

Charlie zipped on the leather jacket. "*Ja.* I need to go for a walk before I get cabin fever." She went over to Kal, who waited beside the front door. After they'd had sex, they napped and woke up to the last hour of daylight. The approaching winter was bringing shorter and colder days. After being in the cabin all day, Charlie needed to stretch her legs, even though it was nearly sunset.

Kal had on her long jacket but didn't bother to button it, plenty warm from the rut. She unbolted the door and allowed Charlie to go first, then sealed the cabin door. "Follow me."

Charlie assumed her lover knew a path or two around the area that they could enjoy. She shoved her hands into her jacket pockets and kept pace. "How many times have you been here?" They left the open lands and followed a path through the woods that had been cut open.

"Since becoming Kal, about a dozen times."

"Maybe more before you were Kal," Charlie whispered while studying the rusty colored leaves coating the ground. She exhaled and watched the white mist form in front of her face. It was colder than she'd expected, but she was determined to take a walk. Even with the chill, it was peaceful and eased Charlie's current worries about the future. "Have you always enjoyed drawing?" she asked and almost slammed into Kal, who had halted in front of her.

Kal pivoted and studied Charlie, as if confused by the question. "Enjoy it?" She shook her head and continued the walk. "It's merely a means to record what I remember."

Charlie pursed her lips and walked closer. "You're a talented drawer. It's a gift to be able to draw."

"You can't put images to paper?" Kal asked, a hint of bewilderment hidden in her tone.

Chuckling, Charlie shook her head and replied, "I suck at being creative, other than maybe putting together a really good rescue plan." She shrugged and whispered, "I'm better at math or learning a new language." Her thoughts were cut off when Kal snared her, and they came to an abrupt stop. Before she could say anything, a hand covered her mouth.

Kal withdrew her hand and pointed ahead of them toward a downed tree with its roots twisted up in the air. Next to it was a furry creature larger than a fox. Its ears perked up, and its fluffy tail swooshed before it started sniffing the air. Charlie knew a locke anywhere she had always been fascinated by them since first coming to Kander. She leaned into her lover and observed the animal, stiffening when it saw them.

The locke hissed low, squatted, and crept away without every losing sight of them. Its honey brown fur was speckled with white tufts that signaled a change of season. Soon the locke would shed its darker fur for a snow-white coat for the winter. As the animal neared the end of the rotting tree, it paused and bared its teeth at them.

Charlie heard Kal's own snarl that warned the locke to back off. She wasn't concerned that anything would happen other than one predator outmatching the other. The locke's pure white eyes flashed red, then it darted off and vanished in the woods. She grinned at Kal's low puff once the minor threat was gone. "Lockes are so beautiful."

"Mischievous creatures," Kal said before taking the lead again. Their walk continued, but they soon arrived at a wider, shallower part of the creek. Along the shore side were boulders that provided a perfect sitting spot. They watched the dual suns kissing the horizon through the trees.

"So it is a little cold," Charlie admitted, pulling her legs closer to her body and hugging them to her chest. "But it's nice." She rested her chin on her knees. "I guess we should return to Tarrak tomorrow." Charlie sighed at Kal's agreeing rumble and wished they could stay hidden longer in the cabin. "It was a nice vacation while it lasted."

Kal grunted and crossed her long legs as she reached into her coat. She retrieved Charlie's most precious valuable and held it in the palm of her hand, offering it to her.

Charlie swallowed against the hard lump in her throat and asked, "You kept it on you the whole time?" She had expected Kal to stow it away somewhere without too much concern.

"It was the safest place." Kal waited for Charlie to reclaim it, her features patient.

Charlie took a deep breath and slid her fingers around it to take it back. She cradled it in her hands and ran her thumb over the cracked glass. "It was my mother's." The quake in her voice was clear. The memories from her last day on Earth bubbled up and burned behind her eyes. "And her mother's before that."

"You tell time with it," Kal said and continued studying it from her higher position next to Charlie.

"*Ja*," Charlie whispered. Again her thumb rubbed the glass before going down the wristband, feeling every tiny metal link. "It's called a *watch*."

Kal hummed, then leaned in closer and asked, "But it no longer works?"

Charlie shook her head and looked up, staring out at the creek. "It used to."

"Why haven't you fixed it?"

Charlie wiped at her left cheek to rid yet more tears today. "Because I broke it." She pulled up her hand with the watch in it. "When they blew up Earth, the shockwave hit the ship and I fell down on it." She tucked the watch into her jeans' front pocket, hiding it away again. "When Earth was destroyed, time ended anyway." She shook but not from the cold. Pulling her legs back up, she clenched her legs until her fingers hurt. "There's no point in fixing it."

Kal exhaled low, straightened up, and studied the babbling water.

"I guess we're not that different in some ways." Charlie combed her hair back before hooking her arm across her leg again. "We both have old lives that we forget." She sniffed from her runny nose, unsure whether it was the cold or her emotions. "My old name was Charlene."

Kal narrowed her eyes, then whispered, "Charlene Larson." She ignored Charlie's bulging eyes. "You told me before you died."

Charlie closed her slackened jaw and said, "That was you. That was you controlling me after I crashed." She lowered her legs and almost slid off the boulder. "I thought it was some kind of dream. But it wasn't, was it?"

Kal lowered her head and nodded before saying, "I can use the Spirit of Kalatas to manipulate a person." She sighed, then shifted her attention to the creek. "It has limitations though, especially if the person is unwilling."

"You can heal a body, bring someone back to life, and control their body." Charlie turned on the rock and faced her lover. "What else can you do with the spirit?" She waved her hand in the space between them. "I saw you sense Magnar's ship in the atmosphere."

Kal released a rumble from deep in her chest, then met Charlie's curious gaze. "What do you know about Kalatas?"

"As much as the next Earthling, I guess." Charlie shrugged and considered what she had learned about Kander's religion. "I mean Dorlon told me some things when we were kids."

Kal nodded and remained quiet for a moment, then a thin smile graced her hard features. "Kalatas is Kander." She indicated the landscape around them. "All of this is Kalatas." She touched her chest. "I am Kalatas, and so is every Alpha and Omega."

"But I'm not," Charlie whispered.

Grinning, Kal leaned in and said, "You may carry your god in you, whereas Kalmar are made from Kalatas." She placed a hand on Charlie's knee and whispered, "But you and your people are becoming Kalatas the longer you stay."

Charlie frowned and considered the explanation until it hit her low in the gut. "We drink the water here. We eat the food here. We breathe in the air."

"And now humans are being born here," Kal added.

"That's why our scent is changing," Charlie whispered.

"It has changed." Kal chuckled at Charlie's realization. She folded her arms and studied the suns' orange light cutting between the trees. "I don't carry all of Kalatas's spirit. It is much too powerful. But I am an extension of it."

"The walking and talking piece of the spirit," Charlie concluded aloud. After Kal's nod, she asked, "But does it weaken you? After you healed Dorlon, you seemed exhausted from it."

"*Ja*." Kal placed both hands flat against the stone and propped up her legs. "I can channel more of the spirit to do extraordinary things, but it can weaken me."

"Makes you vulnerable." Charlie now understood why Dorlon had stayed in Tarrak after she crashed on Kander. It wasn't to watch after Charlie but rather Kal, who had been drained by healing and bringing back Charlie. "So you don't use it often." She clenched her lip between her teeth and ached at knowing Kal had gone to great lengths and taken on huge risks to bring her back to life. "*Tah*, Sumner." She placed her hand over top of Kal's own. "I never thanked you."

Kal turned over her hand and said, "*Motah*."

Charlie slid her fingers between Kal's larger ones, then looked at the last bit of blood orange light streaming through the trees. "Do you feel ready to go back to Tarrak?"

"*Ja*, in the morning." Kal ran her thumb over Charlie's knuckles. "We should return to the cabin."

"What's for dinner?" Charlie smirked at her lover and wiggled her eyes brows. "I know what's for dessert."

Kal grunted low and chuffed after a long moment. "I should have killed the locke for dinner."

Yanking her hand free, Charlie slapped her lover in the side but yelped after being manhandled. Somehow she ended up in Kal's lap, facing each other. She gasped and settled into the warmth under her.

"You shouldn't hit me. It could be dangerous," Kal warned her.

Charlie wasn't deterred and instead smirked. "Or you'll rough me up a bit?" She dragged her teeth along her bottom lip and teased, "I might like it."

Kal growled and lowered her head while her hand sneaked under Charlie's jacket. Her warm fingertips teased soft skin hidden under the layers. "I could hurt you accidentally."

"I might be smaller, but I'm not fragile," Charlie whispered, pride thick in her voice.

"*Ja*." Kal's lip curled and revealed the distinct canines. "I noticed last night." She leaned in closer and pushed away Charlie's hair on one side. "You were able to take in all of me."

Charlie moaned when moist lips burned against her throat. "Not quite all." If only she could have had Kal's knot too. She groaned at Kal's heavy rumble and wanted to sprint back to the cabin, shedding her clothes along the way. It was a great plan in her head, but they were in the cold wilderness at dusk. "Do you think you can knot me?"

"If I can, it may be painful for you." Kal nudged Charlie's jaw with her nose. "We should go."

Sighing, Charlie tilted her head back and gazed up at the darkening sky. "We should." Once they were back at the cabin, it would be their last night together in a secluded place. They were safe and free here. She hated to give it up, but people relied on Kal. If the Sworne were coming, then the planet would need their ruling god.

Kal dropped her head back too and secured her hands behind Charlie's hips.

Charlie eyes were aglow with the stars that broke through the darkness one by one. "It's so beautiful out there." She exhaled and felt her shoulders drop down, then she shifted her attention to Kal. Even if she longed for the stars, she was at peace in Kal's arms. "Come on." She slipped free and slid off the boulder, bouncing on her feet.

Kal hopped off after Charlie moved out of the way.

"I can't see much now," Charlie said, scanning the dark forest and making out a few trees. She didn't have anything to light her way, not even her techbit.

"Stay close." Kal laced their hands together and guided the way back to the path through the woods.

Charlie heard a low bird call in the distance, familiar with the flying animal's screech. She blew out a breath and wrapped her other hand around Kal's muscular forearm. "It was cold earlier and now it's fucking freezing." Once the suns were gone, what little warmth was in the air had all but vanished in an instant. Uncontrolled shaking wracked her body until something hard struck her boot tip. With a yelp, she almost went down until Kal snared her.

"How Earthlings survive is beyond me," Kal said, needling Charlie a bit. She scooped up her lover, adjusted her in her arms, and continued back to the cabin.

Not bothering to argue, Charlie snuggled in closer for more heat and hooked her arm across Kal's shoulders. "Says the Alpha who is sneaking around and fucking one." She laughed at Kal's wide grin but became serious. "Dorlon is so mad at me for this."

"She is concerned for us both." Kal's pace had increased now that Charlie was secure in her arms. As a Kalmar, she had superior night vision and the Spirit of Kalatas also helped her. "You are her childhood friend, and she mentored me for many years. Now she's my commander and closest advisor."

"She stands to lose a lot if something bad happens." Charlie peered over her shoulder and spotted the glow from the cabin's window. "She was mad at me for having sex with you. But she wasn't mad that it was us." She shook her head and whispered, "If that at all made sense."

"Dorlon will not be against a human and Kalmar together." Kal exited the woods, paused, and allowed Charlie to slide out of her arms. "You changed her opinion of Earthlings."

"*Ja*. So if you were Sumner and not also Kal, she wouldn't be mad." Charlie was relieved to get back into the warm cabin and blew out a shaking breath. Kal guided her to the fireplace, now only a mild glow from the dying embers.

Kal resurrected it with fresh wood and allowed Charlie to warm up. "I'll make dinner."

Charlie grumbled at not being helpful, but she sensed that Kal wanted to cook—or else they wouldn't be eating tonight. If Kal didn't keep her hands busy in other ways, they would be tangled under the bed sheets. Once warm enough, Charlie went into the washroom and rekindled the fire to wash their clothes so that they would be dry tomorrow. By the time she finished cleaning and hanging them, dinner was ready.

Again they ate in comfortable silence but Charlie's wandering mind reviewed the rescue mission for Starr. There was one small topic they hadn't discussed that continued annoying Charlie; she decided to test the waters and kept her voice calm.

"During the rescue mission, I went after Victor."

Kal paused and gazed across the table, features tight and eyes steely. "But you failed to kill him."

Charlie's poker face cracked, feeling transparent in front of her lover.

"You did mention that he contacted you later and threatened you," Kal reminded.

Charlie huffed low and dropped the dirty spork on the plate. Her lip curled, and she lost control. "I didn't get the chance to kill him because *you* ordered Andren to stop me!" She felt the heat in her face as memories of Andren attacking her made her blood boil again.

"*Ja.*" Kal's response was monotone. She stood and took the plates. For once, the rising tension in her shoulders was visible.

Charlie jumped out of the chair and followed one step behind. "Why did you do that?" She tried holding back the heat in her voice, but it was even more searing. "It was my decision, my choice. We even discussed it before I left."

"*Ja.*" Kal set the plates into the sink, then faced Charlie. "I didn't agree with your choice."

"It was *mine* to make!"

Charlie was panting and kept her fisted hands at her side. She watched the hardness in Kal's face and waited to see what the next move would be between them.

Kal was so much taller than Charlie, who had to keep her head tilted back. Kal's body hummed with more dark energy the longer the silent ticks dragged on. She clenched her jaw, causing her eyes to narrow. "It was also *mine* to make," Kal whispered with finality and power.

Charlie shook her head and warred with the urge to shove Kal, but she knew it wouldn't work anyway. She put space between them, or tried to, until Kal grabbed her waist. She yelped while being driven back onto the empty table. Her ass dragged a few inches over the table top and her legs were forced open. She clutched Kal's hips and rasped from the powerful body pushing into her.

"You made an emotional decision." Kal bared her teeth, revealing her prominent canines. "I countered it with a logical one." She pressed her hand against Charlie's jaw, and her blunt nails scraped into flushed skin at Charlie's neck. "Tell me where you'd be right now if I hadn't ordered Andren to protect you?"

Charlie's eyes fluttered, but the raw intensity in Kal's features forced her to keep watching because it was so beautiful. "H-h-held captive or dead." She shivered after Kal's snarl, then gasped when Kal leaned over her.

"Why are you so determined to kill yourself?"

Kal's question sliced through Charlie's thick skin, and it made her whimper and curl her fingers into Kal's shirt. "I-I-I…." She cracked a little more and leaned into her lover, being anchored by her. "What has this life ever given me?" She peered up, eyes glistening with rawness. "It just keeps taking and taking until I have nothing."

Kal cupped Charlie's cheeks and whispered, "I willingly sacrificed my old life. You were forced to sacrifice your old life." She ran her thumb across Charlie's cheeks, then leaned in closer. "But this time, maybe we can give each other better lives. Ones that are better than the old ones."

Charlie threaded her fingers into dark strands and pulled Kal's forehead against her own. "Why are you willing to risk everything for this?" *For me*, Charlie's mind whispered.

"Because you woke me up," Kal replied in a hushed voice, as if to ensure no one else heard her secret.

Biting her lip, Charlie shifted her head until their cheeks were rubbing together, passing affection between them. "I know. And it kind of freaks me out." She withdrew until she could see Kal's face. "We're playing with fire, Sumner. What if—" Kal's fingertips held her lips still, and she waited.

"You are here for six noreds." Kal waited for Charlie's nod. "Return to outer space if it's too much after those noreds."

Charlie threaded her fingers through Kal's larger ones. "I think it's already too late for that."

"Then we try one day at a time," Kal said; her voice was deep again.

Charlie nodded and squeezed Kal's hand to the point it hurt. "*Ja*. One day at a time." She was then jolted by a sudden growl.

"And stop trying to kill yourself," Kal ordered.

"*Turen!* I didn't blow up my own ship," Charlie argued but grinned at the playfulness in her lover.

Kal released another growl, then yanked Charlie hard against her waist. She gave a pleased rumble when Charlie started grinding against her. "You attract trouble."

Charlie grunted and somewhat agreed with her lover's assessment. "One of my better skills in life." She grabbed the first button at Kal's waistline and pulled on it. "But not my best skill." Raising an eyebrow, she licked her lips and noticed that Kal's attention went to them. "Take me to bed."

Not denying her lover, Kal lifted Charlie off the table and secured her against her larger frame.

Charlie nibbled and licked Kal's bare skin along her chest, tasting the spicy hint to it. Her hands slipped under Kal's tank top, and she moaned when she found toned muscles. "Fuck." She nipped Kal's skin and earned a snarl. Her lover placed her on the bed, and she crawled a short distance before Kal removed Charlie's boots.

Removing all but her skintight pants that barely contained the bulge in her crotch, Kal followed Charlie to the center of the bed.

*Fuck. That has to hurt.* But it was delicious eye candy, and Charlie loved the show. Part of her wondered if the Alpha was doing it for her, preening in a way. She sucked in her breath after Kal snared her waistband and worked the jeans' button. Sitting up with one arm holding her, she hooked Kal's wrist and slowed them. "Will you make love to me before fucking me?" She studied her lover's hungry features and watched them calm.

"*Ja.*" Kal composed herself, and a low but soothing thunder rolled in her chest. "Take off your shirt and lie back down for me."

Charlie nodded, leaned forward, and removed her shirt and breast wrap. After tossing them to the floor, she lowered herself into the soft blanket and released a strained breath. Often they'd wrestle for power until Kal dominated and fucked

Charlie into exhaustion. But tonight, Charlie already sensed Kal reining in her Alpha, and every touch was gentle.

Kal was slow and tender as she peeled away Charlie's skinny jeans. Her fingers twisted in Charlie's black panties, pulled them down, and traced her fingers along Charlie's thighs. Once rid of the satin underwear, she lowered onto her hands and crawled over Charlie. She adjusted her dark hair to one side, then dipped her head until her searing lips burned against Charlie's flushed stomach.

Clawing at the blanket, Charlie lifted her back and moaned as each kiss traveled higher, closer to her breasts. A soft nip to the underside of her breast caused her to gasp. She peered down at the smirking Alpha and whimpered in need. This time she wasn't told to beg or submit but was worshipped by her lover. Kal's rough hand closed over her right breast, rolling and pinching with the pressure. Arousal surged through Charlie, and she hissed after Kal bit her left nipple. She dug and dragged her heels into the bed, and wetness built between her legs.

"Sumner," she demanded, wanting and hot. Freeing a hand, she tangled her fingers into Kal's dark mane and urged her nipple deeper into Kal's hungry mouth. She groaned at the warm but coarse texture of Kal's tongue brushing across her sensitive skin. With her other hand, she grabbed her lover's toned ass cheek and growled at the thick material of the pants that separated her from the skin. She wanted the pants off, but Kal distracted her by switching to her other breast. Charlie moved her hand up and dug her nails into back muscles, earning a growl from her lover.

Kal sucked hard and fast against the nipple before releasing it. A low rumble vibrated deep in her chest as she trailed her nose upward to Charlie's throat. "You smell so sweet." She pushed her hips into Charlie's thighs, then tasted Charlie's burning flesh. Dragging her teeth over Charlie's pulse point, she nipped and bit the same spot.

Charlie sensed it was the location for a permanent bite mark. If their lives were different, Kal would already have sunk her canines in and tied Charlie to her. But the risks hung around their necks, like nooses ready to choke them if they made a mistake. Charlie whimpered at the unfairness of it, even though she felt crazy for wanting it. She opened her eyes and discovered promise in Kal's features.

"One day," Kal whispered, her voice firm and strong.

After a nod, Charlie guided Kal in for a long kiss that carried promises. She moaned each time their tongues danced together, not wanting their night to end. Between gasps she whispered, "Take off your pants." She shivered at Kal's wolfish smile and grabbed the annoying pants' button, but a hand halted her attempt.

"Soon." Kal redirected Charlie's hand to her back, then lowered to her left side next to Charlie. She hooked her left arm under Charlie and drew their bodies together until their heads touched.

Charlie turned toward her lover, touching and grabbing muscles. "You're so beautiful and handsome." She dragged her nails across Kal's toned stomach and felt every ounce of strength. "I don't want to stop touching you." She flushed from Kal's amused rumble and continued moving her hand closer to the prize. Sneaking her hand past the waistband, her fingertips grazed the base of Kal's penis until Kal hooked her wrist.

Kal snarled in Charlie's ear, warning her one last time. She returned Charlie's wandering hand to her stomach, then reached between their bodies. Her fingers slipped between the wetness and toyed with Charlie's swollen clit. She growled when Charlie started moaning and writhing beside her.

Charlie rolled onto her back and spread her legs open to give her lover better access. She cut her nails into Kal's outstretched forearm while her other hand wrenched into raven hair. "Oh gods." Panting, she screwed her eyes shut and struggled to be patient as Kal learned her clit. Kal had explored her body once before, but this was still new.

"You are so wet," Kal whispered into Charlie's ear with slight wonderment in her voice. She pressed her fingertips against Charlie's clit and rubbed it, hard and fast.

Crying out, Charlie rocked her hips to the motions. Passion curled low in her gut, and she clawed Kal's arm. "D-don't stop!" She gasped when teeth latched onto her ear, almost holding her still. A hungry growl caused her to tremble and scream until the orgasm sliced through her. Gasping for air, she latched onto Kal's hand and pressed it against her sex. "I just need a tick."

Kal pushed in closer and nibbled at Charlie's nape, purring near her ear. She inched her fingers lower until she found Charlie's entrance and spread the folds. She pushed a little, earning a moan from Charlie.

"Go inside, *krafka*." Charlie rolled her hips, urging Kal to take her. One finger slid into her, slowly but steadily. She held her breath, then released it after Kal went still. "Add another," she whispered her plea for more.

Kal pushed a second finger through the slick, velvet walls until they were both in deep. She gazed down at Charlie and watched her expressions. "You're always so tight." She grinned at Charlie's whimper, then slid her fingers toward the entrance. "Right here." She rubbed her fingertips against a certain spot that caused Charlie to melt beside her. "It's rough but sensitive here."

Charlie moaned long and hard until Kal paused to allow her to speak after a deep breath. "I-it's my G-spot." Saying it in Kalmarese sounded strange, but it was easier than using English. "That's what we call it." Her eyes rolled up when Kal started rubbing it again. "Oh gods, please." She arched her back but collapsed after Kal pushed her fingers forward.

Kal drew her fingers back, then drove them in and sent shockwaves through Charlie. She kept a steady pump and built Charlie's orgasm again.

Charlie jerked her hips and ground down on Kal's hand. She cried out each time Kal curled her fingers, wiring her body even more. Lifting her head, she crashed her lips into Kal's own. Her walls spasmed, then clenched around Kal's fingers when they plunged deeper. Charlie tried to break the kiss, but her scream was swallowed whole. Her body jerked and shook from the orgasm wracking her. She gulped for air and clung to her lover.

Kal nuzzled golden hair, inhaled deeply, and growled with intensity. Charlie continued quivering against her, and she pulled out her fingers with care. She rolled on top of Charlie and sheltered her while the orgasm's aftershocks faded away.

Charlie held onto Kal's broad shoulders and calmed her fluttering heart with deep breaths. She didn't want to lose this feeling, so she burned it into her memory, knowing she would need to remember one day. She wanted to stay here forever and hide away from the dangers. Charlie buried her selfish desires and peeked out from her safe place to discover Kal's insatiable but patient features.

"I'm going to check the fire," Kal whispered, a hint of question in her tone.

Charlie nodded and withdrew her hold, allowing her to go. "Don't be long." She grinned at the responding growl. Turning to her side, she watched Kal load wood into the fire to ensure it would burn for a few more hours. She wasn't quite used to the level of care that Kal offered her in several small ways. It was new and unfamiliar, almost foreign, to Charlie after so many years of being alone.

Kal returned to the bedside and paused next to Charlie. A slight furrow dug across her brow, as if thinking through a puzzle. "Are you tired?"

"*Joh.*" Charlie wanted to stay awake all night and fuck between naps. She suspected her tired body wouldn't allow it, but she would try her best. Tomorrow their relationship would revert to being a secret hidden in the shadows under everyone's noses. If nothing else, she could talk to Dorlon about it, at least she hoped.

"Good." Kal flashed a wolfish smile, then opened the first button of her pants. She reached for the next button but hesitated after her eyes locked with Charlie's own. "You enjoy watching me."

"Can you blame me?" Charlie indicated Kal's gorgeous body. "You're fucking ripped from head to toe."

Kal lifted an eyebrow and said, "It took me many years to become this."

Charlie smirked and licked her lips. "All your hard work is greatly appreciated on my end." She followed the line of muscles down to the fingers poised to undo another button. "And I love how hard you get there too." She jumped from the Alpha's throaty growl. "Those tight pants have to be killing you by now."

Kal freed the second button of the five. "This is helping." She freed the third button, then slid her left hand into the opening.

With wide eyes, Charlie watched on and moaned when Kal clutched the handful between her thighs. "*Vuk*," she whispered and gripped the side of the bed. "But it's not helping me." She grumbled at Kal's smug look.

Still, Kal worked the second to last button with her right hand, the extra room offering her the chance to move her hand more. She groaned, tilted her head back, and continued the movements hidden by the pants.

"Sumner," Charlie hissed, close to getting off the bed. She settled when Kal seemed to take pity on her and came over to the bedside.

Kal unhooked the last button, then pulled out her left hand with the hard shaft springing free. She massaged the tip, which was swollen and red with need. She lifted her dark eyes to Charlie, grinned, and extended her hips that brought the head closer to Charlie.

Accepting the invitation, Charlie grabbed the middle of the shaft, then brushed her lips over the sensitive tip. She kissed the head, tasting the spicy scent that was her lover. She wanted more, but Kal withdrew a step and continued massaging her cock. Pausing, she stripped the pants off and kicked them aside before coming to the bed again. "Get on your back."

Charlie didn't hear authority, not yet at least. Things were still slow between them, even playful. She wanted it to continue, so she rolled onto her back; then Kal grabbed her hips and turned her body until her ass nudged the edge of the bed. Peering down, she saw her lover standing between her legs.

Grabbing Charlie's right leg, Kal positioned it on her shoulder, then gripped Charlie's left ankle. She pulled Charlie an inch off the bed and rubbed the head of her cock between her slick folds to coat it. With hooded eyes, she grinned at Charlie's lustful whimpers.

"Oh fuck." Charlie rocked her hips and rubbed her clit against the tip of her lover's cock. "Oh gods that feels so good." She moaned louder when Kal pushed her hips forward but up, making the underside of her thick shaft massage Charlie's sensitive clit. She clutched Charlie's thigh near her chest to secure her. Yet Charlie managed to roll her aching clit against the hard length. With her head back, she kept working her clit and noticed that Kal remained still for a moment, letting her enjoy herself.

Unable to satisfy her craving, Charlie growled and dropped her ass down. "I need you to fuck me." She felt her heated demand pull at Kal's Alpha, and yet it wasn't enough. There was promise in Kal's eyes for later.

"Soon," Kal whispered. She then slipped the head past the entrance, spreading Charlie open. With gentle movement, she pushed forward until she found Charlie's G-spot and paused there, as if memorizing the spot.

Charlie lifted her head and peered down at the thick length protruding from her. She was greedy and ached for all of it. Confusion twisted her features when Kal didn't fuck her and didn't pound into her. Instead, her lover rocked her hips and started to rub the swollen head against Charlie's G-spot. Her heart leapt forward, and she squirmed from the beautiful sensation near her entrance.

"Oh gods, Sumner." Charlie clawed at the blanket and gulped for more air as she tried to survive the heat lancing through her body. "What are y-you doing?"

"Sit up and watch," Kal ordered without halting the short strokes of her cock inside Charlie.

Urging her strength, Charlie propped up her body with her elbows. Her eyes were fixed on Kal's cock easing in and out of her entrance, hitting her G-spot over and over.

"Does it feel good?"

"*J-ja.*" Charlie held her lower lip between her teeth until she was panting again. "It feels so good." It was new and different for her. Every shockwave raced up from her sex and burned in her chest, and she gasped louder. She tilted her head back and focused on the amazing sensation. Her moans were long and deep, until a single, sharp thrust made her scream. The strokes returned to short and delicate, building the pleasure at an intimate pace. Charlie loved every tiny bit of friction, and the pressure from the swollen head of Kal's cock hit her perfectly.

Earlier Kal had been focused and tested Charlie until she found the best rhythm. Now more confident, Kal increased the pace and gritted her teeth.

"Oh gods, fuck." Charlie shifted and watched the swollen head pushing and pulling near her entrance. She moaned and panted, noticing that Kal was echoing her. "Don't stop, please." She met Kal's gaze, then that invisible thread around her heart clenched with a different kind of need. "Don't ever stop," she whispered, a rawness cutting into her voice.

Kal responded with a deeper pump that elicited a cry from Charlie. "Mine," she growled and buried her nails into soft skin. Her Alpha shined in her eyes, and her canines flashed in the firelight. She jogged her hips faster, insisting Charlie orgasm on the head of her cock.

Charlie craned her neck and cried out as her lover drove her to the top. She was almost sure Kal's cock had swollen more as it banged harder against her G-spot. Her cries were harsh against her aching throat, but she didn't want this to end and fought off the orgasm. The rutting Alpha could have slammed into Charlie violently and without restraint. But instead, Kal remained in control and pleased her lover with a precise motion, stroking Charlie to her limit.

As her cries grew louder, Kal snarled and panted like a determined hunter. She increased the pressure against Charlie's G-spot with a rise of her hips. With three more hard strokes, Charlie broke in half and yelled, clawing at the blanket. Kal bared her clenched teeth and shoved her cock deeper during Charlie's orgasm.

Breathless and shaking, Charlie fell back and allowed the orgasm to envelope her. She felt her walls clench around Kal's cock to remain full and whole. After several deep breaths, she opened her eyes and looked up at the Alpha towering above her. She wanted Kal beside her or even on top of her.

Kal tested Charlie's tightness, pulling out with gentle movement. She dragged her nails along Charlie's thigh before releasing both legs and climbing onto the bed.

Charlie whimpered when her lover drew her farther into the bed and hid her from the world. Closing her eyes, she promised them both that she was going to rest for only a minute before she collected on the promise for a good fuck. But the security and warmth around her lulled her into a deep, peaceful sleep.

# Chapter 4

The dual suns hung low in the sky, announcing the start of a new day on the cooling planet. Charlie didn't mind it, even if she preferred to be in bed. Instead, she was guiding the two tacked horses from the stable to the front of the cabin. She stood and held the reins while she waited for her lover.

Everything around her was peaceful and whispered to her to remain here longer. A piece of her felt five years old again, wanting to stay at the cabin in hopes her parents would arrive soon. But she knew they were in the afterlife and ready for her return. *One day*, she told them, *just not right now*. Her thoughts were fragmented by the cabin door's creak, and she straightened up when Kal exited it.

In her hands, Kal held a large, iron padlock and an old key she inserted into it. She twisted once, then twice, and the padlock's shackle swung free. She turned to the door, jerked on the its handle, and worked the padlock into place.

Leaning to her right, Charlie watched her lover set the padlock, hindering anyone wanting to get into the cabin. There was very little to steal from the house or property, but a random person might take residence if they found it. The property's secret location reminded her of the cloth map in her jacket, which she fished out from the inside pocket.

Kal approached Charlie while tucking the padlock's key into her pants' pocket.

"I almost forgot." Charlie held out the abused map.

Kal accepted it and put it in the same spot as the key.

"Are you sure you're ready?" Charlie asked, zipping her jacket back up.

After a low rumble, Kal rested her hand on the sword hilt at her side. "*Ja.*"

Charlie gave a faint nod, and her attention traveled back to the locked cabin.

"You are not," Kal said.

Charlie sniffed, thanks to the cold air bothering her nose. "You think I want to give this up?" She signaled the beautiful landscape that hid them away from the scariness of Tarrak. "I could stay here… with you." She and Kal started putting the reins over the horses' heads, then mounted them. "For a long time," she whispered to herself.

Kal was first into the saddle, adjusting her body until she was comfortable. She peered over at Charlie and promised, "We'll return." She tapped the horse's side while saying, "And so will my rut."

Charlie frowned, still trying to get situated in the saddle. She hadn't ridden in the many years since Dorlon taught her, but most of the lessons returned to her. "Wait. What?" She urged her horse to follow the much larger, darker one. "Aren't you going to take suppressants now?"

Kal looked over at Charlie, who rode behind her along the trail. "Do you wish for me to take suppressants?"

"I feel like this is a trick question," Charlie replied and ducked under a low branch. "Do you really think you'll rut again? What if it was just a one-off thing?" She was rambling while her mind launched into thousands of directions at the idea of Kal rutting once every two noreds.

"Can you get more blockers?" Kal asked, peering over her shoulder at her lover.

Charlie blew out a breath, then urged her horse to ride next to Kal. "*Ja.* I can get more." She narrowed her eyes at Kal's thoughtful look. "Why?"

"Dorlon will want me to take the suppressants," Kal explained.

"To hide that you're rutting now," Charlie said, then shook her head. "But you don't want to. Why not? If people find out that you're rutting, then they'll ask why."

"Or who," Kal whispered and glanced at Charlie. "But I'm an Alpha."

Charlie's shoulders fell, and she sympathized with Kal's need to be an Alpha. "*Ja.* You're more than just a god." She stretched out her arm, squeezed Kal's knee, and withdrew when the horses distanced themselves. "So you want to use the blockers as a compromise. Do you really think that'll get Dorlon off your back?" She was startled by Kal's snarl, then she realized how her question sounded to an Alpha. "I meant to get Dorlon to stop hassling you about suppressants."

Kal chuffed and glanced at Charlie. "*Joh.* But it's the only option I'm willing to take."

Charlie worked her jaw a few times, almost ready to speak as she tried understanding Kal's intent with the blockers. "You want to be an Alpha and rut into me." She blushed and squirmed in the saddle when Kal revealed her wolfish smile. "Sumner, I…." She had no idea what she wanted to say and faltered for a moment.

"I will take the suppressants if that's what you wish," Kal offered, her tone neutral again.

"*Joh.* I don't want you taking something you're against," Charlie argued as her heart beat harder.

"But if you—"

"I'm not against it," Charlie interrupted, then sighed and stared straight ahead. "I'm just worried it's an increased risk that someone will find out what's going on."

"I can manage it," Kal promised.

Charlie peered over and studied her lover's confident features, then put her trust into Kal's abilities. "All right." She nodded with firmness and said, "We'll go with the blockers if you rut again."

"I will rut."

Licking her lips, Charlie eyed Kal across the space between them. "How sure are you of that?"

"Completely." Kal was smug and prideful, a true Alpha at her core.

Charlie blew out a breath, and her body hummed from Kal's cocky attitude. Her eyes dropped to Kal's crotch in search of the bulge behind the saddle's horn.

Kal snarled and leaned in the saddle toward Charlie. "Don't make my ride back any more uncomfortable."

Smirking, Charlie bit down on a snarky reply. "We can always take a break if you need one." She jerked after another growl, but she shrugged it off. "Just a thought." She urged her horse to the front when the path narrowed again, passing orange and yellow leaves.

* * *

Charlie guided her horse up to Kal, who was seated high on the stationary gelding. She frowned at Kal's serious demeanor and pulled back on the reins when close enough. "What's up?"

Kal raised an eyebrow at the Earthling slang, but replied, "We're not far from the main road." She tilted her head when she turned her gaze forward. "We'll need to separate."

"Right." Charlie frowned and whispered, "We can't ride into Tarrak together." She shifted in the saddle and considered the options. "Well, I should probably find Raine and see if she has any idea where I'm staying. I kind of blew out of there without saying anything." She had a guilty smile. "I'll go through the Koblenz Gate."

Kal responded with a rumble, then narrowed her eyes at Charlie. "You have your weapons?"

"*Ja*. I'll be fine."

After a single nod, Kal said, "Then you should go now."

Charlie parted her lips, but she sighed and returned the nod once she accepted their separation. Already they were shifting to their former roles as ruler and mercenary, and it sliced into Charlie. She toyed with the reins and tapped the horse's sides, urging the animal to take her to the city.

"Charlie?"

Pulling on the reins, Charlie peered over her shoulder at her lover. A spark of hope grew in her while she studied Kal, who was both beautiful and strong. She almost crumbled at the idea that they would have to pretend they were nothing to each other, even after unlocking each other's secrets.

"I will find you after I arrive."

With a faint smile, Charlie urged the horse to go before she broke down and asked for more. She rode the horse at a hard canter now that the trees and brush were thinning out. The ride to the main road was only ten minutes; then she continued the fast pace toward Tarrak, putting distance between her and Kal.

The cobblestone road was dotted with other travelers, mostly people hauling supplies between cities, towns, and villages. The goods and wares were stored in wagons, pulled by different animals like horses or a larger animal called a *pooren* that was a cross between an ox and bear from Earth. They were large, furry beasts with horns and the strength to pull heavy loads. Often the *pooren* provided a level of security due to their razor teeth and claws. Charlie had forgotten the size of the beasts when she passed a double wagon towed by three of them. She slowed her horse and gave them a wide berth, then greeted the two Alphas merchants.

After passing several small merchant wagons, she counted three hover vehicles with patrolling soldiers. She wasn't far from the city, so she kept her horse at a steady walk. In the distance, she could see initial signs of buildings of the old capital beyond the trees. If she continued on this path, she would enter the through the Great Gate, but Charlie steered the horse to a side road that wrapped around the city and went to the other southern gate along the Koblenz River. The southern gate was used by merchants bypassing the city's busy streets.

Foot soldiers at the Koblenz Gates eyed the travelers but hassled few, including Charlie. Once in the city, she was forced to dismount and guide the horse through the traffic. But luck was on her side as she neared the bustling market and found Raine at her usual spot. She noticed Raine was busy talking to a customer, so she located a spot to hitch her horse. Removing her techbit from her saddlebag, she turned it on and reconnected it to the planet's satellite communications.

Chewing her lower lip, Charlie watched the applications and notifications load, including a message from Sallarus. She almost tapped it when Raine's voice made her lower the device.

"Well, look who surfaced." Raine stood with her arms folded, head tilted, and eyes narrowed. "Here I thought you changed your mind and had Magnar pick you up after all."

Charlie pocketed the techbit and glared at her friend. "I made a promise." She warmed her hands in her jacket's pockets and shrugged at Raine's suspicious look. "I had to take care of some business." *Gods that sounds so lame.*

"Right." Coming closer, Raine didn't believe Charlie's excuse and indicated the horse with a chin nod. "Nice horse too."

Charlie patted the horse's neck and said, "She's Dorlon's ride."

Raine rolled her eyes and dropped her arms. "Of course she rides instead of using hover transportation."

"Sorry for vanishing," Charlie offered in hopes that Raine wouldn't push the conversation. "Something came up that I had to handle."

Raine held up her hands in defeat, then dropped them. "I get it. It's cool." She glanced over her shoulder to check her stall, but Chris wasn't swamped by customers. "So what now?"

"I was going to ask you the same thing." Charlie lifted her shoulders high and rocked on her boots. "I don't know where I'm staying or what I'm doing for the next six noreds."

"I have room for you at my place." Raine pointed at Chris from over her shoulder and said, "I rent out a place outside the city for me and Chris." She lowered her hand. "It's on a farm."

"A farm?" Charlie echoed.

Raine sighed and glowered at Charlie's attitude. "We just stay there. Repair some of the tech there, then sell shit here. We go back to New Earth for a nored or two at a time to see family and friends."

Scratching her nose, Charlie tried imaging such a life, and she shook her head. "No wonder you're still single."

Raine sputtered and went wide eyed before pointing at her chest. "Me? How about you?" She laughed, then teased, "I'd date me before I'd date you."

Crinkling her nose, Charlie said, "Same." She puckered her lips and asked, "So what am I supposed to do for the next six noreds?"

"Oh. Well, that's more your problem than mine," Raine replied, her voice playful and eyes gleaming.

"Raine, come on." Charlie held out her arms while keeping her hands in the jacket pockets. "I will get bored out of my mind."

"Fine, fine. You can help me with my business." Raine nodded toward it and revealed, "Chris has been talking about taking a long break and staying in New Earth. I think his girlfriend is over the long distance thing."

Charlie chuckled, then peered around Raine at the busy stall that had a variety of Alphas and Omegas poking through things. "Sell tech, huh?" She pursed her lips and considered her ability to sell things besides mercenary jobs. "I can do that." *At least for now*, she thought, *until I get really bored*. She wanted to ask more, but Raine's attention shifted to something behind Charlie. Her heart thrummed and a low hum grew stronger in her body. She already knew who it was but confirmed Kal's presence with a glance.

All around them, the crowd of people paused upon seeing their godly ruler; then they continued their business in the market. Raine was staring at the ruler like she was a foreigner among them. Charlie was almost inclined to jab her friend in the ribs.

"*Turen*, Charlie."

Dipping her head, Charlie said, "*Turen,* Kal." She frowned at Raine's awed look, then cleared her throat. "I guess you didn't really get a chance to properly meet my friend the other day."

Kal stood tall with her hands in front of her body and stony features set on Charlie before she turned them to Raine. "*Joh.*"

Charlie nodded and indicated her childhood friend. "This is Raine Ramos. We met as kids on the *Liberator.*" She let go of her tension when Raine worked herself out of her stupor and held out her arm to Kal, who clasped it.

Kal's grip was firm, showing her respect to Raine.

With a curious stare, Raine held longer than necessary and asked, "Have we met before?" Her eyes seemed lost in the past.

Kal released arms and replied, "Not that I'm aware of."

Charlie frowned after the strange introduction and eyed Raine, who was working through something. She made a mental note to ask Raine about it later. "So Raine and I were just going over what I'll be doing for the next six noreds while I'm stuck here." She held down her body's natural response to Kal's throaty rumble. "Apparently she needs help selling more tech."

"A lot more," Raine joked, grinning at her friend.

Charlie nodded, then turned to Kal. "And I'll be staying with her at a farm. She rents housing there."

Kal stood rigid, her hands linked in front of her again and features indifferent. "What farm?"

With a raised eyebrow, Charlie looked to her friend and wondered the same thing.

"It's a farm to the east," Raine replied, her tone stern now.

"Who is the Alpha?" Kal asked further.

Charlie heard her lover's authority seeping into her voice. She hoped Raine gave a clearer answer, or else Kal's meager self-control might pop.

"His name is Taden." Raine folded her arms, and a furrow creased her brow. "I rent a small cabin on his property."

Kal responded with a low rumble, then said, "*Ja,* I'm aware of Starlight Farm." She turned to Charlie and canted her head. "Dorlon requires her horse so she can return to Kardos."

"Right," Charlie whispered and turned to her friend. "What time do you leave?"

"About an hour before sunset. It's a twenty minute walk to Taden's farm." Raine smirked and said, "Tell Dorlon I said *turen*."

Charlie grinned but nodded. "All right." She unhitched the horse's reins. "I'll be back by then." She guided the horse away but overhead Kal and Raine's final exchange.

"*Tah* for assisting Charlie on her rescue mission."

"It's what family does for each other," Raine said, pride coloring her statement.

Charlie smiled to herself and blinked away the sting in her eyes from Raine's sentiment. She continued walking toward the Great Tower, and Kal came to her side after a moment. "How is Dorlon?"

"She wishes to speak to us both," Kal replied.

Frowning, Charlie glanced up at her lover, but Kal wore a neutral mask. "That doesn't sound good." She raked her fingers through her hair and sighed at the pending conversation. Kal's silence confirmed her suspicions, but she kept a cool head while they walked to the stable near the barrack. She untacked the horse, shouldered her saddlebags, and followed Kal to the Great Tower's main entrance.

They went to the lift on the next level and rode it up to the office. As the quiet minutes passed between them, Charlie fidgeted more with her jacket or belt or anything within reach. She wanted to ask what Dorlon needed to talk about, but they would be there soon. Following Kal out of the elevator, they entered the office, which was left unguarded for the first time.

Inside, Dorlon was standing beside the burning fireplace and was staring in it until Charlie and Kal arrived. Kal sealed and bolted the two doors, then took Charlie's saddlebags and placed them on the desk. Charlie swallowed when Dorlon approached them, but Kal's presence halted her worries.

"So what happens now?" Dorlon asked, breaking the strained silence. Her piercing gaze flickered from Charlie to Kal, expecting an honest answer. "You didn't knot her." She ignored Kal's displeased rumble and asked, "When will you return to outer space, Charlie?"

"Actually, not any time soon," Charlie replied. "I'm here for the next six noreds." She held back a laugh at Dorlon's bulging eyes. "I made a promise to Raine that I'd stay if she helped me rescue Starr."

"What?" Dorlon snapped and neared Charlie with a curled lip. "You're joking." But Kal halted her advance by moving behind Charlie in warning. "This can't happen," she said, her voice tight. Her attention went to Kal, and she said, "Charlie has to return to space. She's can't stay on Kander."

Charlie closed her eyes when dark heat rushed through her veins, and she grabbed Kal's forearm in time. She stilled Kal's initial reaction to Dorlon's demands. "I don't think that's really going to be an option." Struggling to keep her tone even, she looked at Dorlon and whispered, "We've decided to continue our relationship." *Or whatever it is.* Somehow announcing it as a relationship cemented it in Charlie's mind.

"Are you both suicidal?" Dorlon asked, baring her teeth.

Withdrawing her hand, Charlie allowed Kal to handle Dorlon, because she wasn't considered anyone of importance on Kander. She was a piece of space trash that crashed on the planet. In need of distance, she separated from the pair.

"Charlie is welcome on Kander," Kal declared, thunder filling the room. "And she will continue sharing my bed."

Charlie stood next to the sofa's side, turned, and watched the two warring over her in a battle of wills. She rubbed her brow and almost spoke up, but Dorlon beat her.

"This will only fuel the revolt," Dorlon hissed.

"*If* word spreads."

Dorlon shook her head, then asked, "Does anyone besides me know about this?"

"Andren," Kal replied.

"Andren!" Dorlon growled, moved away, and spun around toward Kal. "What are you thinking with bringing her into it?"

"She doesn't know know," Charlie cut in but faltered when Dorlon's fiery gaze turned to her. "Well, she probably does know because she's taken me to Kal's quarters at night or been there when I left in the morning."

Dorlon snarled with certain venom, canines on display, and looked between the pair. "Is there anyone else that *might* know?"

Charlie flinched and whispered, "Probably Lurain and the Carnec Omega who guarded me."

"Rybeck," Dorlon supplied, huffing and hissing at the news before focusing on Kal. "You could have any Kalmar for a lover. Any!" She was fuming and glanced at Charlie once before she whispered, "Why?"

Charlie clenched her hands at her side and tensed as Kal approached Dorlon. She tried calming her pounding heart, but she had no choice but to watch and listen.

"Because Charlie gave me back pieces of my old life," Kal whispered softly that Charlie almost missed it.

Dorlon closed her eyes, bowed her head, and whispered, "Sumner." She peered up and studied Kal for a quiet minute. "I remember the first day we met outside your village. You were so different from most Alphas I'd met before."

Kal tilted her head and seemed intrigued by the past dancing along Dorlon's features. "You remember it."

"Only after Charlie spoke your old name to me. Before that, it was gray and broken." Dorlon went silent, but her stare with Kal never wavered. "This could kill you both." She revealed a frown to Charlie.

"*Ja*, maybe." Charlie folded her arms and leaned against the sofa. "Or maybe it'll work out okay."

"What makes you think it'll work out?" Dorlon asked, her features both open and worried.

"Faith," Charlie replied. "Something has to go right in my life *for once*."

Dorlon's shoulders fell, then she sighed and went over to the lit fireplace. "When this gets out…" She looked between the pair. "… and it will get out."

"I will handle it," Kal said, authority seeping into her statement.

Dorlon scrubbed her face with her palm and said, "We need to get suppressants."

Charlie cringed and waited for Kal to handle that detail. If Dorlon didn't implode now, it would be a miracle.

"I won't take suppressants."

Dorlon started to growl, but she was outmatched by Kal's snarl. She was forced to surrender, turning her head to the side.

Charlie groused at the posturing between her lover and childhood friend. Her grip on the sofa was the only thing keeping her from inserting herself between them. It was dangerous to step between two battling Kalmar. Once Dorlon submitted to Kal, Charlie released a breath and said, "Sumner agreed to take the blockers."

Dorlon was quiet and returned Kal's hard stare, but she held back her aggression.

Sighing, Charlie neared them and hoped to calm them both before relationships were damaged by the argument. "Dorlon, I think we can manage this."

"What if you're wrong?" Dorlon tore her eyes away and looked at Charlie. "*You* could jeopardize everything that Kal has worked toward."

Charlie's eyes fluttered a few times, then she shook her head and whispered, "Maybe you're right. Maybe I should return to outer space." Her lover's growl caused her to flinch, but she pushed the conversation further. "I mean, who I am to fuck up this planet's peace and wreck everything Kal has done to move it forward?"

Dorlon slumped and whispered, "Charlie."

Looking up to Kal, Charlie said, "I'm being selfish and stupid about this. Nothing ever goes well when I get involved." She swallowed, but her voice became hoarse. "I belong to the stars." She broke away and headed to the sealed doors until her escape path was blocked by her lover. Tilting her head back, she met the piercing green eyes that touched her spirit.

"You belong to me."

Charlie's heart jumped into her throat before it started drumming in her chest. Kal's possessive declaration twisted the string in Charlie to the point that she started to tremble. "Sumner, I—"

"You agreed." Kal shifted closer, invading Charlie's space.

"I know, but I can't be the cause of your people's self-destruction," Charlie whispered. Even the idea was weighing on her and crushing her shoulders.

Kal chuffed, then said, "Dorlon is wrong. I have faith that this will work."

Gazing up at her lover, Charlie was able to pick out the confidence and certainty in Kal, who was usually reserved. "You wouldn't risk your people if you thought it would end badly," she murmured in realization and lowered her head, thinking about the future.

"But if you truly wish to return to the stars, I will not stop you."

Charlie bit her bottom lip, then clenched her hands at her side and resisted the need to touch Kal. The more she considered leaving Kal, the more her heart felt like it was being ripped apart by a torture rack. "I want you," she said, her voice rasping after confessing the truth.

Kal's heavy rumble broke the silence, and she drew Charlie into her body.

Ignoring Dorlon's presence, Charlie hooked her arms around Kal and leaned into the comfort. She inhaled a few deep breaths, which settled the shaking in her limbs.

"Stay," Kal breathed into Charlie's ear. After Charlie nodded, Kal purred low and nuzzled her temple.

After separating from Kal, she faced Dorlon and felt Kal pressing against her back, still relying on her Alpha instincts to support Charlie. "Dorlon, we need your help." She watched how Dorlon's attention flickered between her and Kal. "*Krafka.*"

Dorlon sighed and shook her head at them. "All right." She held out her arms and asked, "What do you need me to do?" She raised an eyebrow, directing it at Kal.

Charlie peered over her shoulder at the ruler, who had an evil smile.

"I need you to return to Kardos." Kal remained behind Charlie, even though her presence filled the room. "We need to handle Alpha Prime first."

Pursing her lips, Charlie listened to them and held back her questions about Alpha Prime. From Kal's tone, they were a problem, possibly a major one.

Dorlon nodded. "I do need to return, now that you both are healthy." She came closer to them, revealing tight facial lines. She studied them for a moment and said, "I don't want to lose either of you, let alone both of you." Her eyes cut up to Kal. "I also don't want what you've worked toward to fall apart now."

"We've worked for," Kal argued. "Your teachings and support have gone a long way."

Dorlon bowed her head, then she smiled at Charlie. "So you'll be here for the next six noreds. I hope you come visit me in Kardos."

"That's part of the agreement," Charlie said. "By the way, Raine says *turen*." She noticed a slight pinkness dust Dorlon's cheeks, and she almost questioned it until Dorlon stepped around her.

"I should be going."

"When I receive word from Alpha Prime, I will message you." Kal walked Dorlon to the doors, unbolting them. "Continue with double patrols."

At the mention of messages, Charlie fished out her techbit and recalled the unread response from Sallarus. She ignored Kal and Dorlon's chatter as she opened the message and skimmed through it. Frowning, she jerked her attention to Dorlon, who was saying goodbye to her. She pocketed the device and hastened to her friend, giving her a hug. "*Tah* for your help, Dor."

Returning the hug's strength, Dorlon whispered, "Stay strong." She offered a last smile before she departed the office.

Charlie noticed that Kal didn't ask her to leave and was sliding the latch back into place. She retrieved her techbit and pulled up Sallarus's message. "Take a look at this." She handed it over to Kal, whose larger hand dwarfed the device. "Sallarus said there hasn't been any talk about the Sworne. There's actually more talk about Serrato Corps buying supplies in every quadrant of the galaxy. In the past rotation, they've ramped up selling slaves for stills or trade."

Kal grumbled, then returned the techbit to Charlie. "Can Sallarus find out what kind of supplies?"

"Possibly." Charlie rubbed her chin, then started responding to Sallarus's message until another thought came to mind. "If I keep asking for information, he's going to want stills." She watched her lover approach her desk, noticed Kal's hesitation, and lowered the techbit. "You have something on your mind."

Kal turned, sat on the corner of the desk, and folded her arms. "I have another mission for you."

Charlie narrowed her eyes and pointed the techbit at her lover. "Not that I'm against a job and more stills, but I'm kind of shipless and crewless."

"I can take care of that," Kal said, thunder rolling in her chest.

After putting the device in her pocket again, Charlie approached Kal and bit her lower lip. "All right. I'll bite. What's this job?"

"I want you to kidnap Victor."

Charlie felt her jaw loosen, but she snapped it shut and continued to stare at Kal. She laughed in surprise and asked, "You're serious?"

"*Ja.*"

Blowing out a huff, Charlie combed her fingers through her blond strands. Her mind reeled at the idea, and part of her was already scheming how to kidnap him.

"I need to know what he knows about the Sworne and Serrato Corps's plans," Kal said.

Charlie folded her arms and considered Kal's goal, nodding after a moment. "*Ja.*"

"How quickly can you obtain a ship?"

Charlie frowned and replied, "Well, I have to find a buyer for that darakar before I can purchase a ship." She rubbed the back of her neck.

Kal pushed off the desk, went around it, and pulled out a tablet from the drawer. While tapping on it, she asked, "How fast can you get a ship if you already have the stills in hand?"

Charlie blinked, then eyed her lover. "Three to seven days, no more than a nineth."

Looking up from the tablet, Kal said, "Kander will purchase the ship. You'll captain it."

Again, Charlie's jaw slackened before she shook away the awe. "Um, and a crew?"

"Raine will join you. I'm sure she'll be concerned about your returning to Kander to fulfill your promise."

Sputtering, Charlie realized that Kal had already thought through all the hurdles. "How long have you been planning this?"

"Since my ride from the cabin to the city." Kal returned her attention to the tablet, tapping the screen.

Shaking her head, Charlie neared the desk and stood opposite her lover. She admired Kal's ability to work through a problem and prepare for the future, such as the Sworne. "I need to figure out how to get to Victor." She was more used to rescuing than to kidnapping. In Victor's case, he was surrounded by military personnel, which made it a hundred times more difficult. On top of it, Charlie had already hit Serrato Corps, so they would be more vigilant now. But there was one advantage Charlie could exploit. She smirked and whispered, "Starr. I can use Starr to draw out Victor."

Kal had a smug look and cradled the tablet between her hands. "*Ja* that will work well. I suggest setting up a meeting point."

"Then ambush him," Charlie whispered, liking the plan formulating between them. "Only problem is that he'll come with soldiers. Between me, Raine, and Starr that won't be enough."

"You'll take a unit with you," Kal said.

"A unit of your soldiers?" Charlie asked, stunned that Kal would send more Kalmar into outer space. "Sumner, I don't know if—"

"It's the best option. You will need trained soldiers to apprehend Victor."

Charlie admitted it ensured the capture of Victor, so she conceded with the idea. "All right. But it needs to be a team that'll listen to me and those I can trust. I don't want the same shit that happened with Andren repeated."

Kal dipped her head, seeming to accept Charlie's rules. "And Andren will accompany you."

"*Joh*." Charlie fisted her hands and started to fume at the idea. "There's no way I'm taking her after what happened last time."

Kal set the tablet on the desk and moved into Charlie's space. "She is someone you can trust with your life."

Looking away, Charlie tried to get a grip on her temper and folded her arms. "I know I can trust her with my life. I just…." She clenched her hands against her body. When she noticed Kal's patient features, she realized the ruler always gave Charlie the chance to open up. "I'm kind of used to being in command on my ship and with my team. Everyone listens to my orders. The fact that your orders superseded mine really got under my skin."

"I understand now." With a straight back, Kal said, "I apologize for preempting your command."

Charlie sensed that Kal, as a leader, understood Charlie's distress and concerns with giving secretive orders to Andren. Kal's sincere apology loosened the weight from beneath the suffocating anger. "*Tah*. I'm sorry you felt you needed to go to those lengths to protect me from myself. I won't be so reckless from now on." She mirrored Kal's slight smile after they worked through their differences, but then she sighed and said, "Andren can come. I'll kiss and make up with her." She nearly jumped out of her skin from Kal's ferocious snarl and realized her mistake. "It's just an expression!" Holding up her hands, she hastened to explain herself. "I'm not really going to kiss her."

Kal huffed deep and low before picking up the tablet again, tapping it. "Will five hundred thousand stills be enough for a ship?"

Charlie held her breath at the huge amount of money and thought about the various spaceship options on the market. "It depends on what you need it to do. If I'm taking soldiers, then it should be a transporter ship large enough to hold everyone. They build ships that are like mini barracks with sharable quarters." She leaned against the desk, still deep in thought. "I'd say anywhere from two hundred to three hundred thou."

"Let me know what you find, then we'll make the purchase," Kal said. "I'll give the seller extra if they bring it here sooner."

With a raised eyebrow, Charlie realized the urgency Kal felt to get her hands on Victor. "All right. I'll send out messages to a few of my contacts." She narrowed her eyes, unable to stop herself. "What are you going to do with this ship after the job is done?"

"Prepare for a war," Kal replied and walked around the desk.

With a slack jaw, Charlie turned toward the ruler. "Wait. Wait." She held out her hand toward her lover. "You just can't say that and end the conversation."

"It's too early, and I don't have enough information until you get Victor for me." Kal set the tablet on the desk, then picked up the saddlebags. "You should return this to Dorlon. She will need them soon."

"Right," Charlie whispered as she picked up the bags and shouldered them. "I'll let you know what I hear about ships for sale." Kal was in ruler mode, and Charlie would have to prod Kal another time. "Sumner…?" When Kal focused on her, she insisted, "There's time to get ready and be ready." If the Sworne weren't in the galaxy yet, then there was hope.

"I know."

Charlie nodded, then headed to the doors. Just as she pushed one open, Kal called to her.

"We'll discuss the price for this job later."

Charlie turned halfway and gave Kal a smug look. "Oh, I already know what the price will be."

# Chapter 5

After a brief visit with Dorlon, Charlie exited the Hall of the Commanders and returned to Raine's stall in the market. There was only an hour left before sunset, and Charlie felt drained from the busy day. Raine and Chris shut down the stall, packaged up their wares, and loaded them into a wooden cart. Chris took it upon himself to walk the cart so that Charlie and Raine could talk during the journey to Taden's farm.

"When do you want to go to New Earth?"

Charlie was uneasy to answer, given her new job from Kal. She wanted to discuss it with Raine but didn't know if Chris was trustworthy. "Maybe in a nored. What you think?"

"Well…" Raine glanced back at Chris, then shrugged and replied, "Chris wanted to take time off and go up there. I was thinking when he comes back, we could go. We could stay through Christmas."

At the mention of the holiday, Charlie nearly tripped on the gravel as they passed the Great Gate. "C-christmas?" She sputtered and tried imagining celebrating the holiday she gave up after Earth's destruction.

Raine lifted an eyebrow and eyed her friend. "Look, I know it's not your favorite, but I think it'll be good."

"You're really taking this to the bank for helping me rescue Starr."

Raine walked closer to Charlie and teased, "I thought it'd be nice for two sisters to spend the holidays together." She hooked an arm across Charlie's shoulders, jerking her closer.

Charlie growled and broke the contact before she said, "Fine." She couldn't argue, especially with the upcoming kidnapping mission. She prayed that Raine would join her, even though Chris wouldn't be around to watch the stall in the market. "Just don't expect me to sing Christmas carols."

Raine laughed and shook her head. "*Joh*. I remember how horrible your singing voice is."

Rolling her eyes, Charlie elbowed her friend, then mentioned, "I told Dorlon you said *turen*." She bit back a grin and watched Raine's passive features, searching for a hint.

"How is she?" Raine asked.

Charlie shrugged. "She is her usual self. Dramatic and worried about the future."

Raine grunted and slipped her hands into her pockets.

Recalling Dorlon's voiced concerns, Charlie struggled with getting more involved with the uprising in Kardos that was trickling across the planet. She preferred to keep her head in the stars, but her relationship with Kal was grounding her. Always too nosy, she allowed her curiosity to get the better of her. "Do you know anything about a revolt going on in Kardos?" When Raine frowned, Charlie had her answer.

"It's just another ripple in the pond," Raine replied. "Each year, it seems like the ripple is getting smaller."

"What if it's not?" Charlie countered. "What if this one is bigger?"

Raine sighed and shrugged. "Well, the fighting in Kardos has stopped. But the tensions are still there." She tilted her head and studied Charlie. "Have you heard something different?"

"Just what Dorlon told me." Charlie mimicked Raine's shrug, then said, "I heard it's the Alphas that are stirring the pot."

"*Ja*. It seems to be only the Alphas who are arguing with Earthlings. They were the ones to start calling us Betas." Raine swept a piece of curly hair behind her ear. "There's been hate crimes and murders against Earthlings."

"Rape?" Charlie asked. As a kid, there were countless incidents of male Earthlings being kidnapped and raped by Alphas. It was rare that a female Earthling was taken and raped, as they didn't want to sire a hybrid bastard. The memories caused goose bumps to prickle across her back.

"*Joh.* That stopped after this new Kal took power," Raine replied. "There'd always been an unspoken law that Alphas couldn't rape Omegas, but they didn't see it that way with us. When the new Kal took power, she made it a law that Alphas would be publicly castrated if they raped any human."

Charlie cringed and whistled low at the punishment. Alphas would never cross the line and lose their most precious piece of equipment. "Kal doesn't fuck around." She flushed at the accidental innuendo.

"*Joh.* She's actually pretty badass," Raine said. "It was cool to meet her."

"Have you met her before?" Charlie asked, recalling how Raine acted when she met Kal in the marketplace.

"Maybe?" Raine had a furrow across her brow. "She seemed really familiar but not sure why."

Charlie didn't push the conversation. Raine led the way onto a well-traveled road meant for one-way traffic. The cart's wooden wheels fit perfectly into the deep ruts. The road cut through a pasture on one side and a farm field on the right. About halfway down, trees stood tall like guards on either side of the road. Ahead was a large, stone home with falling white plaster on the front that showed its age. The black shutters were closed, blocking the already cool evening.

"It's beautiful," Charlie murmured. "Does the family just farm or…?"

"Actually they train and sell horses. They also grow crops, vegetables, and fruits to sell in the market." Raine pointed to the right of the main house and said, "Over there is a small cabin that I rent from Taden."

Charlie recalled that Taden was the Alpha, who owned the farm. "What's the name of the farm again?"

"It's called Starlight Farm," Raine answered, grinning at Charlie. "I call it Middle of Nowhere Farm."

Charlie laughed and shrugged at both the name and nickname. "I think that's most farms around here."

"It's home sweet home." Raine turned around and walked backwards. "Go to the barn first?" Chris agreed, and they went to the left of the house, passing more tall trees until they came upon the open barn.

After Chris tucked the cart to one side in the barn, Charlie snared her duffle bag and joined them outside. "So what's for dinner?"

Raine laughed and hooked Charlie again, pulling their bodies together. "Nothing but the best. *Cheeseburgers*, *fries*, and a cold *soda*."

Chris laughed, indicating that Raine was lying to Charlie.

"I was hoping for *pizza* honestly," Charlie teased.

"I call it in for delivery," Chris bantered back. His smile was big and playful as he walked alongside them.

Charlie groaned at the idea of eating pizza again after loving it as a kid. "I want to eat just one last *pizza* before I die." *Die again*, her mind whispered.

Raine squeezed her friend's side and said, "Maybe you'll get lucky."

Rolling her eyes, Charlie followed Raine and Chris to the A-frame style cabin set behind the main house. Once inside, Charlie took stock of it and decided quaint was the best description for it. The door opened into an entryway that led to the kitchen, which had a wooden table. The kitchen's open space spilled into a great sitting room with a stone hearth and tall windows exposing the dense woods. Off to the right was a short hallway with two doors. One was to a bedroom and the other to a washroom. A second bedroom was located in a loft over the kitchen. The loft was Raine's space and where Charlie would stay during her visit.

Standing at the foot of the large bed, Charlie realized she would be sharing it with Raine and folded her arms. There was plenty of space, but Charlie was accustomed to sleeping alone—mostly. She felt Raine's judgmental stare behind her.

"Or you can sleep on the sofa downstairs."

Toying with the duffle bag's strap, Charlie considered the hard-looking sofa downstairs, then shook her head. "*Joh* this is great." She ignored Raine's smirk and whispered, "Cozy."

"You still suck at lying." Raine turned and pointed at the wide dresser against the far wall. "There's room in there for your stuff." Thumbing over her shoulder, she said, "There's also a trunk that has space too."

Charlie nodded and took the hint to unpack.

"I'm going to cook something for us." Raine headed to the wooden, spiral stairs that went down to the sitting room, but she paused at hearing Charlie's voice.

"*Tah*, Raine."

* * *

After sipping on her drink, Charlie set the wooden mug on the table to her right. She continued typing out a message to several dealers, who could provide her, or rather Kander, with a new ship. She was unsure how Kal planned to purchase a spaceship, but once word spread that Kander owned one, rumors would fly around the galaxy. Kalmar were not a space-faring species, and anything different would fan the gossip windmill. Setting aside her concerns, Charlie looked away from the dancing flames in the fireplace and finished the message, while the others chatted on the sofa.

Charlie reread the message she wrote. It made no mention of Kander purchasing a new ship; she'd only explained that she needed a replacement. It was best to make it look like the purchase was coming from Charlie, not the ruler of Kander. As her finger hovered over the Send button, she realized the satellite signal was weak at her spot in the living room; so she moved to the closest tall window beside the fireplace. Once the signal increased, she sent the message to her contacts.

"Charlie, what are you doing?" Raine had a raised eyebrow and suspicion darkened her features.

"Work." Charlie shut off the techbit's screen and shoved it in her pocket. "Looking into a new spaceship for later."

Raine shook her head.

"Raine said you're staying here for several noreds," Chris said.

Charlie dipped her head in agreement. "*Ja*."

"Sorry your ship got blown up." Chris sat with his mug and studied Charlie. "I saw when it happened."

Charlie suspected many people on Kander saw the explosion after the *Pacifica* lit up the sky from its spot in orbit. She tried to keep the memories of the crash landing at bay.

"You're lucky you made it." Chris had a sympathetic expression that eased Charlie's nerves about him.

"Just a rough landing." Charlie hoped to brush it aside, but Raine's piercing gaze told her that she failed to convince her friend. They'd known each other for far too long, and it made Charlie vulnerable and transparent. She looked away and studied the fire before Raine said something.

"I think I'm going to get some rest." Chris finished off his drink, then offered to take Raine's mug too. He deposited the two dirty cups in the sink and called goodnight to the women.

"See you in the morning, Chris." Raine watched him before she turned her hard stare to Charlie.

Swallowing the last of the *kello*, Charlie whispered, "What?"

"You know what," Raine replied, then stood up. "I'll be upstairs when you're ready to talk."

Charlie listened to her friend's heavy boot steps going up to the loft. She stared into the fire and sipped on the last bit of the herbal drink. It was nice to be alone for a moment and consider recent changes in her life. She grabbed the techbit, popped out the headphones, and inserted them in her ears.

After finding one of her mother's favorite songs in the music library, she tapped it.

Tori Amos's beautiful voice filled Charlie, but the song made her heart ache. She hummed Crucify's lyrics and stared into the fire, lost in her memories. Somehow her life had altered course, and she was still shaken by it. Peering down at the techbit in her lap, she tapped the screen and searched for the Kander clock.

The first clock on the screen was for the galaxy, which was created by the Jerothian, who based it on the black hole at the center of their system. Swiping up, Charlie frowned at the useless clock that tracked Earth time as if it still existed. Today was September twenty-eighth on Earth in the year 2046, only months from Charlie's birthday.

Charlie brushed past the Earth clock and looked at Kander's calendar, which was much more simplistic than Earth's Gregorian system. The Kalmar favored numbers rather than naming each of their "months." On Kander, the date was 2152.8.40.3, and it took a moment for Charlie to reconfigure the dating system in her mind. The first number indicated the year, the second number was the nored of the year, the third was the nineth of the year, and the last was the day of the nineth.

Kander was in their last nineth for the eighth nored, and there were nine total noreds per year. All of it totaled to four hundred five days, nothing more or less. The nineth nored was also the start of the planet's long winter season. But as Charlie's attention went back to the current year, it sank in just how long she had been gone from Kander. She left in the beginning of 2136, which was sixteen years by Kander standard time. But as Raine pointed out, Charlie had been away for eighteen years in Earth time. Rubbing her brow, Charlie closed out the clocks and decided looking at the different date references was annoying.

Staring into the flames, Charlie felt time pressing down on her shoulders. In outer space, it was easy to lose track of life, because time seemed infinite among the immortal stars. But on a planet it was impossible not to see faces age, buildings crumble, animals die, and plants cycle with the seasons. Charlie was infinitesimal and unseen in outer space, but living on Kander forced her eyes open to the shortness of life. Her chest clenched in pain, and she almost dropped her mug as a fiery need to be near Kal washed over her. Somehow a thirty-minute walk to Kal felt too far.

Charlie forced herself out of the chair and deposited the empty mug in the sink. She allowed the fire to burn and went upstairs to the room shared with Raine. At the top, she paused and removed the earbuds. She tucked them back into the techbit and smiled at Raine seated by table, reading a tattered book under the candlelight. "Brushing up on your *Linux* coding skills?"

Raine rolled her eyes and lowered the book to her lap. "Funny." She closed the book after inserting a marker in it. "So what's up?"

Coming around the bed, Charlie decided to be up front rather than test the waters. She pulled the second chair around the table and sat in front of her friend. "Something came up."

Raising an eyebrow, Raine placed the book on the table and leaned forward toward Charlie. "You're leaving Kander."

"Sort of, but I need you to come with me."

Raine shook her head. "I can't leave—"

"I really need your help." Charlie prayed that Raine would at least listen before giving her final decision. She could make the mission work without Raine, but after the last one she loved having her adoptive sister at her side. Raine's sighed, and Charlie took her opening. "You remember how we overheard two Serrato soldiers talking about the Sworne?"

"*Ja.*"

"One of those soldiers was Victor, the guy who blew up my ship."

"I remember." Raine tilted her head, and she hummed with curiosity.

"The High Commander asked me to kidnap Victor," Charlie whispered.

"What!"

Charlie held out her hands and hushed her friend after the outburst.

"Tell me you're fucking kidding me," Raine hissed, leaning toward Charlie again. "Why the fuck does she want him?"

Charlie sighed and swept loose hair behind her ear before replying, "She wants to know what Victor knows about the Sworne and Serrato Corps's plans."

Raine was quiet and studied Charlie for a moment, then massaged her temples. "Okay I have to agree that whatever is going on with Serrato Corps, it's pretty fishy. But isn't she the least bit worried that kidnapping one of their higher-ups could cause trouble?"

"Serrato Corps kidnapped and ransomed a Kalmar," Charlie argued. "I think Serrato Corps started it first."

Raine rolled her eyes. "You know tit-for-tat never ends well." She frowned and started to rub her face now. "How can you even kidnap him? They'll be on you like white on rice if you show up anywhere near Serrato."

"I know." Charlie grinned with an evil glint in her eyes. "But I can give them something they still want."

"Like what?"

Charlie wiggled her eyebrows and replied, "Starr."

"You're not going to really—"

"*Vuk joh*," Charlie cut off. "There's no way I'd give them Starr. But I can use her for bait to draw Victor out."

"How sure are you that they still want Starr?"

Charlie chuckled, leaned back in the chair, and grinned wider. "Pretty damn sure. When we were traveling back here from Serrato, Victor contacted me and demanded I return Starr to him. After I told him to go fuck himself, he said that the Grand Marshal was sending down a kill order and bounty for me."

"God," Raine whispered and slumped against the chair. "So all you have to do is offer Starr in exchange for the Grand Marshal to remove the kill order."

"*Ja*." Charlie lost her smirk and dove into the rest of the rough plans. "The High Commander is giving me a few soldiers to take with me so that I can ambush him. They won't expect Kalmar soldiers there. Once he's captured, we'll transport him back here."

"Will the High Commander return him to Serrato Corps?"

"I don't know. I didn't ask." Charlie hoped that Victor would meet his end after Kal was done with him. "But I could really use your help."

Raine shook her head, then asked, "What could I possibly do that several Kalmar soldiers can't?"

Charlie lifted an eyebrow and replied, "Fly a ship." She had another plan in mind for Raine, but it required getting her hands on a certain piece of special tech. For now, she kept that to herself until she heard back from her contacts.

"You need a ship first before I can fly it," Raine teased.

"I'm working on that," Charlie assured her. "I don't think the exchange will take long. I'll pick a halfway point between here and Serrato."

Raine stayed silent for a few moments, then said, "I can't ask Chris to man the stall alone after the last trip. But I can leave it empty for a few days."

"I can give you stills to cover the loss in business," Charlie offered and frowned when Raine shook her head.

"A few days won't ruin my business." Raine appeared certain of herself and grinned at Charlie. "Are you sure you want to go to outer space in a small boat with a handful of Kalmar?"

Charlie laughed and joked, "We'll have to take extra barf bags."

Raine returned the laugh and agreed with her friend. She stood from the chair and went to the dresser, her limp more noticeable now that her brace was off for the night.

Charlie returned the chair to the table and paused; her shoulders slackened after a worrisome talk. Still, she had another concern and neared her friend next to the dresser. "There's also an infiltrator on Kander that's helping Serrato Corps."

"Or infiltrators," Raine said, peering over at Charlie. "They could also be the ones stirring up the revolt."

"Maybe when we go to New Earth, we can look more into it." Charlie tensed after having blurted out what came to mind rather than thinking it through. *Why am I getting myself anymore involved in this?*

Raine huffed and eyed Charlie with a doubtful look. "Like you of all people poking around and asking questions wouldn't set off alarm bells around New Earth." When Charlie opened her mouth, she held up her hand and said, "Let's just focus on the kidnapping mission first."

"Right," Charlie whispered, knowing Raine had a good point. She and Raine finished getting ready for bed. Both were happy to crawl under the blankets and furs. Already the fire in the sitting room was fading, and darkness settled over the loft for the night. Gazing out the tall windows on either side of the chimney, Charlie stared at the twin moons that were slivers beyond the limbs of the black trees.

Next to her, Raine was breathing heavily. Her friend's presence was a minor comfort, but Charlie longed for her lover's warm, strong body. Tomorrow she expected to see Kal again so they could discuss both the ship offerings and Charlie's price for the job. She also wondered how many more days Kal had left of her rut. Most Alpha's rutted for five to seven days, and today was Kal's fourth.

As Charlie closed her eyes, she focused on the gentle pull in her chest that she'd first noticed about the same time Kal's rut would have started. It was less demanding than it had been when she found out Kal was rutting, but it was constant and solid inside of Charlie. She wanted to ignore it, but its needy presence followed her every heartbeat. Giving into her weary state, her mind whispered, *Goodnight, Sumner.*

* * *

Charlie sent out multiple messages during the walk to Tarrak from Starlight Farm. Her first one was to Starr, hoping she could convince her to return to the quadrant and help with the kidnapping mission. It was a huge risk for her friend, but Charlie needed her or else Victor might not believe that she could deliver Starr to him.

Her second message was to an old mercenary friend who had connections with bounty hunters. She was curious to learn whether Serrato Corps had placed the reward on her head. According to Victor's threat, yesterday had been Charlie's last chance to return Starr to Serrato Corps, the offer expiring with a guarantee of her death.

The last message was a brief one to Kal that asked when they could meet today. Charlie had already worked out a firm price for the mission. When they entered the market, Charlie's techbit dinged with a message from Kal.

*This afternoon. I'll be in my office.*

It was a simple response with nothing underlining it. Charlie sensed her lover's formality, so she replied with an agreement. Tucking the techbit away, she noticed the market was strangely quiet. But it was still twenty minutes before sunrise, and they had a few things to organize in the stall.

Raine went over everything with Charlie, and numerous times Raine reminded Charlie to be patient, especially with Alphas. She instructed Charlie to keep her lectra gun hidden in her jacket at all times. Raine was authorized to carry and use a gun, if necessary. It had taken Raine a lot of effort, agreements, and pulling of strings to be allowed to carry an advanced weapon. Some part of Charlie wondered if Dorlon had helped Raine, but she decided to ask another time.

By the end of the crash course, Charlie wanted a stiff drink—even a tiny shot of the Kalmar's *mkin* alcohol. Instead, she took some of Raine's herbal drink from an old, dented canister, and it warmed her inside. When a few early customers arrived at the booth, Charlie stood aside and watched how Raine and Chris handled them. She noticed that Raine took care of the Alpha while Chris helped the Omega.

As the morning wore on, more people arrived at the market, which was the central focus of the city. Charlie was pushed into helping a few people, trying to sell a tablet here or there. Just as she thought she had her first sale, the Omega was pulled away by her mate.

Raine gave her an encouraging smile, patted her on the back, and went to attend a new customer.

Charlie stood to the side again and watched the people, including those on the street. She noticed one curious person who appeared to be human instead of Kalmar. Just as the burly man passed the stall, Raine nudged her to handle a new prospect at the table.

*Beep. Beep. Beep. Beep.*

"*Vuk*," Charlie muttered under her breath as she fished around in her jacket for the techbit ringing for attention. Beside her, Raine shot her a glare, but she glanced at the name on the screen. "I have to take this, Raine. It's Starr." She didn't wait for a response before she stepped away from her friend and the stall.

*"Hey, Starr,"* Charlie greeted in Jero when she answered the transmission. She peered back at Raine's stall that was busy with three customers.

*"Charlie,"* Starr said, features stern on the screen.

Charlie crossed the street, found a nook between two buildings, and hid in it, away from onlookers. "*You got my message about the mission?*"

"*Yes. I already talked Magnar into bringing me back to the fifth quadrant.*"

Charlie was relieved. She had planned to contact Magnar next, but already having Magnar's agreement saved them time. *I'm going to owe her again.* She tried not rolling her eyes and focused on her conversation with Starr. "*How far are you?*"

"*It'll be a few days.*"

"*All right. I'm working on getting a ship.*" Charlie paused and bit her bottom lip. "*Are you sure about this?*"

Starr folded her thick arms and leaned back in a chair. "*It's not at the top of my list, but you won't be able to draw him out without me.*"

Charlie agreed; she had to show proof she had Starr captured and ready to hand over to Victor. "*I know, and I'm sorry to bring you into this.*"

Starr shook her head and said, "*I wouldn't be free right now if it wasn't for you.*"

"*You also wouldn't have been captured if I—*"

"*Don't even finish that sentence.*" Starr narrowed her eyes in warning, then leaned closer to the screen. "*Listen, Magnar told me the bounty went out about three lumens ago.*"

"*Shit,*" Charlie whispered. "*Does she know what the bounty says?*"

Starr shook her head. "*She's trying to get her hands on a copy to see if she and her team are on it too.*" She hesitated as her eyes darkened with worry. "*You need to be extra careful, Charlie. There could be bounty hunters already in your quadrant.*"

Charlie reached into her leather jacket and fingered the hidden lectra gun, but it wasn't enough to ease her nerves. "*I'll be fine, promise.*"

Starr had a furrow across her brow but nodded and reached toward the screen. "*I'll keep in touch about our location.*"

Charlie thanked her and exchanged a goodbye. As she pocketed the techbit, she noticed the same hulking guy from earlier coming down the street. This time, she had a better view of him from her hidden spot and was able to study him.

He was a male human, if his matching, new clothes were any indicator. From his attire, he wasn't an Earthling from

Kander. His body was muscular, and his thick biceps were exposed by his sleeveless shirt. He was about a foot or two shorter than some of the Alphas on the street. A glint of metal shined at his hip, revealing a double-edge battle axe that, at least in Charlie's case, required two hands.

*What a meathead*, Charlie thought and continued watching him. She was curious where he came from and why he was here. The meathead neared Raine's stall, stood there, and surveyed it for a minute. A moment later he approached Raine and started talking to her.

Charlie narrowed her eyes and reached for her techbit, preparing to take a photo of him for later. But she felt a cold stare and froze until she looked over her right shoulder to see who had found her.

"*There she is!*" A female human called in Jero, indicating Charlie in the hiding spot. "*Max, she's between those two buildings*!"

Wide eyed, Charlie cut her gaze to the meathead and paled when he started toward her. "*Vuk*!" She shoved the techbit back in place, then followed her gut and ducked into the streets rather than run down the tiny alleyway that might be a dead end. Charlie heard Raine yell for her, and she took off to the right, closer to the female human who had spotted her first. She liked her chances of getting past the woman than the meathead, Max, who was barreling through people in the busy street.

Charlie rolled around an Alpha, who hollered at her, then pushed through two more Alphas. Behind her she heard the woman and Max yell for her as they gave chase. They were bounty hunters looking to cash in on Charlie or her head. Hopping off the sidewalk, Charlie dodged an Alpha towing a handcart, then danced around an Alpha and Omega walking a horse.

Glancing over her shoulder, she realized the woman was gone but Max was still on her tail. She cursed and decided she needed a better plan than just running through Tarrak. She knew bits and pieces of the city, but now wished she'd had a proper tour of it. There were also too many people around for Charlie to use her lectra gun. Charlie went right at the fork in the road, then cut down a residential street. Overhead lines ran from side to side with clothes hanging out to dry.

Luckily, the street was quieter than the market. Charlie was able to run faster and put distance between her and Max. Her pounding boots matched her raging heartbeat as she worked out a plan to deal with the bounty hunters. If she could locate Kalmar soldiers, they would help her. The best locations would be the Great Tower, the harbor's port, or maybe the temple. But right now, Charlie had lost her bearings and needed more time.

To her left, she spotted a niche between two homes and tucked into it. She tore free her lectra gun and peered around the side, aiming for her pursuer. Charlie pulled the trigger and hit the ground at his feet after he jumped over a fallen barrel.

"*Fuck!*" Max stumbled back and tumbled behind the barrel for protection.

Charlie continued firing on him until he returned a few shots. She pushed back into the alcove and looked at the local people down the street. She hoped they hid before the reckless gunfire hurt them. Kneeling, Charlie crawled around the corner and held the trigger, sending repeated lectra shots at Max. If nothing else, she was certain their shootout would get everyone's attention in the city.

Max howled and cursed, then fired above Charlie's head and caused chunks of stone to fall off the building. He laughed at Charlie's desperation to jump out of the way, then he took the opportunity and shot at her again.

Charlie howled in pain after a lectra shot cut into her right leg, burning through her jeans. After falling onto her stomach, she gritted her teeth, hissed, and rolled onto her back. She dug the Grasshopper gun from her pants' pocket, then turned to her side and pulled the trigger.

The Grasshopper screamed its sound wave through the air and sent Max flying backward, slamming him into the cobblestone street. He groaned once before going still, unconscious for the next fifteen or twenty minutes.

Whimpering, Charlie peered down at her injured leg, which radiated searing heat. At the center of the hit, the flesh was melted and twisted with blood and sticky skin. Lectra burns were some of the ugliest hits, but Charlie could tell Max was trying to slow her down, not kill her. She returned the Grasshopper to her pocket, then collected her lectra gun. Climbing to her feet, Charlie limped a few times, then forced herself to move faster. She still had to deal with the other bounty hunter.

Cutting down a side street, Charlie hoped she was headed toward the Great Tower. She managed a weak jog and stumbled every few yards, then was forced to stop at a four-way intersection. She leaned against a building's corner and bent forward, gasping from exhaustion and pain. Lifting her head, she gazed at an unusual structure at the end of the next street. Its round bell tower and domed roof rose above the homes as if to watch over the people. Charlie was certain it was the temple dedicated to Kalatas.

Charlie gathered her strength, pushed off the building, and continued toward the temple. She grunted at a few Alphas who backed away from her, uninterested in helping a human. In the distance, the white-washed, stone temple grew taller and beckoned her, as if reeling her to it. After another block, the street ended at the temple's grounds, which were similar to the Great Tower's landscape. The lush grass swept toward the structure, then transitioned to delicate moss that had crept up the side of the temple. Even with its cold stone face, it was inviting to Charlie, and she limped to the open doors.

The stepping stones guided her to the entrance, but she hesitated and scanned her surroundings. A few Kalmar were walking by the temple grounds and noticed Charlie. There was still one bounty hunter in the city searching for her. But she had no idea where the bounty hunter went or why she had separated from Max. However, staying in the open wasn't in her best interest, so she slipped into the temple, hoping she was allowed in.

Charlie entered the heart of the ancient round temple that held simple beauty. The building was constructed from the same white marble as the Great Tower's throne. Black veins in the marble spread out like lightning bolts bursting along the walls, traveling left and right until they met on the opposite side. Charlie was standing at the highest level; there were nine small steps down to the empty main floor. Each step wrapped around the entire structure and reminded Charlie of the ancient Greek theatres. But what both fascinated and bewildered her was the floor. Soft-looking grass covered every tiny space.

Charlie was tempted to walk down and touch it until a quiet sound drew her attention to the opposite side. A single door creaked open, and a lithe form slipped into the sanctuary, closing the door behind herself.

"*Turen.*" It was an Omega by her tender voice. She floated down the steps and glided across the green span that separated them. Her robe was similar to the one Lennox wore, except it was an emerald shade. Once close enough, she offered a smile and said, "Welcome to the Temple of Kalatas." Her eyes traveled over Charlie and halted at the leg injury. "You are hurt."

Charlie limped down the steps, dragging her burned leg with her free hand. She stood on the last step and said, "*Ja,* and I need help." She looked sidelong at the entrance and pulled out her techbit with her left hand. She still carried the lectra gun in her other hand. "I need to call Kal," she muttered while tapping the screen.

"She's already on—"

"*Drop it!*"

Cursing, Charlie froze and glared at the female bounty hunter who entered the temple.

"*Drop your gun and techbit,*" she ordered in Jero, smirking. "*Or I'll burn your hands off. Serrato Corps didn't say anything about keeping all your limbs.*"

Charlie gritted her teeth and calculated her options, which were next to nothing. The bounty hunter was close enough that if she even twitched the hit would strike her. She was foolish to come into the temple and get the priest involved. If she could buy time, then maybe she could come up with a plan. "*All right.*" She held both the techbit and gun up to show she wasn't using them.

"*Toss them far enough away,*" the bounty hunter ordered.

Biting her lip, Charlie formulated a partial plan in her head. "*I'll toss them and come with you if you keep the priest out of this.*" She watched the bounty hunter's grey eyes cut to the priest then back to Charlie.

After a nod, the bounty hunter ordered, "*Tell her to back off. Over there but in view.*" She pointed to the left with her freehand.

Charlie agreed after determining the bounty hunter just gave away the fact that she couldn't speak Kalmarese. She looked over her shoulder at the priest and said, "I need you to go over to the side where she was pointing."

"What is she going to do?" the priest asked.

"Spare you, as I asked her," Charlie replied, then sensed the priest's hesitation. "*Krafka.*" She sighed when the priest took small steps away from her. She turned back to the bounty hunter and said, "*I'm putting my stuff down now.*" At a slow pace, she started to kneel and asked, "*You have a name, kid?*" From the long silence, she wondered if she'd get an answer.

"Clio."

Charlie tossed her weapon and techbit, grateful that the grass cushioned it. "*I'm sure you know already that I'm Charlie.*" She inched back up, hands open and out.

"*The washed-up Galaxy Master,*" Clio taunted, her eyes bright with mischief.

Blowing out a breath, Charlie narrowed her eyes at Clio, who had to be in her late teens or early twenties. "*There's a difference between washed up and antisocial.*"

Clio huffed and came down another step, pointing the gun closer to Charlie's face. "*That's not how they tell it.*" She shrugged. "*Doesn't matter now. Your hide is finally worth something.*" She tilted her head. "*You must have really pissed off Serrato Corps.*"

Charlie revealed all her teeth in a wicked smile. "*You have no idea.*"

Clio grunted and shifted to the right. "*Time to go.*" She checked on the priest, who remained in the same spot.

Going up the first step, Charlie hissed from the pain in her leg but continued ascending the steps. Almost to the top, she faltered from the sudden, warm pulse in her chest that gave her hope.

"*Move*," Clio snapped and shoved Charlie forward.

Collapsing, Charlie hit the stone step but lifted her head and saw the long shadow rushing toward them through the main entrance. Her heart thundered to life, and she reacted with fire to Clio's demands. She rolled onto her back and drew her knees to her chest, then drove her boots into Clio's stomach.

Clio was launched into the air, cursing and screaming. She collided into the ground but then scrambled to her feet and pointed the gun at Charlie.

Sitting upright on the steps, Charlie watched Clio's features grow pale. Charlie felt the heated darkness pouring and sweeping around her, filling the temple. A ferocious growl reverberated off the walls and echoed in everyone's ears. She was warmed by it, unlike Clio, who stumbled backward.

Clio attempted to open her mouth, but she only managed a peep before tumbling to her knees. Still determined, she raised the lectra gun at the immense threat behind Charlie. Her first shot bounced off her target, followed by a roar.

A massive body leapt over Charlie's head, landed in front of her, and lunged to end the entire fiasco with one clean swipe. She cringed as Clio's head separated from her neck, slid off, and fell to the grass. *I fucking hate decapitation!* But it was over, and Charlie slumped against the steps, watching her lover spin around to her.

Kal knelt next to Charlie and lowered her sword nearby. "Are you all right?"

"I'm great." Charlie forced a smile, sensing it didn't make the grade. "There's another bounty hunter."

"He's already been dealt with."

Charlie considered whether that meant the bounty hunter Max was dead or arrested. "You have perfect timing as usual."

Kal chuffed and started to inspect Charlie, hissing at the leg wound.

"It's nothing serious." Charlie sat up on the step and stretched her injured leg. "I've been hit plenty of times in the past." She ignored Kal's displeased rumble and peered up when the priest drifted over to them.

Kal tilted her head back and said, "*Turen*, Tas."

Charlie lifted an eyebrow at hearing the priest's name for the first time. The name Tas had to be a title, similar to the High Commander's being Kal. It was too coincidental that the priest's name was the last portion of Kalatas's name.

"*Turen*, Kal." Tas slipped her hands into the green robe but shifted her attention to the entrance.

Charlie twisted her head around and watched the four soldiers march into the temple. She started to get up until Kal pushed against her chest, telling her to stay.

Kal stood and ordered, "Remove the body. Two of you remain at the temple's entrance and do not let anyone pass."

"*Ja*, Kal," one soldier agreed, then started the process of dragging the body while another picked up the head.

Kal grabbed the sword, sheathed it, and knelt on Charlie's right side. Leaning closer, she spoke in a softer voice. "After the soldiers leave, I need you to lower your pants enough so I can heal the wound."

Charlie sighed and said, "I'm okay. I'll get Brexton to look at it." She stiffened from Kal's low snarl and submitted with a head bow. "I don't want to weaken you."

After the temple became quiet, Kal touched Charlie's leg and studied the injury. "It won't require much energy to heal it."

"Sum—" Charlie was cut off by Kal's dark glare. But she was unsure if it was for using Kal's old name in front of Tas or being argumentative about the wound. Maybe it was both, and she grumbled at the losing battle. She suspected Kal would use a blade to cut the jeans if Charlie didn't take them off. Giving up, she reached for the belt buckle but stopped and glanced at Tas.

Clearing her throat, Tas nodded and turned, then gave them some privacy. Charlie unclipped the utility belt, worked the zipper, and peeled the jeans off, but she grimaced when the clothing brushed the raw, bubbling wound. "I hate these fuckers." She seethed at the bloody flesh sticking to the material. Once they were low enough, the oozing flesh glistened.

Kal's rumble was long and heavy. She raised her hand, letting it hover over the wound. Her eyes were a fiery emerald, and black mist poured from her palm, covering the mangled, charred skin.

Last time, Charlie had watched in awe when Kal healed Dorlon and brought her back. This time, she studied the dark, smoky force that seeped into her skin, blood, and muscle. First the burned muscle started to heal, then the ripped, charred skin pulled and stretched causing the opening to close up. As the wound continued to heal, the pain intensified until Charlie fell back on the steps and cut her nails against the stone under her palms. She let out a low cry, digging her heels into the soft grass. Her entire body strained, and her heart wanted to burst from her chest.

Charlie held her breath until the dark heat vanished from her body. With her head against the top step, she panted and slumped after relaxing her hands. When she opened her eyes, she met Kal's stern features and saw no signs of weariness.

Reaching for the unbuttoned pants, Kal pulled them up to Charlie's waist and left them open while Charlie caught her breath. "How does it feel now?"

Charlie sat up and groaned from the awkward position on the steps. She shifted, then inspected her leg through the hole in her jeans where the burned spot had been. "It feels normal now." She took Kal's offered hand and tested her leg once on her feet again. Keeping her balance, she flexed her leg a few times and smiled at it. Nothing hurt, and no scarring remained other than the damage to the jeans. "*Tah.*"

"*Motah.*" Kal turned to Tas, who remained several steps away with her back to them. "Tas," she called.

By the time Tas joined them, Charlie had zipped her pants and clipped her belt into place. She cleared her throat and swept her wild hair back with her fingers.

"Tas, this is Charlie." Kal hooked her hands in front of her body, legs parted, and stony features locked on Tas. "She rescued the Omega who was kidnapped during the first nineth."

Tas's smile was warm and genuine to Charlie. She slipped her hands into the green robe's sleeves and asked, "You are from Kardos?"

Charlie shrugged and replied, "Once upon a time, *ja.*" She studied Tas's features and suspected that Tas was close to Kal's age. "Have you been the priest long?"

"For about eight years now," Tas replied. "I am the High Priest of Kander, as Kal is the High Commander of our planet."

"So is 'Tas' your title?" Charlie ignored Kal's low huff, which had a note of amusement in it.

"*Ja.* My name is Sallow, but it is spoken by few."

Charlie was intrigued and wanted to ask more, but Kal interrupted them.

"I must go." Kal looked at Charlie with a hint of concern in her eyes.

Charlie nodded and fisted her hand to keep from touching her lover. "Are we still on for our meeting later?" She went over and collected her lectra gun and techbit, coming back over while Kal spoke to her.

"*Ja,* I will be in my office at the fourteenth hour."

Considering her mental clock, Charlie decided it would be good timing between now and when Raine liked to return to the farm. "I'll see you then." She watched Kal and Tas exchange a goodbye, then she was left alone with the High Priest. She pointed a thumb over her shoulder and said, "Sorry about the mess earlier."

"It is not the first time blood has been spilled in this temple," Tas said. "It will happen again."

Charlie frowned and zipped up her jacket, chasing off the chill in her body. "I've never been in this temple. I knew it was here but…." She scanned the interior, then tilted her head back and gazed around the dome that opened to the bell tower. Streams of light cascaded into the temple, lighting up patches of grass around them. "It's beautiful."

"Our temple is the oldest structure in the city." Tas watched how she took in the details. "Before it was a temple, it was the *alping* for the region. Then later the Great Tower was built and became the new *alping*."

Now awed, Charlie focused on Tas and digested the new information. She recalled that an *alping* was both an event and structure in Kalmar society where people assembled for law, hearings, judgments, and announcements from their leader. She hadn't realized the temple held such long history. The stone walls had seen and heard many things over the centuries. "That's amazing." She frowned after a worry came over her. "Am I even allowed in here? I'm not Kalmar."

Tas gave a soft laugh but smiled and replied, "Kalatas does not judge based on species but spirit. You are welcomed here at any time."

Charlie nodded and decided it was time to go, until the wall behind Tas caught her attention. It glowed and flickered from a constant flame that ran along the wall, but only a portion of it. Intrigued, she was drawn across the distance and went up the steps to the wall. Behind her, she sensed Tas following her.

Getting closer, Charlie peered up toward the top of the wall that connected with the dome ceiling. At the top, there was a single name, then under it another and another and then more. They continued downward toward the fire trough at the bottom. She wanted to touch them, feel how they were etched into the white marble. Turning toward the High Priest, she whispered, "Who are they?"

"They are all the High Commanders of Kander." Tas climbed the steps and stood beside Charlie. "Their old names before they became Kal." She spoke in a soft voice and sighed low. "This is how we remember them after they speak their old name upon their death."

Charlie nibbled her lower lip, thinking of her lover. "What if there's no one to hear their name?"

Tas tilted her head, studying Charlie with a thoughtful look. "There is always at least one listening."

Looking at the wall again, Charlie followed the list until she found the most recent, and she glared at it. "I remember him." She held back a growl, but she heard the venom in her own voice.

Tas studied the last Kal's name too and whispered, "At the end, he became a troubled Kal." She looked at Charlie and hesitated, seeming to weigh something. "He did many great things for our people. But when your people arrived, he was unbalanced and unstable." Tas shifted her attention back to the name etched into the wall. "Yukon was driven mad by Kalatas."

"Wait. What?" Charlie narrowed her eyes and said, "Kal said that the last Kal died from the civil war."

"*Ja*, it did kill him."

Frowning again, Charlie sensed that Tas would hold back the details about the last Kal's demise. She filed it away for another time when she could ask her lover about what really happened to the last ruler. "I should be going. My friend is probably freaking out right now."

"I understand." Tas indicated the direction of the main entrance. "Our paths will cross again."

"Hopefully for a better reason than a bounty hunter chasing me," Charlie argued.

Tas followed Charlie closer to the main entrance and said, "But it was a reason nonetheless."

# Chapter 6

"Damn it. I need to go, Raine." Charlie had about ten minutes to rush to the Great Tower after closing a sale on two tablets and a smart watch. "I'm going to be late." She shoved the techbit into her pocket and started to reverse out of the stall.

"We'll wait here for you," Raine promised.

Charlie nodded.

"Don't forget your business blocker." Raine pointed at Andren, who was standing at attention beside the stall. She'd had a sour look about Andren ever since her arrival at the stall.

Charlie didn't bother asking Andren who sent her, and before leaving she swore to Raine that she would handle the situation during her meeting with Kal. Having a soldier stationed at the stall was bad for business, and thus bad for Charlie's employment.

Andren shot a weak glare at Raine before following behind Charlie. She carried a spear, wore her normal dark uniform, and had a laser rifle strapped across her back.

Charlie jogged to the Great Tower, hating to be late. By the time she made it to the fifty-second floor, she had one minute remaining. The double office doors were closed and under guard. Like previous times, Charlie hurried down the hall between the elevator and the office, but she noticed that farther past the office entrance was the other, mysterious door. For the first time, it was open and light was streaming out of it, but there was no time to peek.

After a guard pushed open the left door, Charlie entered Kal's office and expected to find the ruler behind the desk, but the office was empty. Looking to her left, she spotted

Kal seated in a wingchair beside the roaring fireplace and a familiar tattooed, bald-headed figure on the sofa.

Kal rose and came around the sofa, greeting Charlie. "Just on time."

Charlie grinned and joked, "Still working on the early part." She watched Lennox stand and exchanged a greeting with him.

"Lennox and I were discussing your upcoming mission. He has a few questions for you."

Charlie tried to remain calm, even if she was unprepared for the meeting to include Lennox. "Right." She took Kal's offer to sit down in the opposite wingchair, grateful for the warmth from the fire.

Like Kal, Lennox returned to his seat in the center of the sofa. He ran his hand over his neat beard. "Kal has informed me that you will be taking a unit of soldiers into outer space to capture the human responsible for kidnapping the Omega."

"*Ja*." Charlie refrained from looking at Kal, holding all of Lennox's attention.

"How do you plan to kidnap him?" Lennox was calm and his voice rather soft, making it easy to forget he was an Alpha.

"Ambush him," Charlie replied. "There's a planet in our quadrant called Eos Minor that skirts quadrant six. It's inhabitable, but no intelligent race lives there. It would be a neutral place to meet." She recalled it was inhabited by various small creatures similar to reptiles and dinosaurs that had once been on Earth. "Anyway, the terrain is like here. There's plenty of trees and landscape to hide the soldiers." She grinned at Lennox. "I'll give him my crewman in exchange for Serrato Corps to drop the bounty on my head. At least that's the ploy to get Victor to meet me on Eos Minor."

Lennox was quiet for a beat, then narrowed his eyes though his features remained calm. "And how can we be assured you won't have other plans? You may wish to go through with the exchange with Victor. Or perhaps you'll want to kill Victor yourself rather than return him to us, since he was the one that destroyed your ship."

Charlie clenched her hands and resisted her initial reaction to Lennox's list of accusations. He had a point after all, and she wanted to earn the job. She took a deep breath and held his steady gaze. "I might be a merc, but I have honor and a reputation at stake. I lose clients if I don't hold up my end of the agreement."

"*Ja,* but in this situation it's your life at stake, thanks to a bounty," Lennox countered.

Charlie flashed a grin. "I'll tell you a secret." She leaned toward him and whispered, "My life is always at stake." She straightened up after he chuffed at her. She wanted to say more and explain that the mission's purpose was bigger than she. Victor held information about the Sworne and what could be coming their way. However, Charlie was unsure whether Kal had disclosed to Lennox about the Sworne's potential arrival.

Lennox rested back in the sofa and slid his hands into the arms of his robe. He continued a staring contest with Charlie.

Kal shifted in the wingchair, which drew Charlie's attention to her. "Lennox, as part of the payment to Charlie, I will be offering her Victor's life after I've finished interrogating him."

After a low rumble, Lennox looked over at Charlie and asked, "Does such an arrangement agree with you?"

Not expecting the offer, Charlie took a beat to weigh it and lifted an eyebrow at them. "Don't you want to return him or ransom him back to Serrato Corps?"

Kal remained silent and looked at Lennox when he spoke up. "It would be unwise to freely return him, Kal. He's been a threat to us."

"Nor is there anything that Serrato Corps can offer us as a ransom," Kal said, a low rumble rolling in her chest.

Looking back at Charlie, she said, "His life will be yours to take."

Charlie hadn't calculated the offer and worked her jaw a few times, unsure what to say. But the expectant gazes from both Alphas made her sigh. "All right."

"Kal has made me aware of the possibility that the Sworne are returning to our galaxy," Lennox said. "You overheard this from Victor during your mission to save your crewman?"

"*Ja.*" Charlie shifted in the chair and crossed her legs.

"We know very little about the Sworne." Lennox frowned and worry etched his features. "Only bits and pieces from your people."

Charlie swallowed as childhood memories tried to bubble to the surface. "I'm not an expert on them. I was a kid when they attacked my home planet. But I can tell you that their technology far outweighs anything here on Kander." She glanced at Kal, then said, "It's possible that their tech has even improved since they were last here."

Lennox made a disapproving sound, then asked, "Are there any among your people who are knowledgeable about the Sworne?"

Blowing out a breath, Charlie wondered about the best answer when she knew so little about the Earthlings in Kardos. "During the war, I'm sure my people studied the Sworne and learned everything they possibly could so that they could find their weakness and stop them." She felt Kal's dark gaze lingering on her. "The people who are going to know the most about the Sworne will be those left from the military, probably the US military."

"US military?" Lennox repeated.

"The United States," Charlie replied. "It was a government body on Earth. The US was kind of a province, but it was its own separate power. There were hundreds of governments like that around Earth." She didn't know if there was a Kalmarese word for country, but it was the best interpretation she could provide. "At the time, the highest power in the US was the *president*, but he died on the *Liberator* about a year after we left Earth."

Lennox looked at Kal and said, "I don't believe their current leaders have military background."

Charlie didn't know who the current leaders were of the Earthlings in Kardos, or if there was one single leader. After the president died, the government's structure was reshaped on the *Liberator*, and a council was formed to govern the ship. "Actually, from what my friend told me, I know one person that has military background that was a leader. Her name is Melissa Hoyt."

"I have met her twice. Is she trustworthy?" Lennox asked. "We must limit the news about the Sworne."

"I don't know." Charlie hooked a lock of hair behind her ear. "I mean I knew Hoyt as a kid, and she was a good person. My friend Raine seems to still be friends with Hoyt and would know more." If Kal had the information, then she could better understand the new enemy. "Someone in New Earth is bound to still have data on the Sworne."

"It is only a matter of asking the right person," Lennox said to the High Commander.

Kal rumbled in agreement, then looked at Charlie. "Can you speak carefully to Raine about Melissa Hoyt?"

Charlie glanced at Lennox before she nodded at Kal. "I'll talk to her tonight."

Kal seemed pleased and looked at Lennox. "Is there anything else you wish to ask Charlie?"

"*Joh*." Lennox scooted forward as if to stand, but he paused and held Charlie's gaze. "*Tah*." He stood, filling out his massive seven feet.

Charlie hesitated but managed to respond. "*Motah*." She earned a nod from him, then he departed the office with the door sealing behind him. She blew out a breath now that she was alone with her lover.

"How is your leg?"

"Like I was never hunted down by bounty hunters," Charlie joked, receiving an annoyed huff from Kal. "What happened to that other bounty hunter?"

"He was interrogated and killed," Kal replied. "There are three hundred thousand stills on your head."

"*Vuk!*" Charlie was wide eyed in complete awe. "I should collect the bounty on my own head. Serrato Corps must really hate my guts."

"Four hundred thousand stills if you're alive," Kal said.

Charlie whistled low, then sank deeper in the wingchair and hung her head in her hand, trying to fathom how this happened to her. Both the attack and the high bounty triggered Kal to send Andren to Raine's stall for the rest of the day. "I'm not really sure how to get rid of the bounty."

"Perhaps Victor's life is worth yours."

Eyeing her lover, Charlie considered the suggestion and sighed. "Lennox just sat there and said Victor was a threat. Why would you let me return him?"

"If his return removes the bounty, then it is worth it."

Charlie lowered her gaze and decided to table the idea for now. She first had to get her hands on Victor before she could ransom him back to Serrato Corps. Reaching into her jacket, she retrieved her techbit and said, "I received several offers for a ship." She moved to the sofa, sitting on Kal's left. The techbit loaded the files and created a holo screen in front of them so they could review the ship options. "So these first two are pointless. They're old buckets that can barely reach leed one."

Kal leaned closer to Charlie, and their bodies pressed together. "What is a leed?"

Smiling, Charlie looked from the images of the ship to Kal, who was a ruler over a race that didn't consider venturing into outer space. "In space travel, we use leed speeds to measure how fast a ship moves. Leed speeds are tiers of light speed, so the higher the leed, the faster the ship. Most ships out there do at least leed one and usually leed two. There are some that do leed three or four, but they consume huge amounts of fuel and cost too much."

"What speed was your ship able to reach?"

"The *Pacifica* could reach leed two, and sometimes I could push it to leed two and half." Charlie grinned and explained, "Not that a half of a leed is a thing, but when you're trying to get away from someone that half leed matters." She returned her attention to the screen. "The third ship is probably the best option. It's huge — about..." She did the math in her head and said, "It's about thirty-five *varka* in length." She swiped the techbit and watched the holo screen flip to the next vessel. "It's not perfect, but it has the room we need to house everyone."

"How fast is it?"

"It can reach leed two," Charlie replied.

"Can?" Kal repeated and lifted an eyebrow.

Charlie grumbled and swiped to the fourth ship. "This was the other option. It's a newer ship built by the Jerothian race. It's fast and reaches leed three, but it's small. It was designed to quickly move their diplomats through the galaxy." She indicated the ship's spec sheet on the far right. "But the quarters are tight and not enough." Looking at Kal, she asked, "How many warriors will go?"

Kal folded her hands together in the space between her legs, seeming to buy time. "Between nine to twelve soldiers."

"Plus Raine and myself, so that's anywhere from eleven to fourteen." Charlie chewed her bottom lip and pointed at the Jerothian ship. "It only holds five comfortably. Might be able to do eight." She swiped back to the third vessel and said, "This one has room for twelve to sixteen people." She reached up and used her fingers to zoom in on pictures of the interior of the ship. "Plus there's more headroom for your soldiers." She looked at Kal. "One of the reasons I bought the *Pacifica* was because Starr kept knocking her head everywhere on the first ship. Trust me when I tell you that having nine or more big Kalmar in tight and low confines isn't going to go well." She eyed the third ship option that would have to do for them. "It was bad enough with one hybrid."

Kal responded with soft thunder in her chest. "I have concerns that the Serrato Corps's ship will chase after you."

Charlie better understood and lowered the techbit to her lap, distorting the holo screen. "I don't think that'll be an issue. We'll end up killing all the Serrato soldiers. Even if we don't, they probably won't attack our ship with Victor on it."

"And if they follow you back to Kander?"

Charlie toyed with the techbit, knowing Kal had a point. With the Sworne's possible return, she was worrying about what Kal could do to fight back. The Sworne had ships, advanced weapons, and technology that far surpassed what little bit of tech Kal imported to the planet. However, there were more tech advances on Kander, such as hover vehicles, laser rifles, electricity, and even a satellite system for deep space communication. After a sigh, she shut off the holo screen and said, "That's something I wanted to ask you."

Kal tilted her head and waited for Charlie to pose her question.

"You can tell me to fuck off if it's not my business, because it's really not." Charlie bit her lip, then worked up her courage. "Does Kander have any space defenses? I mean Kander has an amazing foot military. But there's no air or space defenses that I can tell." As the silence lingered, she felt her shoulders drop after overstepping her position.

"*Ja.* Kander is not as defenseless as you may think."

Charlie peered over at her lover and warmed from the level of trust that Kal was giving her.

Kal took a deep breath and said, "The satellite array is also our space defense. There are forty-five satellites orbiting Kander. It takes six to link up so that a high-powered focused ion beam can fire at a ship."

"That's the Jerothian's FoSIB System," Charlie whispered, realization hitting her. "The Focused Space Ion Beam System that's like millions of stills."

"Try seven million with installation," Kal said.

Charlie's jaw slackened, and she stared at her lover. Her mind darted in several directions as she pieced together the real changes on Kander, which wasn't so archaic anymore.

"I purchased it shortly after becoming Kal. Your people's arrival made me realize we needed something to protect Kander from other, more dangerous races out there."

Closing her mouth, Charlie sympathized with Kal's worries. "Then why don't you use it to handle situations like Fairlee's kidnapping or those bounty hunters today?"

Kal sighed and leaned back into the sofa. "It is more of a passive defensive system. Without having any kind of air or space patrol, ships can come to Kander and land. I will and have destroyed ships that have come to Kander illegally. Word has spread over time, so hunters hitch a ride with authorized merchants that land on Kander."

"Is that how Max and Clio made it?"

Kal nodded, then indicated the techbit. "Are four ships the only options?"

Picking up the techbit, Charlie allowed the holo screen to re-form in front of them. "No, but they're the only four ships that we can get quickly enough. Otherwise it could be two nineths or a nored before we find the perfect ship." She canted her head, watching her lover think through the direction of the kidnapping mission.

"You will purchase that third ship. I will organize a team to go with you." Kal left the sofa and moved to the desk. "How long before they bring the ship here?"

Charlie closed the holo screen and used the techbit's touch screen to respond to the seller. "About three days. The ship is in the twenty-first quadrant, so it won't take long." She focused on writing a quick message but felt Kal sit beside her.

"What is the price on it?" Kal asked.

"They're asking two hundred thou, but I'll get it under that." Charlie sent the message, then turned to Kal. "I should hear something back in a few hours."

Kal was busy on her tablet, tapping it several times. "Will you be able to tell if anything is wrong with the ship?"

"*Joh*, but ships are sold with an independent inspection. Well, the reputable sellers do that. If you don't get an inspection, then it's at your own risk." Charlie felt her techbit vibrate, and she looked at it. "Damn," she whispered after seeing that two hundred thousand stills were sent to her from Kal. She held up the techbit and promised, "I'll return the change."

Kal folded up the tablet and slipped it inside her jacket. "We have to discuss your price for the mission."

Charlie shut off her own tech and shoved it in her pocket. "Before we do that, can we talk about Andren for a minute?" She pointed a thumb over her shoulder in the general direction of her returned shadow. "I can't have her—"

"*Joh.*"

Grinding her teeth, Charlie clenched the techbit and tried keeping the edge out of her tone. "She's hurting Raine's business. She's about to boot me out of the stall so she can make Andren go away." She pointed a finger at her lover. "And if that happens, I will get into a world of trouble without anything to occupy my time. I don't need a guard all the time."

Kal's low rumble grew deeper, and her voice thickened with authority. "You've already been in trouble."

Charlie blew out a breath and looked away, trying to cool her temper. Kal was trying to protect her from more bounty hunters, but she was used to handling her own bad situations. "Can we meet halfway on this?" She heard the heavy thunder in Kal's chest start to die down, so she took the opening. "Andren can keep guarding me, but she has to be inconspicuous. If she wears regular clothes, gets rid of the spear and rifle, and just carries handguns, then she won't chase off any more of Raine's business."

"That is agreeable," Kal said. "I will speak to her superior tomorrow."

Charlie nodded and relaxed into the sofa after they found middle ground. "*Tah.*" She studied Kal's face and noticed the dark coloring was gone. "How are you feeling? Did you sleep last night?"

"*Ja.*" Kal leaned back and rested her hands on her knees, legs still spread open. "My rut is fading."

"Will it end tomorrow?" Charlie asked.

"Most likely."

Charlie nodded and trailed her eyes down to Kal's crotch, staring at the slight bulge there. She suspected that Kal was still dealing with a constant hard-on. It would explain why she kept her legs apart to relieve the pressure. *But there's better ways to find relief.*

"Charlie," Kal snarled, popping up from the sofa.

Feeling the heat rushing to her cheeks, Charlie looked to the fireplace and cursed her own body's natural ability to give off alluring scents to Kal. She tried to fight the excitement electrifying her, but her clit was already throbbing. "*Perka gi,*" she offered in apology.

Kal stood next to the fire and folded her arms, staring hard at Charlie. "How much do you want for this job?"

Biting her lip, Charlie withheld a smirk, but she was sure that her eyes told her wishes. "Well you're providing the ship and most of the muscle. So it's really my time, Raine's, and the effort to bring Starr back." She hated being the one to give the first price, but things were different with Kal. She leaned forward and rested her elbows on her knees. "I think about ten thousand for Raine will cover the time she's away from her stall. Starr doesn't exactly need payment, but Magnar will belly-ache about the fuel."

"What do you suggest for Magnar?"

Charlie heard the displeasure in Kal's question because it was Magnar. She shook with silent laughter but cleared her throat and replied, "I'd say about twenty-five thou, but I'll handle her."

Kal agreed, then asked, "And how much do you want?" Her gaze darkened and remained locked on Charlie.

Standing up, Charlie wiped her damp palms on her pant legs. "I thought I'd give you a break for using my services again." She neared the rumbling Alpha, who was trying to remain in control. "Everyone likes a good discount." Reaching out, she toyed with Kal's long jacket and inched in closer until they were almost touching. "I'll do this job for free, if you fuck me in the throne room." She was grateful she had locked her knees, because Kal leaned over her and caused her aching clit to hurt more.

Kal kept her arms folded, and a few beads of sweat were visible around her forehead. "When?"

"I'd like to collect the payment before I go." Charlie gazed up into hungry features. "Just in case I don't make it back." She trembled when Kal bared her teeth and growled, but she shrugged at Kal's dislike of Charlie's lifestyle. "The joys of being a merc."

Kal huffed deeply, then leaned lower until her lips were near Charlie's ear. "I'll make the arrangements."

Smirking, Charlie took one step back before one of them became disarmed for the other. Like Kal, she only had so much resistance. "I look forward to it." She turned and started to the door while saying, "I should go. Raine leaves soon." Kal followed her to the door. "I'll let you know what I hear about the ship."

Kal nodded and stood by the sealed doors, close to Charlie. "Andren will be staying with you at Starlight Farm."

Charlie rolled her eyes but accepted the new circumstances. "It'll be tight in the cabin, but we'll make it work."

"I know you will." Kal cupped Charlie's flushed cheek and whispered, "I wish it were me."

Reaching up, Charlie hooked Kal's wrist and frowned at the ache in her heart. She analyzed the meaning in the rare confession from her lover, who was reconnected with her deeper Alpha self. For Kalmar, it was coded in their blood to protect what was theirs. For Kal to resist that natural instinct had to be crushing on some level. Squeezing harder, Charlie said, "*Tah* for sending Andren. I promise I'll be fine."

Kal dipped her head, then allowed her hand to fall away. "Perhaps I will see you tomorrow." She started to the desk but paused when Charlie called her name. Turning halfway, she lifted an eyebrow.

Charlie refused to end their afternoon on a sour note about the bounty on her head. She grabbed a door handle, but didn't open it. "I expect my payment *in full*." She grew smug when Kal revealed her canines in a soft snarl, but she jerked open the left door. As she started out, she heard Kal's final, hungry promise.

"You'll get it, *all* of it."

* * *

For once, the cold weather was perfect against Charlie's heated skin after her visit with Kal. She still needed to purchase a heavier coat and clothes if she was going to stay any longer on Kander. With that thought in mind, she returned to the market the longer way so she could check out which stalls had clothes before meeting up with Raine.

The suns were low on the horizon, signaling the end of the day for the various merchants. She slowed down when one of the stalls tickled a memory. Gazing between the moving bodies, Charlie searched for what had stirred her interest. Then she spotted the familiar animal that captivated her last time.

On an upper shelf, a locke was pacing in a metal cage. But this one was different from the last one, smaller and shrunken to one side. Above it was a sign that read "cheap" in Kalmarese.

Frowning, Charlie weaved through the people and saw the locke being taken down from the shelf. She moved quicker and entered the stall, garnering the merchant's attention while the Omega came down a three-step ladder with the caged locke.

"*Turen*," the merchant greeted. He was an Alpha and already imposing himself to Charlie. "What can I help you with, Beta?"

"Freema," the Omega said, a hint of warning on her face.

The merchant, Freema, shifted on his feet, then clasped his hands behind his back. "May I help you?"

Charlie kept her annoyance at bay, then pointed at the caged animal in the Omega's hands. "How much for the locke?"

Freema chuckled and replied, "It's not for sale."

Fisting her hand, Charlie narrowed her eyes at the outright lie. "The sign said 'cheap' on it." She suspected he didn't expect her to be able to read Kalmarese, only speak it.

Freema bristled and puffed up his chest. "It's already sold."

"Freema," the Omega called again. She had placed the caged animal on the ground behind one of the tables, then appeared by Charlie's side. "What do you have to pay with?" She was looking over Charlie from head to toe. "I can tell you're not from here, but your Kalmar tongue is better than most Earthlings."

Charlie blushed at the compliment and wondered if it was a ploy to get more money. "I can pay in stills." She ignored Freema's grumbling complaint about stills.

"No coin?" the Omega asked.

Shaking her head, Charlie opened her mouth, but a voice behind her cut her off.

"I have the coin," Andren replied.

Freema jumped and looked at Andren, who had materialized at Charlie's side. "You're Guard."

"So I am," Andren stated as her eyes drilled into the Alpha in a challenge.

For once, Charlie was almost sure she was getting overwhelmed by dueling pheromones, even though it wasn't something her nose could scent. "How much?" she asked the Omega, who was probably Freema's mate.

"Thirty coin," the Omega replied.

"*Vuk!*" Charlie hissed and peered over the Omega's shoulder at the balled-up animal. "Look at it. The thing is practically useless and probably starving."

Freema chuffed louder and groused at Charlie. "And what do you plan to do with it?"

Charlie glared back at Freema and replied, "What does it matter? And what good is the locke to you now, like that? No one else will buy it." She turned her attention to the Omega. "Ten coin, that's it." She read the Omega's hesitation to accept such a low offer. *Hell I don't even know if Andren's got it.*

"Twelve and it's a deal." The Omega offered her hand.

"Krisa," Freema said, a growl filling the name.

"Hush." Krisa shot him a final warning before nudging her hand closer to Charlie, trying to finish the sale.

Charlie peered over her shoulder at Andren, who gave a faint nod. She clasped Krisa's arm and sealed the deal.

Krisa hastened to the cage, ripped off the sign, and took the fearful animal to its new owner. She placed it on the table next to Charlie. "We didn't feed it yet."

Andren had retrieved the coin and handed it to Freema.

Picking up the cage, Charlie realized it was heavy, but she didn't let it show. "*Tah.*"

Freema was biting each coin before pocketing it. "Not that it'll live much longer," he joked and grinned at Charlie's scowl.

Charlie held her tongue and a barrage of colorful words for the merchants. She hurried out with Andren at her side. "I'll repay you." She made a mental note to talk to Kal about converting her stills to coin for her stay on the planet.

"I know."

Smiling, Charlie said, "*Turen.*" She and Andren passed a few more stalls and arrived at Raine's. Charlie hurried between the tables and tucked the cage into a corner, praying Raine didn't notice it right away.

"What in God's name is that?"

Charlie was bent over, checking the terrified animal. She cringed, then faced her friend, who was standing with her hands on her hips. "It's a locke."

"I know what it is. But why is it in my stall?"

"I bought it." Charlie wasn't about to mention that Andren had bought it for her. She held up her hands when Raine was about to explode on her. "It's dying, Raine. I can't just let it die." She lowered her hands while Raine stayed quiet. "I'm going to just feed it and then release it."

Raine shook her head and said, "Help us break stuff down."

Seconding the order, Charlie assisted with loading the cart with the storage boxes of tech. They finished about half an hour before sunset, just enough time to make it to Starlight Farm. As they filed out of the booth, Charlie offered to take the wooden cart and rolled it behind herself. The walk out of the city was slow until they were past the traffic beyond the Great Gate.

Charlie, Raine, and Chris chatted for awhile during the walk but then Charlie encouraged Raine and Chris to walk ahead of her. She slowed and waited until Andren walked beside her.

"Need help?" Andren asked, indicating the cart.

"I'm good." Charlie enjoyed the physical labor and decided it would finish wearing her out for the day. "Besides, you have that heavy-ass spear to carry."

Andren laughed and argued, "It's lighter than it looks."

"It seems ridiculous to carry it all over," Charlie teased.

"Until I have to use it." Andren held pride in her weapon that only the elite guards among the Kander military earned. "You can't join the Guard unless you know how to use a spear well."

Charlie smiled at Andren's dedication and loyalty to the Guard. "How long have you been a Guard?"

"Almost six years now."

"I can tell you love it." Charlie tilted her head, watching Andren's features in the setting sunlight. "I'm lucky to have you assigned to me."

Andren held Charlie's gaze for a moment before she said, "You're not angry anymore."

Charlie half shrugged, the cart's weight making it difficult. "I was angry at Kal and took it out on you."

"Then you worked it out with Kal," Andren concluded.

"*Ja*." Charlie chewed on her lip, then said, "I was angry that her order to you outweighed my own." She had a slight frown at the memory of waking up on the *Four Mag* and learning her chance to kill Victor was taken from her. "You were on my team and following my orders."

Andren dipped her head and took a deep breath. "You do realize I will continue to protect you, even if it means ignoring your orders again or letting someone else die if it means saving you."

Charlie swallowed and whispered, "You wouldn't be a very good guard otherwise." She gazed ahead and watched Chris and Raine walk together. "I'm sorry for being a bitch about it."

"I underst—"

"Just take the apology and run with it," Charlie said, grinning.

Andren laughed and nodded. "Very well." They went quiet for awhile until Andren asked, "What are you going to do with it?" She peered back at the huddled locke in the cage that rested on top of the wooden crates.

"Feed it, then release it."

Andren shook her head and said, "That merchant will get another and another and—"

"I get it." Charlie shot a dark glance at Andren. "I know I can't stop him. But at least I saved one." She hated that Andren had a good point. It was true that putting coin into the merchant's pocket only encouraged him to do it more. There had to be a better way to stop merchants from trapping and selling the beautiful animals. "I don't understand why they fight the lockes."

"It is an old tradition," Andren said. "But not a pretty one."

Charlie huffed, then tucked away her annoyance about the lockes. "Have you heard that you, Raine, and I are going on another space mission?"

"*Joh.* When?"

"In a few days. We'll talk about it tonight with Raine."

* * *

"Has it eaten anything?" Raine asked, kneeling beside Charlie.

"*Joh.*" Charlie remained seated on the cold ground next to the cage, willing the locke to eat the leftover food from their dinner. "Earlier I thought maybe it was because I was sitting here. But it hasn't eaten anything over the past hour."

Raine peered through the cage at the curled-up, gray animal. "Has it drunk water?"

"A little bit."

"That's a good sign at least." Raine brushed several thick strands of hair from her face. "It doesn't look healthy at all."

Charlie was frowning and unsure what to do to help the locke. "I think it's cold." She pointed at its body. "It should have a thicker coat coming in by now with winter almost here."

Shaking her head, Raine looked at Charlie and said, "Maybe you should just release it tomorrow and let nature do its thing."

Charlie stared at the locke and felt her heart pitch at the idea. The animal was too weak to hunt and survive in the wild, at least right now. Already it appeared that the locke had been in a previous fight, losing a piece of its ear. She hoped enough food would give it a chance, but in reality, she was only going to be on Kander a few more days before she had to leave. Yet she wasn't ready to accept the truth. "Do you mind if I bring it inside the cabin for warmth?"

Raine sighed and gave her friend a pointed look. "I'll get a damn towel to put under it." She stood and limped to the cabin's door.

"Maybe two, so it can snuggle into one for warmth." Charlie gave a charming smile to her friend, who rolled her eyes and slammed the cabin door behind her. After a sigh, she looked at the locke and folded her arms to ward off the cold. "Come on." She climbed to her feet, picked up the cage, and went into the cabin. She decided to place the locke close to the lit fireplace, hoping it could warm up.

Raine came down with two towels and handed one to her friend. She folded up the second one and placed it on the floor near the cage. "Need help?"

Charlie was leery of opening the cage but didn't have a choice. She slid the latch, then opened the gate with a careful touch. She kept her eyes trained on the locke and prayed it didn't attempt to escape.

"I think it's too scared and weak to do anything." Raine remained hovering over Charlie's shoulder. "Just go slow."

Heeding Raine's advice, Charlie placed the towel into the cage but didn't push it against the animal. She placed it in the middle as an inviting ball and moved the bowls closer to the gate. "There you go." She closed the gate, then Raine helped her put the other towel under the locke's cage.

"Andren should be back from her walk soon," Raine said.

Charlie remained seated next to the cage but peered up at her friend. Andren had left to patrol the area to make sure everything was copacetic around the property. "We can talk then. Maybe up in the loft."

"Sounds good. I'm going to get changed." Raine rubbed Charlie's back for a moment, then left and went upstairs, her limp more noticeable after a long day.

Charlie looked at the locke and grumbled when it hadn't moved a tiny bit. The animal remained balled up with its pure white eyes peeking out between bits of matted fur. She had been certain that the cooked meat would entice the locke, but it was left untouched in the bowl. Charlie went to the kitchen and searched for something else that might be better, but she had no idea until she turned and studied the hatch in the floor.

Grabbing the handle, Charlie lifted the hatch and descended into the chilly cellar. She used her techbit's light while she searched for something else. To the left were several hanging meats that had been salted or smoked for later consumption. But the shelving nearby had wrapped salted meats, which she took for the locke.

After sealing up the cellar, Charlie cleaned and soaked the meat for a few minutes. She returned to the locke and smiled at it curled up on the towel. "Here." She poked a piece of raw meat through an opening. "You might like this better, I hope."

The locke stared at the offering and didn't seem any more interested in it than the cooked meat in the bowl.

Charlie sighed and whispered, "*Krafka.*" She nudged it closer but not in the locke's face, just near its nose. After a long minute, she started to withdraw it, but the locke moved its head closer to the raw meat. She held her breath as the locke sniffed it, then finally touched it with its tongue and front teeth. Holding down a cheer, Charlie waited for the locke to try the food.

The locke continued to nibble, then stretched its neck farther and pulled at the meat strip with the front of its teeth. It took a few attempts, but it accepted the food from Charlie and ate pieces of the strip.

Smiling, Charlie waited until the locke had finished the first strip before offering another one. She was grateful that the animal was eating something and could regain its strength. As they sat there looking at each other, Charlie wondered about the locke's future, knowing she'd have to release it in the next day or two. Digging around in her pockets, she pulled out the techbit, opened a playlist, and selected Something Just Like This from The Chainsmokers and Coldplay.

Charlie sang the lyrics in a soft voice, not wanting to disturb Chris, who had gone to bed early. The techbit rested on her knee as she stayed seated by the cage and watched the locke eat the food. Somehow it was comforting to see the animal eat, as if it wasn't quite broken or lost.

The locke finished the last bite, then settled into the blanket again. It stared at Charlie with its snow-white eyes that seemed ghostly at first, but Charlie deduced they were part of the locke's natural camouflage for the long winter.

"That's a good start," she told the animal, smiling at it. Charlie looked up when Andren returned from patrol, and she shut off the music.

Andren shut and bolted the door, then came over to Charlie. "All clear." For once, she didn't carry her spear, which was propped up against the exposed chimney.

"It's pretty quiet out here."

"*Ja.* But you can never be sure if someone is tracking you." Andren took a seat on the fireplace's hearth as she shivered a few times. She wore a heavier, black jacket, but every night was below freezing now. "It didn't eat?"

Charlie switched off the music, then replied, "It did. It ate some salted uncooked meat Raine had stored in the cellar."

Andren brightened at the news. "That's good." She folded her arms over her lap and leaned forward, bringing her closer to Charlie. "Did Raine go to bed?"

"She's waiting upstairs for us to talk about the mission." Charlie sighed and knew they should go upstairs, but she wasn't quite ready. There was one thing lingering in her mind that she hadn't been ready to ask Andren. She was unsure if she was prepared to hear the answer. Lowering her head, she listened to Andren get up and load more wood into the fire.

"Will you release the locke tomorrow morning?" Andren asked while grabbing another log.

"I don't know." Charlie watched the sleeping animal and realized it was worn out from lack of rest. "I wonder if it's an Omega or Alpha." She wasn't about to turn the locke over to figure it out, but she was curious.

"Omega." Andren sat down again on the hearth but closer to Charlie and the locke. She grinned when Charlie looked up at her. "One way to find out is to piss it off."

Charlie shook her head, and the silent question showed on her face

Andren pointed at the animal and said, "If it's an Omega, its eyes turn red when it's threatened or angry. If it's an Alpha, its eyes turn yellow."

"Really?" Charlie turned her awed features back to the locke. "I always thought all lockes' eyes turned red."

Andren leaned forward again and said, "*Joh.* Only the Omegas have red eyes."

Charlie filed the information away for later. But the conversation about Alphas and Omegas recharged her earlier question for Andren. She took a deep breath and stilled her fears about bringing something so secretive and dangerous to the light. Swallowing and fisting her hand, she turned her head sidelong and watched Andren's profile. "Back on the *Four Mag*, you said Kal wanted to protect me herself but couldn't."

"*Ja.*" Andren narrowed her eyes. "Why do you ask?"

Charlie played with the techbit in her lap, turning it through her hands. "Do you ever wonder why she wants to protect me?" She tried to be direct, but she feared how Andren might react, even though she suspected Andren knew about the ongoing affair.

Andren leaned forward, so close to Charlie's cheek. "Why does any Alpha get protective?"

Hearing an opening, Charlie turned her body around and saw the certainty in Andren's eyes. She warred between relief and worry, then whispered, "You know."

"I know." Andren smirked and mischief shined in her eyes. "Why do you think she chose me of all the guards?"

"You're cute," Charlie joked.

Andren snorted and shook her head. "As a child, I have always had great faith in Kalatas and what our god has planned for all our spirits. The day I gave my oath to serve, I also pledged my life to Kal. By both my faith and my oath I will never question what decisions or actions Kal makes, because I know they are sound ones."

Charlie stopped fidgeting with the techbit and held Andren's serious gaze, feeling the loyalty humming from Andren. "So you're okay with it?"

Smiling, Andren reached forward and clasped Charlie's shoulder. "I accept it." She squeezed hard, and that undid Charlie.

For a beat, Charlie hung her head and allowed another ounce of pressure to drop off her. She had been certain that Andren knew about the affair, but that didn't mean Andren was okay with it or wouldn't turn on them. A sharp sting started in her eyes, and Charlie couldn't fight off a few tears. "So few will accept it or even understand it."

"I must forgive you for being an Earthling," Andren said, a playfulness in her tone. "Your people haven't truly learned the following that Kalatas has on this planet."

Charlie huffed and whispered, "Not even Kalatas could stop a civil war when we showed up."

"But it was a civil war, not a slaughter. There was a divide, and Kal was able to cut out the deeper hatred among our people." Andren squeezed one last time, then drew her arm back to her lap. "Have some faith in Kalatas's will."

Wiping her eyes, Charlie nodded and said, "Maybe it's just all the Alphas that hate us."

"How certain are you it's all of the Alphas?"

Charlie sharpened at the honest question about the Alphas, especially considering that her lover was one of them. Kal was a different kind of Alpha on many levels. Somehow Andren's question challenged what Charlie thought she already understood about Kalmar. She then noticed Andren looked smug, almost too smug.

"Besides," Andren whispered, "How else could all those Kalman hybrids have been born?"

# Chapter 7

Charlie slowed down and lowered the cart. "Think this is far enough?"

Raine scanned the area and nodded.

"Far enough from the farm," Chris agreed, his hands on his hips.

Andren caught up to the three Earthlings and stood at the side of the cart. "It's pretty wooded here too."

Charlie sighed and decided it was the best place, so she went to the rear of the cart. She stood beside the cage and watched the animal continue to pace. This morning, she had checked on the locke; it had eaten the cooked meat in the bowl after refusing to last night. She fed it a larger meal this morning and decided its constant pacing was a positive sign. "Come on," she whispered and picked up the cage.

"Do you need help?" Raine asked.

Shaking her head, Charlie carried the cage and disappeared into the woods alone. She went a short distance, then lowered the cage to the ground and kneeled down. "Time for you to go." She encouraged the animal with a tender smile.

The locke looked at Charlie for the first time, its head tilted to one side.

"Be more careful out there too." Charlie reached for the gate's latch, worked it free, and opened the door. But the animal sat there, staring out of the opening. "Go on," she told it.

The locke dropped its tall ears, then crept out of the cage and tested its paws on the fallen leaves. It sniffed the ground, as if ensuring it was real. Taking more steps, it unfurled from the cage and stretched its body; it peered over its shoulder and held its gaze on her.

Charlie noticed a reflective sheen to the locke's solid white eyes, which soothed the worry she felt for the locke's future. She parted her lips, but she was silent and entranced by the animal's ferocious yet beautiful nature.

Without another glance, the locke bolted off and easily vanished as its gray coat blended in with nature.

For a moment, Charlie stayed there and searched the woods for any sign of the locke, but it was gone. She sighed, picked up the cage, and returned to her friends. "It's gone," she said when everyone looked at her. Raine squeezed Charlie's shoulder in silent support.

During the walk to work, Charlie stayed by herself and handled different messages on her techbit, including one from Starr that showed a copy of the bounty. Much to her chagrin, Magnar was included on the bounty. Nearing the city, she reminded Raine that she wanted to go to the Great Tower to take care of a few things before work. Her most important task was to call Victor and begin setting the trap.

Again, the city was quiet in the morning, and the smell of firewood, horse, and hints of food lingered in the air. Once past the Great Gate, Charlie separated from the group and continued to the Great Tower, Andren in tow. At the front entrance, Andren departed from Charlie's side and went to the barrack so she could speak with her commanding officer.

The Great Tower was quiet inside, other than the occasional guard, who either greeted or ignored her. She decided to try Kal's quarters first, but she wasn't there; then she went up a level to the fifty-second floor. Stepping off the lift, she noticed the last door was open again. Too curious, she wandered down to it but paused upon hearing those all-too-familiar determined grunts. She hesitated as a spark of jealousy burned inside her when her imagination went wild with images of Kal fucking someone else.

Clenching her teeth, she rounded the doorframe and entered the room, blinded by the sunlight that swallowed her. She blinked a few times before her eyes adjusted to the brightness, then took in the large room's contents. Opposite the door was a glass wall that offered a gorgeous view of Tarrak. Spread throughout the room were various exercise machines and muscle-building contraptions. Different ropes hung from the ceiling, and one very thick pair of ropes attached to metal rings that were anchored to the stone wall.

To her right, Kal was flat on her back on the floor with her legs extended and feet pressed against a metal tray attached to a rail. Square discs were piled on each other on a tray that moved up and down as Kal used her legs to push and lower it. However, she hesitated and twisted her head around after she took a deep breath.

Heat flooded Charlie's face while she stood there in awe. She had expected many things but not a workout room. Her memory jogged back to her brief conversation about Kal working hard to build her muscular body. It didn't occur to her that Kal also had to maintain her physique.

*You're such an idiot. Of course she has to keep training.*

Kal lowered the weighted tray until it hit the stopper. She rolled and stood, revealing her exposed body that shined in the sunlight. She wore a black breast wrap with shoulder straps and tight black shorts that hugged her upper thighs. Her only other attire was black leather straps on her wrist and leather shoes. As she approached, her glowing muscles flexed and curled with each step.

Charlie's eyes traced every contour and line until her attention centered on the apparent swelling between Kal's thighs. Earlier she had been cold, but now the room felt like an oven, and she fought with her jacket's zipper. She heard her heart drumming in her ears when Kal stood in front of her, filling her view. Charlie's smile was weak and her voice hoarse when she greeted her lover. "*Turen.*"

"*Turen.*" Kal rested her hands on her hips, a different stance for her. "You are early." Droplets of sweat trickled over her skin, rolled down, and reflected the light against her tan flesh. Her raven hair was tied up, and it was the first time

Charlie had seen it that way. "Charlie," she growled and cut through the staring.

"*Ja*?" Charlie shook her head to rid herself of the drooling look on her face and whispered, "*Perka gi.*" She scanned the workout room again and said, "I didn't realize you had a place like this."

Kal half turned on her heels and looked at the space too. "*Ja*." She turned back to Charlie and said, "This used to be the office, and the other room was for exercise."

"Why did you switch them?"

"I needed more space for training." Kal revealed a playful grin. "And the view is amazing."

Charlie was ogling over her lover's muscular body and whispered, "It is."

Kal narrowed her eyes after she realized Charlie's agreement wasn't about the window view. "Come with me." She directed Charlie through the maze of equipment.

Charlie was plenty inclined to follow behind Kal, whose ass looked so perfect in the tight shorts. She restrained herself from grabbing a handful and digging her nails into the fullness. She cleared her throat and stood next to Kal by the line of windows. Beyond the glass was the city of Tarrak, which was coming to life in the morning hours. But this view was different than the one from Kal's balcony. Not far off stood the Temple of Kalatas followed by homes, another gate, farmland, and then the forest in the distance. "It is beautiful."

"I have spent many hours thinking and planning in this room." Kal placed her palms against the glass and leaned into it. "Can you see the Hall of the Commanders?"

Charlie followed Kal's pointing and smiled at the familiar structure. "*Ja*." She peered up at her lover bent forward against the glass. "How are you doing?"

"Almost normal." Kal met Charlie's thoughtful gaze and said, "My rut is nearly done."

Nibbling on her lip, Charlie sighed and whispered, "That sucks." She grinned at Kal's raised eyebrow. "Earthling slang for when we don't like something."

Kal huffed and pushed off the glass. "Why are you here so early?"

Charlie sensed that she wasn't put off by her presence, but curious. "I need to contact Victor. I didn't really want to do it around the others and needed a private spot." Part of her wanted to perform the transmission near Kal, even though she couldn't understand English.

"You can do that here or in the office."

Turning, Charlie searched the room for a spot that was neutral. She didn't want Victor to read into anything about her location. She found an area of the stone wall that had nothing of importance or any detail for Victor. There was only a wooden table with several chairs. "I'll do it over there." She unzipped her leather jacket the rest of the way and walked toward the far wall, near the burning fireplace.

Kal followed and took a seat at the table while Charlie pulled out a chair. "Will he answer?"

"Only one way to find out." Charlie pulled out the techbit and retrieved Victor's contact information from their first transmission. "Don't say anything or make any noise. My techbit has a pretty sensitive microphone." After Kal's nod, she took a deep breath and prepared to face Victor, who had a talent for getting under her skin. She tapped the button on the techbit, then propped up the device on the table. She cut her eyes to Kal, about to say something until Victor answered the call.

"*Hello,* Charlie."

Forcing her clenched jaw to relax, Charlie narrowed her eyes. "Victor." She swallowed and folded her arms as she leaned back in the chair and returned in English, "*I don't have a lot of time for small talk since I have bounty hunters on my ass.*" She loathed his smug expression.

"*You were given an opportunity to return our property to us.*"

"*She's not fucking property*," Charlie snarled and fisted her hands against her body.

"*She was bought and paid for*," Victor said. "*You stole her from us, killed multiple soldiers, and destroyed our QMT in the process. The Grand Marshal put a heavy price on your head for such crimes*."

"*Yeah five hundred thousand or more!*" Charlie uncrossed her arms and tried ignoring Kal when she shifted too.

"*So you've heard*." Victor's eyes were full of mirth, but then it was gone. "*I warned you*."

"*Remove the goddamn, fucking bounty!*"

Victor tilted his head, then leaned back in a chair. He appeared to be in his office again and had two tablets with him. "*That is out of my control*."

Charlie seethed and grabbed the table's edge with both hands. "*Remove the bounty or—*"

"*Or what? You'll rally the mercenary coalition that you're no longer a member of?*"

Breathing harder each tick, Charlie struggled to remain in control even if she was intentionally overplaying her anger. She was unnerved that Victor knew her history with the mercenary coalition or at least was aware of it. Refocusing on her true mission, she asked, "*What if I hand over Starr? Will the bounty be removed?*"

Victor tilted his head and sat in momentary silence before he said, "*You are on Kander while she is not. I don't see how that's possible*."

"*And if it's possible, can the bounty be removed?*"

Victor was silent and stared for a long moment before he said, "*The Grand Marshal would want proof that you have her*."

Charlie gave a grunt, then dragged her fingers through her hair. "*I think it'll be easy to capture her since she's with Magnar, who also has a short bounty on her head*."

"*Show me you have her in your possession, then we can talk again*." Victor revealed a toothy smile.

Still fuming, Charlie reached toward the screen and ordered, "*Put a hold on the bounty*."

Victor grinned at her. "*I think not.*" His smirk widened each tick until he reminded Charlie of an ugly villain in the comic books. "*Until then, I'll be waiting. Good luck.*"

Charlie opened her mouth, but the transmission ended. "*Bastard!*" She flipped the techbit and peered over at Kal, who had taut features.

"That seemed to go well," Kal said, a rumble in her chest.

"Well enough." Charlie folded her arms on the table and leaned against it. "He seems to be taking the bait at least." She grinned and considered her plan, which was getting the ship and meeting up with Starr. "Now we wait for that ship to arrive. It should be here on the seventh of the nineth."

Kal nodded and leaned back in the chair, a thoughtful look on her face. "Victor's English was different from yours."

Charlie was surprised that Kal noticed the difference between their accents. "*Ja.*" She tucked the techbit in her leather jacket. "There were thousands of languages on Earth. Victor's native language on Earth wasn't English, but he learned it. So when he speaks in English, his native tongue shows through with how he pronounces stuff." She considered their earlier conversation and said, "His English is actually pretty good compared to some of the other Serrato soldiers I heard."

Kal was silent for a moment and tilted her head. "Kander has only ever had one language." She then stood up and went over to one of the machines. "He agreed to remove the bounty if you brought him Starr?" She picked up a cup from the floor and drank from it.

"Kind of." Charlie slouched against the chair and watched her lover come back. "He wanted proof first that I had Starr."

Sitting down, Kal swallowed more from the tall, clay cup. "Have you heard from her?"

"*Ja.* They're less than two days out, but they won't come here. They'll hide out at another location until I can meet them." Charlie was quiet and held Kal's steady gaze. "I talked to Raine last night about Melissa Hoyt."

Kal canted her head and folded her arms, which caused her biceps to stand out.

Charlie swallowed and kept her focus on Kal's face rather than let her eyes wander. "She thinks Hoyt is trustworthy and can get the information." She hesitated while thinking back on the former Air Force soldier. "Having Raine talk to her might be a good idea. We're already planning to go to New Earth soon."

"If there is time for that," Kal said.

Charlie blew out a breath and nodded. "*Ja.* I guess we can see what we get out of Victor about the Sworne." She faltered because her conversations and plans with Kal involved their working together more each time. As she closed her eyes, the conversation with Andren came back to her, and she whispered, "She knows." Lifting her head, Charlie saw her lover's curious stare. "Andren knows about us."

"I am aware."

Sighing and leaning against the table, Charlie rubbed her brow and continued discussing her brief conversation with Andren. "But I needed to know. I needed to find out if she was okay with it or if she was going to turn on us."

"Andren is loyal and–"

"I know." Charlie lowered her hands to her lap and frowned. "I know now. I just…."

"You are scared."

Charlie bristled but then agreed with the truth, even if it was hard. "I'm scared for you." She watched Kal set the clay container off to the side of the table. "Maybe of the future too and what this revolt could mean." They were circling back to the same unresolved topic, and she could see that Kal was unwavering and firm.

"At the moment, it is not a revolt." Kal rested back in the chair. "It is movement by a rebellious group that has been slowly dying since I took power. They are still trying to rekindle the civil war, but they don't have enough support." She paused, then explained, "For the past few years they have been inactive to the point that I thought they were gone."

"But they're not," Charlie said, feeling better that she was learning the details.

"They are not," Kal agreed, "because I haven't found their leader."

"Cut off the head of the snake," Charlie whispered before she sighed and slumped in the chair. "How did you find out they're active again?"

"They're holding meetings and gatherings to build support, always in secret."

Charlie bowed her head and studied her lover, who was agitated by the rebel group.

"They're also threatening, attacking, and kidnapping Earthlings in Kardos." Kal shook with a displeased rumble. "They appear well funded."

"Do they have a name? Is that Alpha Prime?"

Kal's lips curled, revealing her canines. "*Ja.*"

Charlie couldn't hold back a snort. "Is Alpha Prime the best they could come up with?" However, it was clear that the rebel group's name agitated Kal, who was the planet's ruler or the real Alpha Prime. She cleared her throat and said, "All it takes is a wrong move, then you have them."

"Just as they're hoping with me."

Charlie's mind skipped to their secretive affair, which would add fuel to the fire and spark the revolt that Alpha Prime wanted. "*Ja,* but you are the ruler, not them." Andren's reminder echoed in her head about people following Kal because she harnessed Kalatas's spirit. "You are Kal."

For a moment, Kal remained quiet, then released a heavy breath before she glanced at the burning fire to Charlie's right. "I am Kal, but even I have a weakness." Her eyes trailed back to Charlie, lingering with something unreadable.

Charlie softened and shook her head after Kal's meaning struck a chord. "It's not me." She grabbed the techbit, tucked it away, and stood from the chair. She neared her lover, who had to tilt her head back for once. "It's not us." Her voice was strong, grounding them both. But when Kal rose up, Charlie held her next breath and watched the Alpha loom over her. Her clit pulsed in reaction to the power and dominance emitting from Kal.

"Does Raine expect you back soon?" Kal's voice was heady and sent a shock through Charlie.

Gasping, Charlie managed a faint headshake and fisted her hands at her side to restrain herself. "*J-job.*" Already she felt the wetness between her thighs and knew it was exciting Kal's Alpha.

"Take off your clothes," Kal ordered.

Charlie faltered and glanced about the room, unsure of their privacy. Was there even a place for them to shower? Or would they have to sneak down to Kal's quarters to clean and get rid of their mixed scents? A soft growl forced her attention back to her lover.

"Now."

From the first time together, Charlie trusted Kal, and today was the same. She shrugged off her jacket and placed it on the chair behind her, then started to strip away the layers. Kal stood with her arms folded and full attention on Charlie, who became more flushed with each passing tick. Her skin was burning by the time she pulled off her soaked underwear—her last article of clothing. As soon as she tossed it, strong hands picked her up and placed her on the table top, nearly knocking the clay cup over. Charlie moaned and spread her legs, knowing her scent was wrapping around the Alpha.

Kal stepped into the inviting space and bent forward, breathing in Charlie's smell. "I don't have a lot of time."

Charlie smirked and peered up at her lover. "I don't mind rushed." She pressed her hands flat against Kal's firm stomach, whimpering at the muscles fitting into her palms. "But the throne room is above us."

Growling, Kal bit Charlie's neck and earned a sharp hiss. "It's called an *alping*," she whispered and growled.

Squeezing her eyes shut, Charlie managed to register the Kalmarese word, then clawed the hard flesh under her blunt nails and started to pant after Kal released her neck. Slight dizziness washed over her, but large hands on her hips kept her anchored. Then Kal soothed the pain with her tongue, licking the throbbing pulse point. Charlie groaned at the sensation and trailed her hand down lower. Once past Kal's shorts, she wrapped her fingers around the hard shaft and squeezed it.

Kal dragged her teeth along Charlie's vein, higher to an inviting ear. Her rumbles turned into throaty thunder as Charlie played with her cock.

Charlie scraped her nails down her lover's stomach muscles but slipped her other hand into the back of Kal's shorts. She clawed a handful of Kal's ass that she'd craved earlier. With her other hand, she continued to massage and squeeze the hard length. "*Vuk*," she whispered and moaned after the needy sensation sparked in her gut, making her clit throb. "Sumner, *krafka*," she begged.

Kal snarled and nipped an ear, then picked up Charlie from the table.

With a yelp, Charlie hooked her arms and legs around her lover's large frame but whined at losing her hold on Kal's cock. Her soaking clit pushed against Kal's washboard stomach muscles, and she started to grind her hips.

Carrying Charlie, Kal slipped between a few pieces of equipment, then slowed down.

Charlie felt her back press into cool leather. There was a bench between Kal's legs that connected to a vertical back that Kal had Charlie pressed against. She gasped when Kal lifted one of her legs over her shoulder. Without instruction, Charlie lifted her right leg against Kal, then placed her hands against Kal's biceps, latching onto them for support. But Kal freed her right hand and reached down to her shorts.

Lifting her head, Charlie watched the shorts slip down enough and allowed Kal's stiff penis to spring free. She whimpered at the swollen head that brushed near her clit, teasing her. When Kal's hand went back to her hip, she held on again and arched her back in want. She was dripping and turned on since the moment she first saw Kal working out.

Rocking her hips, Kal rubbed the underside of her cock between the slick warmth and growled deep and long. For a tick, she seemed to forget that time was short this morning and massaged Charlie's clit with her cock. But the shift was instant, her hips going back farther, then she nudged the head against Charlie's entrance.

"Fuck," Charlie hissed, rolling her hips to spread her wetness over the head kissing her opening. "Fuck me, *krafka*."

Kal leaned forward but only a little, causing the head to spread Charlie's entrance open. Barring her teeth, she demanded, "Did you think I was fucking someone else in here?"

Charlie was red with guilt and remembered the fiery jealousy in her gut when she heard Kal's grunts. Her tied tongue prompted Kal's snarl.

"Tell me," Kal ordered. She moved her hips just enough to cause the head of her cock to rock in and out of Charlie. "Or I stop."

"*Ja!*" Charlie was panting and clung to Kal's biceps, desperate to be filled. "*Ja*," she whispered with a hint of regret. "I heard you grunting and thought the worst because you could have anyone."

Kal remained still and silent, then growled and plunged half her cock into Charlie, cutting away the separation between them. She bent forward, as far as possible, and hissed, "I could." She was inches from Charlie's face, eyes bright with fire, and half buried in Charlie. "But you are the only one I will have." She pushed her cock deeper, grunting like she had earlier this morning. "Again and again."

Charlie clawed the biceps under her hands and whimpered at the Alpha's promise. She wanted to voice her agreement, but her throat was swollen with emotions. She managed a nod and cried out when Kal drew her cock out, then pushed in again. Finally the rhythmic fucking started, and she dropped her head back on the board. Kal's throbbing length drove in and out of her wet, clenching muscles. Heat and pressure built up through her entire body, making her gasp and tremble. Kal's grunts grew louder and sent shocks up Charlie's stomach.

Kal snarled and continued to rut into her lover, more Alpha than ruler. She forced her hips faster, causing Charlie to scream louder, unrestrained with pleasure.

As spasms started in her gut, Charlie felt the passion constrict in her chest and heat buzzed in her head. She was close and wanted more than just one orgasm, even if Kal was pressed for time. She clawed her lover's biceps, lifted her head, and through clenched teeth, she demanded, "Don't stop!" Her lover's dark eyes were wild and determined, like her ramming hips. The next thrust sent Charlie over the edge, but the Alpha kept pace as promised. She could feel the shaking in Kal, who was close to her own limit.

Glancing down, Charlie noticed the knot at the base of Kal's penis, but it had shrunk enough to make Charlie wonder if she could handle it. But taking it in would mix their scents and cause a permanent change that every Kalmar would smell on them. Clenching her lips between her teeth, she dropped her head against the bench and gasped before crying out again.

"I'm going to *fercher*," Kal said between grunts. Her shaking body grew tenser with each thrust, so close to climaxing. After a furious snarl, she rammed her cock in deeper, sparking pleasure up Charlie's spine.

Charlie trembled as the second orgasm wracked her body. She then sensed Kal pulling out far too soon, and she hissed in both displeasure and pain. "Don't," she snapped and dug her nails into taut muscles.

"I'm about to—"

"I don't care," Charlie snarled, a death threat written on her face. She sucked in the next breath when Kal's cock buried back in her. Then she groaned at feeling the hot *quima* rushing inside her, taking away the tiniest bits of separation between them. Charlie whimpered and dropped her head against the bench, relaxing her body into the aftershocks. She felt the *quima* moving out of her, reminding them of their lack of union.

Kal was panting but still held up Charlie without weakness. She gently rocked her hips, massaging the head of her cock against Charlie's inner walls. They moaned and whimpered together, savoring the sensation. After a minute, she stopped and adjusted an arm under Charlie's ass while the other went behind Charlie, lifting her off the board. "I have to get ready."

Charlie's inner walls were clamped on Kal's cock, smaller spasms carrying through her body. "I know." She had help lowering her shaky legs, wrapping them around Kal's stomach and back.

Kal took Charlie away from the equipment and carried her across the room, opposite direction of the fireplace with Charlie's clothes.

Twisting her head around, Charlie noticed an opening in the stone wall. They entered it to reveal a private bathroom space. To her right was a walk-in shower with an overhead rain shower head. On the left was a frosted, full-length glass window and a toilet tucked in front of it, then a sink with Kal's folded clothes on the counter. She was awed by the niche of a bathroom, and it was enough room for them.

Pressing Charlie's back into the chilly stone tile, Kal stretched her arm and turned on the overhead rain shower that took a minute to warm. "Are you going to let go of me now?" She raised an eyebrow and peered down at their joined bodies.

Flushed again, Charlie tested her body and pulled away from Kal's cock, groaning at the loss. She unwrapped her legs but relied on Kal to help her stand.

Kal groaned while freeing herself from Charlie, who held on as she stood again.

Charlie's legs were sore and so was the rest of her after being stretched and fucked so well. She loved the feeling and stayed close to Kal. "That'll hold me over until my payment is due." She traced her fingertips along the distinct lines on Kal's stomach, then peered up with a wicked smile.

After a grunt, Kal turned and shifted to the other wall, reaching for the shampoo bar, but she hesitated when Charlie encircled her waist and pressed into her back. For a minute, she remained stiff and seemed unsure about being held for the first time. After a deep breath, Kal relaxed against Charlie and rumbled from a few soft kisses on her back. She turned around, broke the contact, and held out the shampoo.

Charlie accepted the bar and smiled. Together, they showered faster than normal and hurried to get into their clothes after drying off with towels. Charlie was tying her boots next to the fireplace when Kal exited the bathroom in her regular attire. She paused and stared at her lover from across the room.

Kal grabbed her long jacket from the hook near the entrance and shrugged it on while walking over to Charlie. "I must go. I have a meeting with three Jerothian engineers."

Snaring her jacket from the chair, Charlie put it on but didn't zipper it. "Really?" She pulled her wet hair out from between her jacket and shirt. "What is it about?"

Kal pivoted and waited for Charlie to go first. "I am considering an electric monorail train between the capitals."

Charlie's jaw went slack, and she stared at Kal for a moment. "That would be amazing."

"It will be a major undertaking," Kal said, following Charlie to the open door to the hallway. "But if the rumors of the Sworne are true, then the project will have to be put on hold."

Charlie combed her damp hair as they went down the hallway. She considered the technology changes for Kander and how much Kal was investing into it. It was well-known throughout the galaxy that the Kalmar had money stocked away due to their resources and frugal nature. If Kal was willing to sell or trade darakar to other races in the galaxy, then the planet's fortunes were heavy. "I guess we'll find out." She tucked her hands into her jacket pockets and turned when Kal stopped by the sealed office doors. "I should receive word today about the ship's location."

"Tomorrow we will discuss the soldiers that'll be joining you on the mission." Kal grabbed the nearest handle, but remained still. "You will also meet them."

Charlie conceded rather than meeting them minutes before they all boarded a ship together. "Roger that." She grinned when Kal narrowed her eyes at the jargon. "*Ja*." She should have left, but the string around her heart pulled her forward into Kal's space.

Kal responded and met her lover halfway, bending down to met Charlie for a soft kiss. But she didn't linger long, so that their scents wouldn't stick to each other.

Charlie entered the lift and blew out a shaky breath while she closed the gate. Getting fucked this morning had been unplanned but exciting and what she needed today. Even now, her sex was pleasantly sore and left her in a good mood. Once she was off the lift, she exited the Great Tower and located Andren, who was smirking.

"You said thirty minutes at the most," Andren chided, taking Charlie's side during their walk on the pathway across the lawn.

Charlie scratched her neck, then zipped her jacket to ward off the cold. "We got into a heated conversation."

Andren responded with a rumble and remained quiet, but amusement was written all over her face.

Charlie rolled her eyes, then took stock of Andren's new attire. She grinned at the change because it meant that Kal took their compromise seriously. "I like the hat."

Andren adjusted the black beanie style hat and grunted at the comment. She also wore a heavy, plain black coat that went just past her waist. It appeared old with its frayed edges and few sewn patches. Her pants were similar to the coat, but weren't as tight as her soldier attire. Andren also didn't carry her spear or laser rifle, but Charlie assumed there were laser handguns hidden somewhere. She also noticed the sword on Andren's left side.

With Andren now dressing and acting like a civilian, the rest of their walk was quiet because the citizens ignored them. As they neared Raine's stall, Charlie fidgeted with her wet hair until she came to an abrupt stop.

Andren faltered and asked, "What's wrong?"

"My hair. It's wet and Raine is going to notice it." She looked toward the stall and saw her friend and Chris talking to a patron. "She'll ask me why." Her gut tightened to the point that she took a step back, and an alarm sounded in her head. She was about to turn away until Andren gripped her shoulder.

"Here." Andren pulled off her hat and held it out to Charlie. "Just wear this and tell her you were cold."

"But—"

"Just do it." Andren shoved the hat into Charlie's chest. "Come on."

Charlie twisted up her hair and put the beanie on. "*Tah.* You're a lifesaver."

"Oh now I am," Andren said, a glint in her eyes.

Charlie sighed and tossed a glare at Andren, but she smiled thinking of their healed friendship, which had grown deeper now that they were both honest and open about Charlie's relationship with Kal. As she neared Raine, her sister, her smile cracked and a pang of regret chewed away at her brief happiness.

*I wish I could share this with her too.*

# Chapter 8

Charlie checked the time on the techbit and sighed loudly enough for Raine to give her a look. "He should be here by now." She continued to pace but paused when she felt like someone was watching her.

Raine was huddled against the side of the old windmill, staying out of the chilly wind. "Well, Kal said they detected the ship outside the solar system, right?"

"*Ja*," Charlie replied, her tone distant. Something earlier had tickled her senses, and she continued scanning the forest on the other side of the creek next to the windmill. Not finding anything, she sighed and gazed up at the skies, expecting to see the new ship any tick. She looked over at Andren, who was walking around and snacking on jerky.

"What's this guy's name again?" Raine asked.

"His name is Sres," Charlie replied and popped the collar of her leather jacket. With her arms crossed for warmth, she did her best to ignore the cold. "Have you met a Gyr before?"

Raine shook her head and looked over at Andren, who had rejoined them.

"They look like a *dragon* or *lizard*," Charlie said. "Sres has this cool mohawk fin over the crest of his head."

Raine grew wide eye and grinned. "Do they talk with a hiss?"

Charlie mirrored the smirk and nodded. "*Ja*, it can get a little hard to understand them at times."

"How do you know Sres?" Andren asked.

"I bought the *Pacifica* off him. He was recommended to me by another merc." Charlie gazed up at the sky and thought back to the first time she'd met Sres. "He sells and trades large equipment, mostly used stuff." She had also made another purchase from Sres, piggybacking off the sale of the ship to get a discount. "I'll do the talking when he gets here."

"Well, you're the only one that can speak Jero," Raine reminded.

Charlie shrugged and said, "True." Then a boom drew her attention upward to the distant but reflective metal. "I think that's him."

Andren and Raine stepped away from the windmill and looked up into the blue sky. But they all were forced to take shelter next to the building as the winds kicked up more from the ship's arrival. They cursed and ducked around the other side when it became too strong. After everything settled and the engines went silent, Charlie came around the side first.

The massive ship was a single haul vessel with four streamline engines on either side that continued humming even after they were shut down. The sunlight reflected off the ship's mirror-like finish as they neared it. At the stern a large door unlocked and started to lower, but the lift was empty.

Charlie made her way inside, then smiled upon seeing the single shuttle inside the bay. "Come on," she yelled back to Andren and Raine as she approached the shuttle and ran her hand along its side. "*Hey*, Sres."

Sres wore all black leather and revealed a toothy smile upon seeing Charlie. "*I guessss I found the right planet, then*." He walked over and held out his arm, shaking her hand once before he yanked Charlie into a one-arm hug. "*It'sss good to see you again*." He then took notice of the others behind Charlie and hooked his clawed fingers on the upper part of his vest.

"*These are my friends*." Charlie turned to them and indicated them each. "*This is* Raine *and* Andren. *They don't really speak Jero*."

Sres nodded, then shook hands and traded smiles with Raine and Andren. He turned to Charlie and asked, "*Did you look over the inspection report for the ship?*"

"*Yes.*" Charlie had spent this morning going over it with Kal, ensuring that Kal was comfortable with what she was purchasing from Sres. They had plans to meet again this afternoon, despite Charlie's attempt to have Kal join her for the tour of the new ship. But Kal insisted that her presence would only spark gossip about Kander purchasing the ship rather Charlie. "*Tour then?*"

Sres's thin lips pulled back, revealing his razor teeth again. "*Yesss.*" He turned toward the shuttle bay's great expanse and said, "*We can start here.*" He pointed at the shuttle and went over the details about it. "*You have room for another shuttle, smaller though.*"

Charlie nodded and started to follow Sres through the bay to the main door that led to the ship's belly. She glanced back at Andren and Raine. "Sres is going to show us around."

"Can't wait," Raine whispered while her head pivoted in every direction, taking in all the interior details.

Charlie grinned and passed the open door into the first hall that she suspected was the berthing area.

Sres was walking slowly but talking much faster. "*So the ship hasss two deckss. It'sss a hundred ten vitesss in length, twenty vitesss beam, and about thirty-two vitesss tall.*"

"*There's four cabins plus a captain's quarters, right?*" Charlie wanted to be certain that the ship had enough room for everyone.

"*Yesss, there'sss four cabinsss with four bunksss per cabin. There'sss two quartersss—one for the captain and one for a first mate.*" Sres paused by a sealed door, rapped on it twice, and entered the room after it opened up. "*Here isss a berth.*"

Charlie took in the berth, which was plenty wide and tall for an Alpha. The bunk beds appeared to be large enough to handle an Alpha's bigger stature.

"*Head isss in the next door.*"

Poking her head in, Charlie saw the sink, stand-up shower, and toilet. "*All the berths are like this?*" She slipped past her friends, who were inspecting the room too.

"*Yesss.*" Sres waited by the door. "*There is enough room for eighteen to twenty people*," he said, stepping out of the room into the hall. "*I'll show you the messss, storeroomsss, and galley next, then the engine roomsss, ammunition compartment, hold, citadel, garden, and we'll end at the bridge.*"

Charlie and her friends continued the tour with Sres, covering the entire ship from aft to bow. After leaving the garden, they entered the bridge last, which was larger than the *Pacifica*'s own. The bridge had five seats—one each for the pilot and co-pilot, then three more chairs behind them on an upper level. The ship was designed for the pilot and captain to be separate roles, depending on the owner's desires.

Sitting in the pilot's seat, Charlie looked over the navigation system; she could tell the AI was advanced enough that the ship could be flown by one person. Such newer technology wasn't original to the ship but had been upgraded at some point. Overall, she was pleased with it and swiveled the chair into Sres's direction.

"*So?*"

Charlie smiled and folded her hands in her lap. "*I'll take it.*" *Or rather Kal will take it.* "*But not for the full two thou, Sres.*" She saw his features twist with annoyance. "*You know I won't pay full price.*"

"*And you're not in the coalition anymore*," Sres said, folding his arms.

Charlie glowered and stretched out her legs, staring at her boots for a moment. "*After all the referrals.*" She narrowed her eyes at him, daring him to argue the number of times she'd pointed clients to Sres for a ship purchase. "*Did you bring the suit?*"

Sres rested his hands on his hips. "*I promised I would include that in the sale.*"

Charlie was excited to see the suit, but she kept a neutral face. "*Okay. How about a hundred ninety thou?*" She stood and offered her arm, hoping to complete the deal.

Sres hissed low and blinked twice, his eyelids sliding from left to right. He grumbled, then took the final offer.

"*Great.*" Charlie smirked, leaned in, and whispered, "*All I need is a test ride.*" She always made sure to get a rundown of the ship's flight systems from the seller. She'd heard too many horror stories in the past of new owners doing something stupid because they didn't ask for a lesson.

Sres sighed and released arms. "*I figured.*" He glanced at the other two next to them. "*Will they fly with usss?*"

Charlie turned to her friends and asked, "Ready to go for a ride?"

"I'll co-pilot," Raine said.

Andren was pale in the cheeks, but she nodded.

Charlie smiled wider and looked at Sres. "*Let's do it.*"

* * *

Standing beside the ship, Charlie studied the exterior and thought about the flight she took with Sres. Everything about the ship was correct and flew well, though a bit sluggish due to its size. The *Pacifica* had been smaller, sleeker, and easier to maneuver. However, the *Pacifica* was designed to be a fast ship to get Charlie to her clients, not move people through space.

Charlie slowed beside the engine port and looked at Sres. "*Was a coat of thermal put on recently?*"

"*Yesss, I had it done before I brought it to you.*" Sres folded his arms and started shaking from the cold weather. "*It wasss due for a new coat.*"

Pleased, Charlie nodded and noticed that Andren and Raine continued walking the perimeter of the ship. "*We can go back in the bay where it's warmer and take care of the documents.*"

Sres agreed and returned to the bay, sighing from the warmth. He pulled out two work stools that were tied under a bench along the wall. He signaled for Charlie to sit with him.

Charlie heard Andren and Raine coming back, but she focused on the paperwork with Sres. As they traded documents between their techbits, she asked, "*Does the ship have a name?*"

"*Yesss. Its former owner called it the… Betty May.*" Sres stumbled over the name, unsure of the English pronunciation.

Charlie's eyebrows hiked up, and she snorted low at the unexpected name. "*You're kidding.*" She hadn't heard of any ships with Earthling-like names besides the *Pacifica.*

But Sres stared at her, then said, "*He told me it'sss named after hisss mate.*"

Charlie lowered the techbit to her lap and asked, "*Was his mate an Earthling?*"

"*I believe so. She died awhile ago.*" Sres continued working on his techbit with the holo screen up.

Puzzled by the history, Charlie wanted to know more about the ship's former owner. "*What did he use it for?*"

Sres tapped a few more things, then looked at Charlie. "*He transported passengersss around the galaxy for a fee. That'sss why he had a garden room for the longer tripsss.*" After Charlie's low sound, he said, "*I believe Earth was one of his frequent stopsss, and that'sss where he met hisss mate. She left Earth to be with him.*"

Charlie shook her head, trying to imagine a female Earthling giving up her home to go to outer space with an alien. It was uncommon for Earthlings to leave their planet, not believing in extraterrestrial life until the Sworne. "*That's quite a story.*" She returned to her techbit and checked over the documents from Sres, then sent her payment to him.

"*I uploaded your data to the ship'sss AI.*"

In ticks, Charlie was linked up with the ship through her techbit and had full control of it. "*Do you need a ride up to orbit?*"

"*Someone isss coming down for me.*" Sres twisted his head when a low rumble filtered into the bay. "*That should be him.*" He slid off the stool and said, "*I have to gather my thingsss.*" He only went a few steps but paused when Charlie called for him.

"*Where is the suit?*"

"*I left it in the closet of the captain'sss quartersss.*" Sres hurried off.

"So it's yours now?" Raine asked, nearing her friend.

Charlie grinned and replied, "*Ja.*" She hadn't told anyone that it was technically Kal's property and had little idea what would become of the ship after the mission. "Get this. The ship is called the *Betty May.*"

Andren looked between them, confused by the name.

"What?" Raine laughed and touched Charlie's arm. "Tell me you're keeping it."

"It's bad luck to rename a ship."

Raine nodded several times. "So how big is this ship?"

"It's a hundred ten *vites*, which is about…." Charlie did the estimation in her head, then said, "Around two hundred fifty feet, more or less."

Raine whistled low.

Charlie turned when Sres rejoined them. "*Thanks for the new rocket.*"

Sres shook arms with Charlie, smiling big. "*Don't blow up thisss one like the last one.*"

Charlie rolled her eyes and ended the shake. "*Safe travels, Sres.*"

Heading to the open bay door, Sres paused at the top of the ramp and turned back toward Charlie. Across the distance, he hollered, "*Sometimesss he would call this ship the Bitching Betty.*" He had a confused expression, turned, and started down the ramp.

"Did he just say *bitching*?" Raine asked, a humorous note in her voice.

"*Ja*, he did." Charlie shook her head and hoped that it was a joke more than a warning. "I need to get back to Tarrak. You're okay with handling supplies?"

Raine nodded, having promised this morning that she would manage getting the ship loaded. Kal already had food, water, bedding, munitions, and other supplies prepared for the mission. Raine would direct the soldiers where to put everything and organize it later.

"*Tah.*" Charlie and Andren left the *Betty May* and returned to the waiting hover truck that they had borrowed from the Guard. Andren drove them back to the city and parked near the barracks. As they walked over to the barracks, Charlie glanced at the suns that were reaching the highest point in the sky. There was enough daylight to get the *Betty May* loaded for the mission tomorrow.

Entering the building, Andren learned that the High Commander was at the commander's office. They crossed the busy training fields and entered the hall on the other side. At the end of the hall, the sealed doors were decorated with ornate bronze symbols of the military. Andren knocked on a door and pushed it open after she heard an order to enter.

Charlie followed and took in the rustic office that was smaller than Kal's. She remained next to Andren while Kal and the commander stood from their seats around the desk. Upon introductions, Charlie shook arms and said, "Commander Akron and I met before."

Kal hooked her hands in front of her and glanced at Akron, who nodded in agreement. She shifted her attention to Andren and ordered her to wait outside the office with the doors closed. Once they were alone, Kal took control of the conversation. "Did you take delivery of the ship?"

"*Ja.*"

Kal retrieved the tablet from her jacket pocket and tapped the screen a few times. After a beep, she ordered someone to have the supplies sent out to the ship. Ending the call, she refocused on their meeting and said, "We have selected the twelve soldiers who will accompany you on the mission."

"Does the twelve include Andren?" Charlie asked, looking between the two leaders.

"*Ja,*" Kal replied.

Akron clasped his hands behind his back and said, "There will be four Omegas and eight Alphas. Andren is the only one from the Guard."

"They are highly skilled and disciplined," Kal said.

Akron gave a low rumble. "Don't plan to make friends with them."

Charlie cut her attention to Akron as he continued to speak to her. "They understand the importance of this mission and will make any sacrifice necessary to capture Victor."

"I just need to know they'll follow my orders," Charlie said, looking between Kal and Akron. "I don't need insubordination on the ship. Or else I'll lock them up."

Akron shook with soft thunder but looked to Kal, who was calmer than he.

"I have instructed them to follow your orders." Kal held Charlie's stare, and something threatening lurked beneath the surface in her eyes. "They have been warned that anything less will result in their life being forfeited."

Charlie blew out a breath, not really wanting to kill any Kalmar soldier for disobedience. But holding up one's honor in the Kalmar culture was the foundation of their identity. She nodded and asked, "What are their ranks?"

"They are all lances except for one," Akron replied. "Their one commanding officer is a shield master."

Charlie nodded and went through her knowledge about the Kalmar military. The lance position was a step above a blade, which was the entry-level role in the military. The shield and shield master was an officer who commanded the lances and blades, but Charlie couldn't recall how many soldiers a shield commanded at one time.

"We will go meet the lances first," Kal instructed, "then the shield master." She departed the office with everyone in tow and headed to the training field.

Akron hollered an order, which caused ten soldiers to break from their training and hustle over to them. He waited until the ten soldiers lined up in a single row before he introduced Charlie to each one. By the end, Charlie had no idea whether she would remember all the names but decided that most of her interactions would be with the shield master.

They left the training field and returned to the hallways of the barracks, then wrapped around a few turns until they came to a door. Akron knocked first, then entered, garnering the nine soldiers' attention. Each of them were in the middle of doing something different, such as relaxing between shifts, hanging clean attire, or changing into fresh clothes. But they all stood and remained at attention, waiting for their leaders.

"Shield Master Laken," Akron called.

Laken was an Alpha, but mere inches shorter than the others.

Charlie raised an eyebrow as Laken marched up from the back of the shared quarters. She glanced at Kal, who seemed indifferent about Laken's appearance.

"*Ja*, Commander Akron." Laken hooked her arms behind her back and stood proud, even though she was only dressed in pants and a breast wrap, caught between changing her attire.

"This is Captain Charlie." Akron pivoted and held out his hand to her. "She will be your officer for the mission."

Laken stepped forward and offered her arm to Charlie, all her prominent muscles on display. She rumbled low and deep, showing her Alpha personality.

Charlie cleared her throat and clasped the thick arm. In a few ticks, she concluded that although Laken was well-built she couldn't hold a torch to Kal. "Great to meet you."

Laken nodded once then returned to her position. Charlie refrained from rolling her eyes at Laken's typical Alpha personality.

"What time will we depart tomorrow?" Laken asked.

"Probably just after the twelfth hour," Charlie replied. "Will you and the unit be ready by then?"

"We are ready now."

Charlie pursed her lips, then stole a glance at Kal, who was every bit the ruler with a calm exterior. "Great. See you tomorrow, then." She was relieved when they left the shared quarters and continued talking about the plans for tomorrow. Charlie needed to spend time with the *Betty May* and familiarize herself with its systems. She could learn everything overnight and head into outer space at first light, but she had other arrangements.

Kal guided them to the front of the barracks that faced the Great Tower. She thanked Akron for his time, then waited until he was far away. She turned to Charlie as they stood by the main entrance. "I must return to the Great Tower." A question lingered in her green eyes.

"Andren and I are going back to the *Betty May*." Charlie grinned at Kal's curious look and said, "That's the ship's name." She hesitated when a few soldiers marched past them, and she watched them turn at the end of the hallway. Her next words were quieter. "I'll be back before sunset."

Kal rumbled low, then looked at Andren. "You will be off duty tonight."

"*Ja*, Kal." Andren bowed her head. "Shall I continue to wear civilian clothing during the mission?"

"*Ja*, I want you at Charlie's side when the attack begins."

Charlie folded her arms and turned to Andren. "They saw your face on Serrato's moon. They'll just think you're part of my regular crew."

"*Ja*." Andren slipped her hands into her jacket pockets.

"Ready?" Charlie asked, receiving a nod from Andren. She grinned at her lover and said, "I'll see you later to collect my payment." She held back a moan when Kal snarled at her, but she was smug and hastened from the barracks.

Andren chased after Charlie and glanced over her shoulder a few times. "I don't think she liked you saying that in front of me."

"Oh, I know she didn't." Charlie bit her lip and noticed the wetness between her legs. *I can't wait for tonight.*

* * *

"You don't have to walk me to Kal's door," Charlie said for the second time and sighed when Andren gave her a pointed look. She shrugged it off, adjusted the overnight bag on her shoulder, and entered the elevator with Andren. "*Tah* for your help this afternoon. Stowing things went a lot faster with three of us."

"*Motah.*"

Charlie felt prepared for their mission and planned to contact Starr before they took off from Kander. She needed to confirm their location before she set course and left the planet's orbit. The flight to retrieve Starr would take nine or eleven lumens, depending on the solar winds. Thankfully Sres left her with full tanks.

After the elevator hitched, they exited it and walked down the torch-lit hallway to Kal's quarters. Charlie's heart started to race when the tautness in her chest jerked against her, but she restrained her needs. "I think I'll be…" She gave up when Andren knocked on the door.

Andren stepped back after the door opened and revealed the High Commander. She lowered her head in respect and said, "Kal."

"*Tah*, Andren. You may go."

Andren nodded, then flashed a sympathetic look to Charlie before grinning at her.

Charlie glowered and swore she'd get Andren back somehow. Once she was alone with Kal, she smiled and indicated the bag on her shoulder. "I was asked a lot of questions before I left the *Betty May*." She had dodged Raine's interrogation, feeling lucky she made it out alive. They were supposed to remain on the *Betty May* tonight rather than go back to Starlight Farm. Instead, Raine was left to sleep on the gigantic ship by herself. Charlie felt guilty… almost.

"Is everything okay?" Kal asked, inviting Charlie into her quarters.

"*Ja.* I just told Raine that we had a lot to go over, and I didn't want to bother coming back so late." Charlie went into the bedroom, deposited the bag, and returned to Kal in the sitting room.

"Are you hungry?"

"Famished," Charlie replied. "I haven't eaten much since this morning." She had been excited about the ship's arrival, and now the mission was only hours ahead of her.

"I ordered dinner for us. It should be here soon." Kal was tossing wood into the fireplace.

"I didn't know a romantic dinner was included in the payment." Charlie tucked her hands into her jeans' pockets as she studied her lover's ass. Kal's rumble was strong and sent a shock down Charlie's stomach.

Kal straightened up and neared Charlie, her eyes alive with darkness. "You will need your energy for tonight."

Charlie ran a finger along the trim of Kal's coat and said, "Here I thought we were moving on to the romance."

"Romance would only cheapen what this really is," Kal whispered, her voice growing headier by the tick.

"And what's that?"

"You falling to your knees before me and presenting yourself to me." Kal had a predatory smile and continued to stalk Charlie, who was breathing harder. "Then you'll beg me and plead with me to fuck you."

Charlie took a step back, but Kal pursued her.

"But I won't." Kal pressed forward and forced Charlie against the wingchair's side. "Not until you make me believe one thing."

Clawing at the chair behind her back, Charlie leaned against it and failed to control the drumming in her chest. "What's that?" Her next breath hitched in her throat when her lover leaned over and warm lips brushed her ear.

"That you are *mine.*"

Charlie restrained herself from falling back into the chair. Her lower jaw flapped a few times, but she only managed a whimper. A boom at the door caused Charlie to jump and dodge to the left, putting space between them.

Kal rumbled in displeasure at the interruption, then went to the door and allowed the two Omegas to enter the room.

The first Omega Lurain offered Charlie a shy smile, went to the table, and set down the tray. She took the second tray from the other Omega and set it down too. They muttered a word to their ruler before hurrying out of the room.

Charlie looked up from the covered trays when she heard several giggles after one of the doors closed. She parted her lips and looked at Kal, about to ask if the Omegas knew something.

"We should eat," Kal ordered, indicating the divan. Together they sat down and enjoyed the hearty meal that had been prepared for them. Kal's plate had a larger portion, but she ate at the same pace as Charlie. Kal's larger cut of meat was also closer to raw compared to Charlie's own. "Do you feel ready to leave tomorrow?"

Charlie nodded a few times between bites. "*Ja*. Tomorrow morning Raine and I will take another flight test in outer space before we go. I want to make sure we're both familiar with it before we take on passengers." She covered her mouth and asked, "How do I get a hold of Laken once we're ready to fly?"

"Call me. I will send her and the unit out to you." Kal dipped a torn piece of dark bread into pale oil with herbs.

Charlie played with the food, then peered up at her lover. "So Laken is a Carnec Alpha?"

"*Ja*. Is that a problem?"

After a shrug, Charlie said, "It just caught me off guard. I had expected an Alpha, not a Carnec."

Kal responded with a throaty sound. "I thought it would be better if a Carnec worked with you."

"Just because we do," Charlie said, a tease in her voice. She grinned at Kal's narrowed gaze and said, "We do work well together, mostly."

With a huff, Kal said, "You are too stubborn at times."

"Me?" Charlie waved the spork in her lover's direction. "You're the Alpha."

"And you think you are one," Kal fired back, her eyes wild with fire.

Charlie didn't react to Kal's ire and just placed a hand over her chest. "You mean I'm not? *Vuk*!"

Kal's lip curled and showed her canines in warning. "Are you mocking me again?"

Charlie grumbled after her bantering fell flat. She set the plate on the table and placed both hands on Kal's taut bicep. "I think I'm making fun of myself, not you." Already the muscle started to smooth over in response. "I like to tease when I feel comfortable with someone. Don't ever take it seriously."

Kal sighed and lowered her head closer to Charlie's temple. "I'm still learning your nature." She trailed her lips lower and nipped exposed flesh under Charlie's jaw. After earning a hiss, she whispered, "You do have an Alpha's spirit."

"Hopefully that's a good thing," Charlie murmured.

Kal pulled away and said, "*Ja*."

Charlie squeezed her lover's relaxed muscle, then picked up the plate again. She decided on a different topic and asked, "How did the meeting go with the engineers for the monorail?"

Kal tilted her head and studied her lover, a curious light in her features. "It went well."

Charlie nodded and considered such a massive project that would benefit the planet. "Do you think you'll move forward with it?"

"*Ja,* but only after I learn more about the Sworne."

Pausing between bites, Charlie lowered the knife and spork to the clay plate. "If they're coming here, what will you do?"

"Prepare for war." Kal finished the steak, then ate the last morsel of bread and put the dirty plate on the tray.

Charlie blew out a breath and stared at the uneaten food on her plate. Her stomach churned from the worrisome conversation. "How?" She played with the light brown grain called *lurr* that she'd liked ever since coming to Kander. "Their technology way surpasses anything here on Kander." She set the plate on the empty tray and said, "Their tech was ahead of ours back on Earth."

"But your people defeated them," Kal said.

"I wouldn't say we exactly defeated them." Charlie toyed with the linen napkin in her lap before folding it up. "It was more like we turned their tech back on them." She shook her head and whispered, "I don't think destroying our home planet equates winning."

"Earth was not your home planet."

Charlie faltered and blinked after Kal's dry statement, then jerked to life. "What?" She put the napkin on the tray and turned toward her. "What do you mean?"

Kal sighed and stared at the space between them, seeming to put her thoughts together. "Remember I said Earthlings are changing because they've been here?"

"*Ja.*" Charlie touched her lover's knee and asked, "But what does that have to do with Earth?"

"Your people were designed to adapt to other worlds." Kal canted her head and studied Charlie for a tick. "When the first Earthlings died on Kander, they were buried and decomposed into Kander's ground. Kalatas was able to learn about your people."

Charlie sat still and tried to process the new information.

Kal developed a slight frown and said, "In every race's blood, there is a language."

Swallowing, Charlie whispered, "DNA. It's like coding."

"*Ja.*" Kal released a soft rumble. "Parts of Earthlings' coding was engineered by someone other than a god."

Charlie sank into the divan until her back touched the large pillows behind her. "This is so heavy."

"Part of that engineering was the ability for Earthlings to adapt to new worlds very rapidly."

Charlie shook her head and asked, "But why?"

"I am unsure," Kal replied.

Sitting in silence, Charlie struggled to grasp the truth behind her people's possible origins. "Does Kalatas know for sure that we're not from Earth originally and were engineered later?"

"It is a slim possibility," Kal said. "Perhaps there were Earthlings that originated from the planet. But typically a race carries a signature of their god."

"We don't have one," Charlie whispered, rubbing her brow.

"If your people did, it has long been lost by the engineering."

Charlie blinked away the sting in her eyes after learning her people were a by-product. "So that's why we're adapting to Kander?" After Kal's nod, she sat up and cleared her throat. "What if a group of Gyrs decided to settle on Kander? Can they…?" She hesitated when Kal shook her head.

"If a race doesn't have the adaption ability, then they will die off." Kal placed her hand against her chest and said, "Just as if all my people left Kander, they would die out as a race."

"Or if they lost Kander," Charlie whispered in realization. Kalmar couldn't risk losing their one planet, not like Earthlings had done. Popping up from the divan, she went over to the warm fire and stood in front of it, staring into the consuming flames. "We're a bunch of fucking freaks without a real home," she whispered and folded her arms. She shut her eyes when Kal stood behind her.

"Your people are special."

Charlie huffed and glared at the fire.

"To adapt to a new world and continue life is an amazing ability." Kal leaned down and took deep breaths. "To live outside the hands of your god is unheard of in the galaxy."

Charlie turned and gazed up at her lover. "Is that why Kalatas is fascinated with us?"

"*Ja*, it's one reason." Kal traced a finger along Charlie's jaw and continued searching for something in Charlie's gaze. "I did not mean to upset you."

Charlie allowed her shoulders to fall, then collected Kal's larger hand into her own. "I'd rather know the truth." She shook off the conversation and squeezed Kal's hand. "*Tah* for dinner."

"Did you get enough?"

"*Ja*." Charlie was full but not uncomfortable. The meal itself was excellent, and she made a mental note to one day thank Lurain or whoever made the food. Folding her arms, she said, "I'm ready for my payment."

Kal's chest vibrated with a heavy rumble, and she ordered, "This way."

# Chapter 9

The ride up the two floors felt like hours while Charlie fidgeted in the elevator. With her back to Kal, she waited to be taken up to the highest level and thoroughly fucked by the Alpha. Each of her last nights on Kander were shared with Kal, like an unspoken tradition between them. She nibbled on her lip when Kal's front pressed into her back.

The lift hitched at the top and released the gate, which Charlie opened up. She was first off but stepped aside and allowed Kal to lead the way. The few lit torches guided them to the open doors of the throne room.

*Alping*, she corrected herself. But she loved the idea of being fucked in the room where Kal ruled over her people. The *alping* room was alive with firelight and warmth. A fire trough similar to the one in the temple lined the *alping* room's walls, wrapping around from one end to the other. A gigantic fireplace roared on each side.

Kal closed the double doors, which groaned in protest and returned a soft boom once sealed shut. She went to her right and bent over, hands wrapping around a long wooden beam.

Charlie turned and hesitated to help her lover, who was much stronger than her. She doubted she could do anything, considering the sheer size of the beam. In awe, she watched Kal lower the timber between four metal hooks on the doors. Once the beam settled into place, Charlie realized she couldn't leave without Kal's blessing. There were no other exits from the *alping* room besides jumping out a window. When Kal faced her, Charlie trembled at the predatory smile.

"I will stoke the fires," Kal said, starting toward the one on the right.

Charlie wiped her palms on her pants and went to the left. She needed a distraction from her pending future and started tossing firewood into the flames. From the amount of wood piled up, they could stay in the *alping* room for a full day. The crackling from the twin fireplaces echoed through the large, empty space.

Turning around, Charlie's wandering eyes looked from the opposite fireplace to the gorgeous marble throne on top of a white dais. Her gaze traveled up the three steps and settled on the statuesque High Commander seated on the white throne.

Kal had both arms on the throne's wide rests and her fingers curled underneath. Her dark, long coat was open and spilled over the white throne, matching the black veins in the bright stone. One leg remained pressed against the chair while the other stretched out. She didn't move until Charlie started to walk over, her head tilting to one side.

Charlie found the same spot where she had stood the first day she met Kal. Facing the throne, she folded her arms and eyed the dark ruler seated high above the floor. She parted her lips, but her words fell short when Kal held up a hand. Charlie's heart started to race again after the realization that they were slipping into roles. With her head down, she took a deep breath and hammered down her nerves, not truly prepared for tonight. She peered up and studied the High Commander, who was the most powerful being on the planet. Tonight she was getting both the Alpha and the ruler. *I asked for it*, she reminded herself.

"Remove your jacket and weapons," Kal ordered in a thunderous voice that bounced off the stone walls.

Charlie's eyelids fluttered a few times, and a groan passed through her. She unzipped the leather jacket and tossed it to her right, then unhooked her utility belt with the holstered lectra gun and sheathed knife. With a careful toss, she put the weapons onto her jacket. She fished out the Grasshopper and repeated the same technique, not wanting to damage any of them. Her arms exposed, a chill ran down Charlie's skin, leaving behind goose bumps. She crossed her arms again and waited for her lover's next move. Her clit pulsed with anticipation and desire. For a nineth, she had fantasized about Kal taking her in the *alping* room.

Kal shifted in the seat, and her piercing gaze never left Charlie. "Remove your shirt next."

Breathing harder, Charlie reached for the hem of her beloved T-shirt but paused and tested the High Commander. "Don't you want to take off your jacket?" Her stomach twisted into a knot when her lover snarled in warning.

"*Now.*"

Charlie gasped and lifted the shirt up, deciding her best option was to go slowly. If Kal was going to sit and watch, then Charlie would make a show of it. Once free of her shirt, she tossed it near the leather jacket and combed her tussled hair with her fingers. She hooked her hands through the empty belt loops. "What next?" She parted her legs a little and watched Kal's eyes travel the length of her body.

"Boots."

During her normal routine, Charlie would prop up her feet to take off her boots. But tonight, she peered down at them as if noticing them for the first time. "Boots," she muttered and nodded. Kal's low rumbles continued mixing with the pops from the fireplaces. Charlie loved every Alpha sound, both the menacing and the comforting ones.

After another few ticks, Charlie mapped out her plan and turned around until her back was to Kal. She kept her head twisted and swept the hair out of her face so Kal could see she was still playing along. Bending over, she untied the first boot at a painstaking pace and kept her ass up for Kal's pleasure. Kal's soft rumbles thundered the longer Charlie took to remove her boots and socks.

Once done, Charlie threw the footwear aside and turned back to Kal with her hands again tangled in the belt loops. Her body was growing warmer, and her skin charged with need. Her hard nipples brushed against the black bra, aching to be freed of the confines. But first, Kal ordered her to take off the jeans, which she peeled away.

Charlie stood before the High Commander in her matching black underwear and bra yet found herself warm enough. The boycut underwear was damp and agitated her with each passing tick. She prayed for Kal to tell her to take them off, but instead she beckoned Charlie closer. With every step to the dais, she was certain her legs would collapse. But she wasn't alone in her anticipation, as Kal was digging her nails into the throne's arms and a significant bulge had formed between her legs.

*At least I'm not the only one that's fucking wired.* Charlie tried to withhold her smirk, but it tugged at her lips. "*Ja*, Kal?" She heard the slight tremble in her tone.

"Now take off the rest."

Charlie reached for the back of her bra, undoing the hooks. Biting her lip, she allowed the loose item to slide down her arms before she threw it to the right and watched it land on a step.

Kal glanced over at it, an eyebrow arcing up at the silent message in Charlie's defiance. She clenched her jaw but snarled anyway. She looked back at Charlie, who twisted her fingers in the black underwear.

At last, the boy shorts were stripped away, creeping down her thighs and allowing the cool air to brush against her heated sex. Charlie groaned after stepping out of them, as she'd needed to be free of them awhile ago. She noticed Kal was leaning forward and breathing heavily, drinking in Charlie's arousal. Biting her lip, she flung the soaked underwear onto the dais and grew smug when they landed at Kal's feet.

Kal's low growl rolled for about a minute before she peered up from the underwear. With a straighter back, she stared at Charlie while her chest continued rising and falling with deep breaths. Each passing tick, her green eyes became darker and hungrier.

Charlie was certain Kal would break any moment, rush her, and rut into her. But her hopes were dashed when Kal leaned back into the chair and calmed.

"Tell me how slick you are," Kal ordered, her voice booming through the *alping* room.

"Pretty fucking slick," Charlie promised, her hands resting on her hips.

Kal snarled and showed her canines. "Touch yourself first, then tell me."

Charlie lost an ounce of her bravado, hesitant to do anything close to masturbating in front of someone. However, the fierceness in Kal's features made her clamp down on her fears. She moved her right hand and dragged a couple of fingertips through the wet heat, groaning at the sensation. "Like I said, fucking slick." She began to withdraw her hand.

"I didn't say to stop."

Swallowing, Charlie returned her hand and continued to play with her throbbing clit. She was unsure how much strength she had left to remain on her feet for her lover.

"How tight are you?"

Charlie gasped at the thought of going inside herself rather than Kal doing it. But she followed the command and slid two fingers past her entrance, whimpering at both the sensation and need for Kal. "Fucking tight," Charlie said, a growl coming out at the end. She clenched her teeth and asked, "You want to do something about it?"

"*Joh.*" Kal's lip twisted up, and she said, "But you will."

Charlie withdrew her fingers and narrowed her eyes. "I didn't agree to this." She wasn't quite prepared to masturbate in front of Kal and needed a minute to accept it. She had never done such a thing for any past lovers, but Kal was different to her. Their sexual relationship always pushed new boundaries, and Charlie loved it. And if she was rewarded with a good fuck, then she would give Kal what she wanted first.

"Then agree to it now or our deal is off." Kal balled her hands onto the arm rest and seemed to will Charlie to defy her.

"The deal was for you to—"

"Last chance," Kal said, a warning flashing across her features.

Charlie snapped her jaw shut and allowed the tension to build between them. She suspected Kal knew she would agree, in fact had already given into the new arrangement. But she still loved to battle with Kal, whose Alpha nature excited Charlie beyond measure. As a kid she'd stayed clear of Alphas and believed they were dangerous. She hadn't been wrong at the time, but as an adult she was falling for this Alpha's dominance.

"What do you want me to do?" Charlie asked, shaking all over when Kal flashed a wolfish smile.

"Fuck yourself." Kal relaxed into the throne, spread her outstretched legs farther, and ordered, "Now."

Charlie sucked in a deep breath and worked up her courage to masturbate for her lover. She was already nude and on display for Kal, something she wouldn't do for others. If she was going to hold up her part, then she would make it easier on herself rather than stand there. "All right," she whispered and rubbed her clit, enjoying the sensation and needing it to ease her into her pending fate. Gazing down, she watched her fingertips circle and rub, then slide lower into the slickness.

"Get on your knees," Kal commanded.

Charlie peered up at Kal and sensed it was more power play over her, but she dropped to one knee and then the other. She kept her legs spread open enough and continued massaging her clit, working it with persistence. Her fingers glided over the swollen nub, sent shocks through her limbs, and made her pant harder. For a moment, Charlie had her eyes closed until she nudged her fingertips lower and hit the perfect spot against her clit.

"*Vuk!*" she cursed and toppled forward, her left hand catching her. She shook from the weak climax and continued to play with her clit, prolonging the small orgasm. Charlie pulled her hand away, holding up her body and sensing her need was worse, not better. Lifting her head, she studied her lover, who was waiting for her to continue.

Grinding her teeth, Charlie ached to have the Alpha come undone and take her. She had been spoiled by the earlier rut and how it had taken away Kal's self-control at the time. She gathered her strength and rose up, sitting back on her heels. Reaching between her legs, she toyed with her clit and watched Kal's face, which was dark and had beads of sweat forming on her brow. They were both affected by Charlie's brief climax and wanted more.

Rolling onto her hip, she continued giving Kal what she wanted right now. Charlie brought her legs forward and sat on her ass, adjusting to the cool stone under her. When she lay down, she gasped from the chill that felt great against her heated skin. Snaking her hand down, she rubbed her clit and opened her legs just enough for Kal to see firsthand. Every one of her lover's growls caused her stomach to twist in excitement.

Charlie slipped two fingers lower, pushing past her entrance. She parted her legs more and gave Kal an even better view. She earned a pleased growl followed by a long rumble. With two fingers deep inside herself, Charlie drove in and out at a gentle pace. She couldn't recall the last time she had touched herself, but tonight's experience was new and fun.

For a moment, she lifted her head and smirked at Kal's fiery features before she dropped her head and worked her hand faster. Her thrusts grew more desperate, wanting both the orgasm and to get closer to Kal. Charlie whimpered as her muscles clenched around her fingers, so close to her limit. With each needy pump, she lifted her ass and curled her fingers to hit the right spot. Her first cry echoed off the walls and forced a snarl from Kal.

Her next cry was louder after reaching her climax and the underwhelming thrill shooting through her body. Her left hand searched for hot skin to claw, but there was only cold marble. Charlie now recalled why she only masturbated during desperate times and sought out trustworthy lovers. Thoughts of Kal riding her dulled her current satisfaction, and she propped herself up with her hands behind her.

Kal was panting and had since placed a hand over the swell between her thighs. Her fingers were rubbing the same spot over and over.

Charlie gloated at Kal's breaking down and sensed that she would receive her payment soon. She kept her legs open for her lover's enjoyment and asked, "What do you wish for me to do now, Kal?" Since learning Kal's old name, she didn't often use her lover's title, but tonight was about Kal's power as a ruler.

"Get up and come here."

Restraining her urge to run, Charlie climbed onto her feet and ensured her leg strength was back before she ascended the steps. One by one, she neared Kal but paused in front of the undisturbed underwear. Like Kal, she peered down at it, and she grinned at how much her wetness on the boy shorts probably drove Kal insane. She swiped it aside with her toes, then moved into the opened space between the Alpha's legs.

"Kneel again."

Charlie raised an eyebrow and lowered her eyes to the bulging crotch that would soon be eye level with her. Again, their initial arrangement was being denied, but she liked why. Once on her knees, she had a perfect view of Kal's hand massaging herself until Kal shifted and lifted up a little. Charlie softened at being offered a cushion, similar to the first time they had exchanged oral sex. She took the offer and placed it underneath her knees, finding it plenty warm after having been under Kal.

Withdrawing her hand, Kal threaded her fingers into golden locks and whispered, "Undo my pants."

Charlie took the permission and unfastened each button with an occasional glance at Kal's face. She grinned at the exposed desire in Kal's eyes. After freeing the last button, she pushed a hand against the underside of Kal's crotch and asked, "What now, Kal?"

"Pull out my cock." Kal slipped her hand behind Charlie's neck and dug her nails into tender flesh at her nape.

Without hesitation, Charlie pushed between the flaps and grazed the hardened length with her fingertips. One of the veins brushed along her fingers as she clutched Kal's penis with a firm grip. She pulled it free from the tight confines and trembled from Kal's thunderous rumble. Looking up, she questioned her lover and received a nod followed by a light push to the back of her head.

Kal strained against the throne when Charlie pressed her lips against the swollen head that was seeping with droplets of clear liquid. The rut, along with the white *quima*, were long gone—until the next cycle peaked for them. Charlie noticed a less spicy hint but craved it nonetheless. She dragged her right hand up and down the shaft, working Kal's need higher.

"*Charlie*," Kal snarled and tangled her hand in her blond hair, but she never forced herself on Charlie.

Giving in, Charlie opened her mouth, leaned forward, and spread her lips past the pulsing head. While her hand continued stroking most of the length, she sucked and played with the sensitive head. She reveled in the Alpha's growls and hungry grunts for more. Charlie swirled her tongue over the tip, then flicked it several times. She increased the thrusts of her hand and earned a brief hiss between the snarls. The faster she went, the louder Kal became, filling the *alping* room.

But just as Kal neared her climax, Charlie slowed down enough to prolong it. Kal threatened her with a sharp hiss and baring of her teeth in warning. Still Kal maintained her self-control in place and didn't pressure Charlie. "You're j-just delaying me fucking you."

Charlie groaned at the truth, then doubled her efforts. Her grip around the shaft tightened and elicited a jerk from Kal's body. She sucked on the head, knowing that was Kal's favorite. Under her, she felt Kal tense and strain against the throne. A few times she flicked her tongue over the weeping tip, collecting the drops. As she drew up her hand, she yanked harder than before, then did it again after Kal quaked.

"*Vuk*!" Kal gripped both of the throne's arms with her hands and released a roar that went beyond the sealed doors.

Pulling away, Charlie watched her lover topple back into the throne and appear vulnerable for a minute. She stood and crawled into Kal's lap, certain she had Kal's Alpha unleashed. Burning, strong hands brushed along her back, one set of fingers digging into her ass cheek. Charlie whimpered in reaction, then leaned in until her forehead pressed against Kal's damp one. "Please fuck me."

Kal shifted and brought her lips to Charlie's ear, nipping at it.

"*Krafka*, Kal," Charlie pleaded and snaked her hands under the dark shirt. She moaned when her palms pressed against the solid, sweaty muscles. Her lover's growls deepened, and Charlie ached even more. She was crazy with need and desperate to be fucked, to be claimed, and finally to be whole. Tilting her head, she offered her neck to Kal, who was licking and biting her way lower. "Why won't you—"

"Tell me," Kal ordered, her heady voice vibrating against Charlie's throat. She took a long breath before clamping her canines around the flesh at the base of Charlie's neck.

Charlie yelped and clawed at Kal's hard skin, but the commanding bite was undeniable. She locked her thighs around Kal's waist and knotted a hand into midnight hair, crying out from the bite mark that would not claim her, not in body. Her spirit wrenched in reaction, jerking her back to her brief death when Kal called out to her. She slammed her eyes shut and gasped at feeling the bond between them. It was a bright and sharp strike to her racing heart, and she finally whispered, "Yours."

Kal's hold softened, then she started to lick the bruised skin. For a moment, she purred and hummed against Charlie's throat before lifting her head. "Mine." She squeezed the underside of Charlie's ass. She rose from the stone seat with Charlie still in her grasp but lowered her once they were up.

Charlie was trembling and grateful for Kal's hands on her hips. She peered up and saw the authority back in Kal's features, making her almost curse.

"Face the throne." Kal switched spots with Charlie.

Charlie was impressed by the throne's sheer size, which had to hold an Alpha. But she put aside her appreciation for later and instead peered over her shoulder at her lover behind her. She spotted Kal's long jacket coming off and being dropped to the dais beside the throne. A soft push to her back was the only command given. She was expected to present herself to Kal, who was an Alpha at her core. Everything about Charlie was rekindling the Alpha's basic needs and desires, and she loved it.

Leaning forward, Charlie placed her hands on the wide armrests and curled her fingers around the edges. She bent lower and spread her legs until she was certain her ass was high enough. Her invitation to be mounted and fucked was the last push for the Alpha. The hard tip of Kal's cock started to rub across her sex. She sucked in her breath and rocked her hips, coating the head and enjoying the minor friction.

She gasped when the head nudged against her entrance. Charlie clawed the marble under her nails and whimpered before hanging her head. Her walls were already clenching with anticipation, but with nothing inside her, she was hollow. But then she was given a few inches… finally. Charlie moaned at the girth stretching her open and hitting her G-spot. "Oh gods. I need more."

Kal answered with a soft push of her hips and allowed a little more to fill Charlie. "How much more?"

Panting hard, Charlie yanked her hair to one side and twisted her head to the right. "All of you." She hissed when the hard shaft reached deeper in her. "Fuck that feels so good." She held her breath while Kal gently rocked and stroked Charlie's inner walls. Her moans filled the air, and she rolled her hips with Kal's motions.

Kal bent over Charlie without ever breaking their dance. She hooked an arm under Charlie's stomach and rested a hand farther up the armrest. With her lips so close to Charlie's ear, she whispered, "This throne has never been defiled until now."

Charlie closed her eyes and whimpered at the truth. She prayed that Kalatas would forgive her for asking Kal to fuck her here, a sacred location. But while Kal's cock stroked her, she was certain the strongest Alpha on the planet had every right. Being this close to Kal couldn't be wrong, and Charlie needed to believe it.

Kal's soft pushes sent shocks through Charlie's gut, and she wanted Kal buried in her, connecting them entirely. She only needed a little bit more and after a pause, Kal drove the rest through her. "Fuck!" She clung to the throne for support. Long fingers twisted in her hair, jerking her head up to the Alpha's face. She didn't fight back, enjoying her lover's dominate nature.

"Was this your fantasy?" Kal whispered, her breath hot against Charlie's ear.

Charlie managed a weak nod and trembled from Kal's strong rumble.

"Hold on, tight." Kal untangled herself from Charlie and straightened up, both hands hooking Charlie's hips.

Charlie's knuckles turned white, and she locked her knees. She started to pant when Kal dragged her cock out and paused for a tick. After a silent prayer, she readied herself and felt the slickness sliding down her thighs. "Kal, *krafka*," she pleaded, and it was met with the first strong thrust. Charlie cried out and dropped her head forward.

Kal plunged into Charlie, pulled back, and sank into her again. The pace started gentle, then became desperate. Her nails pierced Charlie's skin and sent a shot up her spine. Her grunts started low but turned hungry, like a predator.

At first, Charlie tried to match Kal's thrusts and rocked her hips back but lost focus. Pleasure sparked through her entire body, and she began to scream when Kal increased the pace. Her yells filled the room, and she felt lightheaded from the heat. Her inner walls clenched with tension and desire, connecting her to Kal. She could feel them rise together with the passion and become tangled in their most basic need to claim.

Kal didn't slow, didn't let go, and didn't deny Charlie's demands. She propped her booted foot on the throne and bent over Charlie again with one arm hooked underneath to hold her in place. With a snarl, she pumped harder into Charlie, and they matched cries. With slick and slapping skin, they yelled and grunted until they were shuddering.

The brutal rhythm was all Charlie needed to orgasm. Her cry wrenched free, filling the entire room. Kal paused, then sank into her twice more and climaxed. Charlie felt her body clutch and hold onto Kal's full length, locking them together. Her heart was slamming against Kal's palm, and the aftershocks weakened her.

For a moment, Kal remained bent over Charlie and kept a hand on the throne's armrest near Charlie's own. She growled for a long moment and gently rocked her hips, allowing her cock to massage Charlie's inner walls. Then she picked up her lover, turned them both, and retook her seat in the throne with Charlie in her lap. They were still joined together.

With her head against Kal's breast, Charlie groaned, took deep breaths, and tried to relax her body. Kal caressed Charlie's stomach and inner thigh, rumbling into Charlie's ear as she did so. Lifting her head, Charlie peered down at the bit of Kal's exposed shaft through the opening of the pants. She smiled like a cat and wondered when Kal planned to remove her clothes, other than just the coat. With her right hand, she clawed and tugged at Kal's pants. "Don't you want these off?"

"Later," Kal replied, her voice heavy and firm.

Charlie tilted her head back, meeting the darkened eyes above her.

"Are you tired?" Kal traced her fingertips up Charlie's thigh and her left hand paused under Charlie's breast. "Or would you like more?" She lifted her hips and nudged her cock deeper into her lover.

Charlie groaned, then whispered, "This mission is a big job." She smirked at her lover, who raised an eyebrow at her. "And I need to be compensated properly." She loved the dark glint in her lover's eyes.

"I agree." Kal slid her hand up and covered Charlie's breast. "I like to pay well for good service." Her left hand shifted to Charlie's lower stomach, fingers seeking out Charlie's aching clit. She and Charlie shared a moan when Kal touched the swollen bud.

Charlie jerked after Kal's fingertip hit her sensitive spot, but she groaned long and deep as Kal massaged her breast and rubbed her clit. Both were rhythmic and just the right amount of pressure. She noticed Kal's legs were wide open, so she stretched her own and hooked them over Kal's thighs. Dropping her head back, she watched Kal play with her clit before gazing out over the dais and the entire room. Her fantasy was more than met, and she moaned with pleasure at being worshipped on the throne by the High Commander.

Kal seemed to sense her lover's heightened arousal and satisfaction from tonight's fucking. She responded with a thick rumble, rolled her hips, and massaged her cock inside of Charlie's slick walls.

Gasping, Charlie grabbed the armrests and arched her back until Kal's muscular arm snaked across her chest, holding her down. "*Vuk!*"

Kal snarled and hissed, then pushed harder against Charlie's clit.

"Faster, *krafka*!" Charlie ground down onto Kal, who ground up into her. She pushed and pulled against the iron hold across her stomach, but it was impossible. Her skin was fiery, and she was peaking quicker than last time. Every stroke of Kal's cock and flicker across Charlie's clit was driving her mad. Just as her straining body peaked, she hissed, "Don't stop!"

The short pumps of Kal's hip became harder, and she circled her fingers over Charlie's clit with feverish demand. Her growl erupted when Charlie screamed, but she kept going and pushed Charlie to her next limit.

After the first climax, Charlie was swept up in the harsh drives inside her. She clutched Kal's shoulder behind her and begged for her lover to make her orgasm again. Her body strained and clenched, ready to explode. A final thrust tipped Charlie, and the stronger climax tore through her. Under her, she felt the Alpha quake with echoing satisfaction.

Charlie slumped against her hot lover, both of them panting together. She closed her eyes and waited a few minutes to allow her muscles to relax. After another deep breath, Charlie lifted her body, and Kal helped her separate themselves. She whimpered after the head of Kal's penis popped free and the delightful soreness became apparent. It would be a little while before she was ready to be fucked again, but they could do plenty of other things until then. Settling back in her lover's body, she shut her eyes and soaked in the aftershocks.

*We totally defiled the throne*, she thought with a smug look.

* * *

Charlie climbed onto Kal's bed and said, "Okay. So how does this work again?" She looked at Kal, who was seated on the side of the bed, waiting for Charlie.

"We'll move to the middle."

Charlie supported her lover's idea and crawled to the center with Kal, then faced each other. They were naked and worn from their long night in the *alping* room. But before they left, Kal had suggested trying a special form of meditation that Kalmar couples often shared with each other after or before sex. Charlie was unaware of the ritual and was intrigued from the start.

"First, we both sit with our legs crossed."

"Facing each other, right?" Charlie shifted and sat cross-legged in front of her lover, who mirrored her.

Kal then stretched out her arms, turning up her open hands.

Charlie took the invitation and rested her palms flat against Kal's larger ones.

"Now just breathe," Kal instructed.

Charlie closed her eyes and focused on her breathing pattern. After awhile she noticed where her skin touched Kal's. Their knees were pressed together, thighs brushing, and their hands connected. Kal's constant presence was reassuring and anchored her.

Kal's next breath was deep and long, as if she were lost in another world. Charlie wondered if Kal was somehow connected closer to the Spirit of Kalatas when she was calm like this. Opening her eyes, she saw Kal studying her with a strange expression that Charlie couldn't place. It was gone in a tick, but Charlie had caught enough of it.

"Try to listen to my breathing," Kal instructed. "You're not trying to match it."

"Just listening," Charlie said, knowing that their breathing patterns would be different due to their body sizes. At first it sounded simple, but she was having a hard time centering herself. "I don't think *meditation* is my thing."

"*Meditation*?" Kal repeated in English.

Charlie looked at her lover and shrugged. "That's what humans call this." She pulled her hands away and rested them on her thighs. "Sitting still isn't my best skill."

Kal tilted her head, then gave a faint nod. "It is late, and you have a mission ahead of you." She uncrossed her legs and turned her body to get off the bed, then went to her dresser and pulled open a drawer.

Frowning at her lover's sudden shift, Charlie toyed with her hair, then hopped off the bed and searched out her clothes. Goose bumps were forming on her body from the chill in the air, and the clothes were welcoming. She waited until Kal was done in the bathroom before she went into wash up and get ready for bed. The suns would rise in less than four hours, and Charlie groaned at the long day ahead of her.

Back in the bedroom, Kal was under the blankets and welcomed Charlie into the warmth. In the beginning, they had each slept on their sides; then the invisible barrier melted away one night, and Charlie half slept on top of Kal. Tonight was similar, and Charlie sighed into the heat radiating off her lover's larger body. With her forehead pressed into Kal's temple, she relaxed but grinned when Kal squeezed her ass cheek.

"You can practice the bonding by yourself," Kal whispered.

Charlie was on her stomach, pressed against Kal's left side. She nudged Kal's head with her nose and whispered, "How can you practice that by yourself when there's supposed to be two of you?" She chuckled at Kal's displeased rumble.

"Many Kalmar practice it before they find someone," Kal replied.

"Oh." Charlie tightened her arm across her lover's chest, then asked, "Do you?"

"*Ja*."

Charlie nibbled on her lip and considered whether she was willing to keep trying the meditation. Just in their brief conversation, the meditation had sounded important to Kal, who was sharing it with Charlie. "I'll practice," she whispered, hoping she could keep her promise. A shiver raced up her spine after Kal's pleased rumble that turned into a purr. The rhythmic, soft sound was pulling Charlie closer to sleep when Kal's last words caught her ear.

"Mine."

Charlie's lips spread into a genuine smile after her lover's tender claim that made the line around her heart hum in delight. After a content sigh, she whispered, "Yours."

# Chapter 10

Charlie finished putting her things away in the messenger satchel, then grabbed her leather jacket. She swung it on and looked over at Kal, who was coming out of the washroom. She admired her lover, who wore her usual black pants and frayed shirt. Every article of clothing was simple when it came to the Kalmar. On rare occasions they dressed up for special events, which Charlie hadn't witnessed yet.

"Do you have all the supplies you need for the trip?" Kal asked, walking over to claim her coat from the hook on the wall between the bedroom and sitting room.

"*Ja.* We have plenty, enough for a nored." Charlie had requested food for two nineths, but Kal doubled the supplies. It didn't surprise her, considering most Kalmar's nature to be over prepared for things. "*Tah* by the way." She hooked the messenger bag across her chest, then neared her lover. "Raine and I are going to practice more with the ship." She watched Kal pull the belt around, about to buckle it, but Charlie grabbed it. She hesitated, unsure why it felt natural to her, but she cleared her throat and started to buckle it herself.

Kal didn't stop her and instead lowered her hands to her side. "Then you will be ready for my warriors."

"*Ja.*" Charlie played with the belt after buckling it and looped it through once like the old knights did with their sword sheaths. Kal never wore it that way but didn't argue with Charlie's decision to do something different. Peering up, she asked, "Did you give any of your soldiers secret commands that I should know about?"

"They would no longer be a secret if I tell you," Kal replied, lifting an eyebrow.

Charlie grumbled and folded her arms. "I guess I'll just have to trust they won't start a mutiny on the ship."

"They cannot fly or navigate the ship," Kal said.

Charlie hummed at the truth and understood that the soldiers' lives were her responsibility. She nodded once, then shifted to another topic. "Will I see you before I take off?"

"*Ja.* I will see you off," Kal promised.

Nodding twice, Charlie almost backed away until Kal leaned down and kissed her first. Startled by the affection, she froze for a tick, then returned Kal's tender kiss. She tangled her fingers in jet black hair and moaned when their tongues brushed together. It had been since the cabin that they shared a kiss, and its intensity drew her into Kal's body.

The first kiss they had ever shared had been immature and clumsy but still special to Charlie. Now, Charlie found the kisses alluring on every level, and she hated breaking them. She was nearly sure that Kal took another piece of her with each one. Gasping for air at the end, she clutched Kal's biceps and lowered her forehead against Kal's breasts.

"You must be strong on this mission," Kal whispered, bent over Charlie. "Victor will attempt to goad you."

"I know." Charlie swallowed and curled her fingers into Kal's jacket. They couldn't stay this close much longer before their scents smeared onto each other's clothes. "I won't let him get to me. I'm better than him."

"Spoken like an Alpha," Kal said, a teasing hint in her voice.

Charlie lifted her head and grinned at the sparkle in Kal's bright green eyes. "*Tah*, I think."

* * *

"Okay. Hold it there," Charlie ordered her friend.

Raine continued to control the aircraft, hovering it high above the ground. "How am I looking?"

"Really good this time." Charlie was watching the ship's readings and glanced at the cameras' screens to her left. "Now just take your time."

Raine gritted her teeth while she maneuvered the *Betty May* to land back on Kander. The ship shuddered twice, and several times the AI squawked at them. "Goddamn it! Can you silence that thing?"

"It's a warning system," Charlie said, an edge in her words. "Just focus on landing. You're doing better than last time."

"Fucking hate gravity!" Raine's left hand swept across the screen, tapping a few things. With her right, she guided the gigantic ship to the ground.

"This is why we take shuttles in," Charlie muttered under her breath, then held it. So far, her friend's landing was a hundred times better than the last ten. The eleventh time seemed to be a charm. When the landing system came to life, they were just shy of touching down in the same spot they had taken off from this morning. "Ease it down."

"Easy for you to say!" Raine wiped her palms dry on her pant leg, then finished lowering the ship. "You can land perfectly on the second attempt."

"That's because I've been flying a lot longer than you." Charlie smiled at the improved readings and watched the ground come up to the belly cameras. "Engage the landing anchors."

"Engaging." Raine switched them on and huffed after they latched onto the ground. Once the *Betty May* settled onto the planet, she blew out a huge breath and slumped into the co-pilot's chair.

"Nice job." Charlie took care of shutting down the engines, and the bridge became quieter. At least until she heard a dramatic groan from behind them. She spun around and smirked at a pale-faced Andren, who was seated in the captain's chair on the bridge.

"Why did I come on these test flights?" Andren rubbed her sweaty face.

Raine turned and chuckled at Andren's distressed features. "You survived."

"I puked." Andren indicated the barf bags at her feet. "Twice."

Charlie switched over to the comms but paused and looked over at Raine. "Both times were from you putting the nose to low."

"I did kind of almost put the ship into a spin."

Charlie rolled her eyes, then switched her headset to the comms. Unsure who to hail first, she decided on Kal. "High Commander, High Commander this is the *Betty May*." After a few ticks of silence, she opened her mouth and prepared to call Blade Perras next.

"Go ahead, *Betty May*."

It was the first time that Charlie heard her lover over the radio, and she stared at the screen. Clearing her throat, she replied, "We've completed our flight tests. We're ready to take on the crew."

"We will arrive at the *Betty May* in twenty-five minutes."

"Roger that," Charlie replied. "*Betty May* out." She transferred the comms to her techbit in case there were any calls later. "They'll be here in twenty-five."

Raine tilted her head and asked, "What did Starr have to say earlier?"

During their test flights, Charlie and Starr shared a transmission while Raine piloted the ship in outer space, near Kander. Their transmission had only lasted a few minutes, but it was good news. "They were taking on fuel, then headed to Eos Minor. She thought they'd arrive a lumen or two after we get there."

Raine nodded and said, "It's coming together."

Charlie agreed and climbed out of the chair. "Come on. Let's go get things ready." She ordered the AI system to open the cargo bay door for the soldiers' arrival.

Charlie and her team finished prepping the ship for the oncoming crew. By the time they walked to the open shuttle bay, the trucks had filtered into the bay and announced the start of their mission. They left the *Betty May* and met the Kalmar soldiers beyond the mouth.

The High Commander was in the lead with the unit of soldiers behind her. She halted several hundred paces from the entrance and waited for Charlie to join them.

"Do you want a tour?" Charlie asked once in earshot.

Kal gazed past Charlie and replied, "Perhaps another time." She pivoted and signaled for Laken to join them.

Laken stood at attention beside the pair and kept her attention trained on Kal.

"Shield Master Laken, you are to now follow all of Captain Charlie's orders and instructions. Failure to do so will be a mark on your honor and your unit's honor." Kal remained calm, but a familiar fire showed in her eyes. "Is that clear?"

"*Ja*, Kal." Laken bowed her head and said, "We will not fail you or our people." She turned to Charlie and lowered her head again. "Your orders, Captain Charlie?"

Frowning at the title, Charlie handled the request. "Your unit is to board the *Betty May*. Raine and Andren will show all of you around the ship and to your quarters."

"*Ja*, Captain Charlie." Laken took one step back, then hollered commands to the waiting unit. She was about to join them when Charlie caught her.

"And shield master," Charlie ordered, "Do not touch *anything* on my ship except for what's in your quarters."

Laken shifted on her boots and puffed up a little but nodded before joining her unit.

Charlie watched them march past, then shook her head and gazed up at Kal. *Damn Alphas and their egos*. Not that she hadn't grown used to Kal's Alpha ego, but she wasn't about to tolerate all the Alpha egos on the planet. She waited until they were alone and out of hearing range from the soldiers.

"They will serve you well," Kal said, pride coloring her statement.

"I know." Charlie put her hands into her pockets, trying to ward off the cold. "I'm not worried." She caught Kal's pleasure about her acceptance of the unit. "I need you to do the same favor for me again."

Kal lowered her gaze when Charlie offered her closed hand.

"*Krafka*," Charlie whispered.

Nodding, Kal accepted the watch from Charlie's smaller hand and tucked it inside her jacket's inside pocket. "We'll both be waiting for your return."

Charlie nodded, then hesitated to go before saying, "I won't be gone long." She started to go but paused after hearing her name.

"Be strong, Charlie."

Walking backward a few times, Charlie teased, "Like an Alpha." She winked at her, turned, and hurried up into the illuminated mouth of the *Betty May*.

* * *

Charlie lowered her gaze, shifted on her boots, and listened to the soldiers march into the shuttle bay. Raine and Andren took her side and reported that the soldiers had been shown the layout of the ship and their quarters.

Laken stood in front of the soldiers, arms crossed, and waited for further instructions.

Charlie stepped forward and studied the soldiers' faces, accustomed to their stony features. "On this mission, I am your captain and your leader. Any disobedience will be more than just dishonorable; it could be fatal." She searched their eyes for signals of agitation or anger. "Fatal for all of us. We are going into outer space where a mistake could endanger everyone." She approached the unit and said, "Don't be that mistake."

Laken turned her head toward the soldiers, seeming to gauge them as well. She looked at Charlie, who spoke again.

"As you know, our mission is to capture a soldier from Serrato Corps, who has been plotting against Kander." Charlie hooked her hands in front of her. "We will spend about one day traveling to another solar system and orbiting a small planet called Eos Minor. Once there, another ship will meet us and bring the bait we need to bring Serrato Corps to us." She tilted her head when she heard a few Alpha rumbles. "Later we will discuss the plans to capture the Serrato soldiers."

Each soldier moved their head in agreement and said, "*Ja*, Captain Charlie!"

*This title thing has got to go*, Charlie decided. "In the meantime, you may use the galley, go to the viewing deck, your quarters and the garden, and practice in the one cargo bay." She had made sure that one of the holes remained empty so that the soldiers had something to do in their spare time. "Understood?"

"*Ja*, Captain Charlie!" the soldiers replied.

Charlie kept from rolling her eyes and was about to dismiss them until a last thought came to mind. "Oh." She held up a finger and flashed a wicked smile at them. "And when you puke on my deck, be sure to clean up after yourself, or you'll be scrubbing toilets for the rest of the trip." Turning away, she called, "You're free to go."

Raine was smirking and wiggled her eyebrows. "Time to fly."

"But first, we need an entrance song," Charlie said and chuckled at Raine's curious glance. "We can't do anything without proper music."

Raine placed her hands on her hips and stood patiently by the open door to the hall.

"Nova, play 'Physical' by Olivia-Newton John. Pipe the song through the entire ship," Charlie ordered. "Volume level forty."

Raine snorted but started rolling her hips to the song when Nova patched the song through all the ship's speakers.

"Now it's time to fly!" Charlie step had purpose and bounce to it as they hurried through the halls and decks to the bridge. Together, she and Raine danced and sang the song together. The stars were calling to her heart, and she would answer them. "*Betty May*," she called over the comms, "warm the engines."

"Initiating start up protocol for engine bay one," the *Betty May* reported over the comms in Charlie's earpiece. "Initiating start up protocol for engine bay two." She continued to ticking off each engine until all of them were ready and warming up.

Charlie and Raine entered the flight deck took their spots in the chairs, prepping the ship for takeoff. Charlie relayed their status to Andren through the comms and made a mental note to give Laken a comms earpiece later.

"All systems are green," Raine said.

"Andren, Andren this is Charlie."

"Go ahead, Charlie."

"Get everyone prepared for takeoff," Charlie ordered. After a few minutes of silence, Andren hailed her back and confirmed that the crew was ready to take flight. She grinned over at Raine and nodded, both of them sliding the throttle up on the touch screen.

"Anchor system released," Raine reported.

Charlie maneuvered the huge ship straight up and gained altitude, departing from the ground. She gripped the yoke with one hand and continued adding more power to the engines, then turned the yoke to the left to aim for the right direction once they were in space.

Raine operated the engines' direction, guiding the ship's nose up and down. "Ready to jump throttle."

"Here we go," Charlie whispered, sliding the throttle faster and launching the ship upward through the atmosphere. "Keep an eye on the heat."

"We're good."

Charlie smiled when the ship's haul started vibrating and humming from the battle against gravity. "Nova, play my Oldies List. Start with 'Born to Be Wild' by Steppenwolf."

"Playing 'Born to Be Wild,'" Nova replied.

"And reroute it through the flight deck's speakers. Volume level twenty," Charlie ordered.

Raine perked up at the initial rhythm of the song, then grinned at her friend. "*This is our song, yo*!" she cheered in English.

Charlie laughed before singing the opening lyrics, then Raine joined her. Together, they continued flying the ship through the layers of atmosphere, nearing the outer limits of the planet. Just as the ship pierced the atmosphere, she and Raine sang, "Boooorn to beee wiiiiild!"

Once in outer space, the *Betty May* sailed away from Kander and vanished into the dark reaches that had stars for lighthouses. After putting enough distance between the ship and Kander, Charlie engaged the light speed systems and pushed the ship to leed one, then leed two. Raine finished mapping out a route to Eos Minor and locked it into the navigation system.

For about a lumen, Charlie and Raine stayed in the chairs, ensuring the *Betty May* was operating normally. So far, the vessel was a solid investment, even if the real owner didn't know how to fly it. Whoever the previous owner was, he had taken pride in maintaining the ship, and Charlie was thankful for that.

After a lumen, Charlie unbuckled from the chair and announced, "I think autopilot can take it from here. I'm going to give Laken an earpiece and check on the soldiers."

"I'm going to hang out here for a bit." Raine's attention was on the long streaks beyond the ship's nose.

Charlie nodded and touched her friend's shoulder, getting her attention for a moment. "Catch up with me later at my quarters. I have something for you."

Raine narrowed her eyes and asked, "Like a present?"

Chuckling, Charlie patted Raine's shoulder once, then headed up the steps to the upper flight deck. "Something like that." She departed the bridge and went in search of Laken, who was at the viewing deck with a few other soldiers. "How's everyone holding up?"

Laken nodded and replied, "Only a few dirtied your deck."

Charlie grinned and folded her arms. "I'm surprised it wasn't more of them."

"Several soldiers have experience on ships," Laken said.

"Ships on water are different than in air or outer space." Charlie was still impressed but expected other soldiers might become motion sick later or not eat. At least they had downtime at Eos Minor so the soldiers could eat and rehydrate before a fight with Serrato Corps. "Listen, I want to give you a comm." At Laken's confused look, she said, "It's an earpiece that's tapped into the communication system in the ship. We'll be able to talk to each other from anywhere in the ship or outside of it."

Laken rumbled low and said, "I understand now."

Charlie held out her hand with the sand-colored earpiece and waited until Laken had it fitted in her ear. "Okay, so all you have to do is call one of our names twice to activate the comm. So for example, I'll hail Raine." She cleared her throat, then called, "Raine, Raine this is Charlie."

"This is Raine."

"Just testing the comm. Thanks." Charlie ignored Raine's huff and said, "Charlie out." She looked at Laken, who seemed to understand it. "You have to say 'out' to shut off the call. Then to hail everyone on one comm, you say 'Hailing all' twice."

"Who has a comm?" Laken asked.

Charlie smiled and replied, "Raine, Andren, and me." For a few more minutes, she spoke to Laken, then parted ways. On the walk to her quarters, she realized how drained she was after a late night with Kal and now starting the mission. She promised herself she would get several hours of sleep before arriving at Eos Minor.

In the captain's quarters, Charlie took off her boots, jacket, and utility belt. She didn't bother with her knife or

Grasshopper and collapsed into the huge bed that was enough for three humans. On the *Pacifica*, her captain's quarters had been about half this size. At some point, the *Betty May*'s former owner had combined two smaller quarters to make the larger room. Charlie approved of his remodeling choices.

Charlie was about to doze off, but the door chirped and signaled Raine's arrival. She rolled off the bed and called for the door to open for her friend.

"Sorry I woke you."

Charlie finished rubbing her face and said, "I wasn't quite asleep yet."

Raine crossed her arms and had a toothy smile. "Late night at the Great Tower?"

Before she blushed, Charlie turned toward the closet and replied, "I sleep better in space." At least once upon a time it was true. With a darker blush, she admitted to herself that sleeping on top of Kal out-rated any bed, ship, or planet.

"So what did you have to show me?" Raine asked, following Charlie a few steps.

Charlie took a deep breath and cooled the heat in her face, glad Raine couldn't see her. She slid the closet door open and searched the floor for the special item. She grabbed it by the handle, pulled it from the closet, and turned to Raine, who stared oddly at it.

"What is that thing?"

Charlie had a wide grin and held up the metal item. "It's a battle suit." She watched how Raine's eyes turned into saucers bigger than a planet. "This specific one is called the Galactic Hammer."

"Wait, wait. Hold up." Raine pointed at the oval-shaped pod-like object. "You said battle suit."

"*Ja*." Charlie's grin started to hurt, and her amusement seeped into her next words. "It's a suit of armor that you wear."

"Like fucking Iron Man?" Raine asked, her voice reaching a high-pitched note.

"*Ja*."

"Oh my fucking god!" Raine launched forward and snared the suit from her friend, looking over every inch of it. "How does it work?"

Charlie laughed and steered Raine over to the bed. "Set it down for a tick." Once it was safely on the bed, she said, "You put it on like a backpack. It'll automatically tighten up around your back and waist. Then you activate it with a voice command when you're ready to use it."

Raine was gushing and petting the suit. "Does it cover your body like Iron Man's suit in the movie?"

"Pretty much."

Raine snared Charlie's wrist and said, "I have to try it. *Pleeease*!"

Charlie chuckled and picked up the suit from the bed. "Turn around." After complying, Charlie helped Raine slide her arms through the straps, which then shrank to fit her shoulders. "Clip this around your waist."

Raine hooked the pack's belt around her hips. "Okay, so how do I active it?"

"Just say 'Galactic Hammer activate,' and it'll go." Charlie put space between them and smirked when Raine held out her arms like a dork.

"Galactic Hammer active," Raine ordered.

Charlie was awed by the battle suit coming to life and how its metal sheathing covered Raine within a few ticks. "Not bad," she whispered.

Raine squealed from somewhere inside of it and started to move around in the room, her steps heavier now.

Charlie watched Raine dance in the white suit with bright red accents. It was designed to improve one's strength and eyesight, as well as protect them. She folded her arms and waited until Raine came off her high. "So what do you think?"

Raine hurried over to her friend and replied, "This is so badass!" She rested her hands on her metal hips and asked, "How do I look?"

"Like a total badass." Charlie laughed at Raine's superhero stance and shook her head.

Dropping her arms, Raine asked, "Does this thing fly?"

"*Ja*, technically." Charlie touched her friend's arm and heard another squeal.

"It just gave me a read of your vitals!"

"Breathe, Raine." Charlie sighed and considered whether giving Raine the suit was a good idea. "Okay so listen…" She faltered and said, "Tell the suit to remove the helmet."

"Um, how do I do that?"

Charlie rolled her eyes. "Just say 'retract helmet.'"

Raine repeated the order, then the helmet's plates receded down into her collar and revealed her face. "Wow."

Again, Charlie attempted to redirect Raine's focus. "Just listen for a minute." She finally had Raine's undivided attention. "The suit gives you strength, protects you from four to six laser shots, and lets you fly for about an hour. But you can't take it into outer space because it doesn't have onboard oxygen. It does regulate inside temperature to a point so you stay comfortable."

"Okay, so extra strength, armor protection, and limited flight." Raine ticked off her fingertips. "And no outer space or super hot and cold places. Got it."

Charlie continued to hold up her hands, keeping Raine's attention on her. "My plan is that you'll be wearing the suit when we ambush the Serrato soldiers. You make the first move, grab Victor, and fly him away from the fray before he can get hurt or killed."

Raine smiled at the idea, but it cracked after a tick. "But I don't know how to fly this thing."

Charlie grinned and said, "We'll have plenty of time at Eos Minor for you to practice. And you'll have time now to learn the suit and the onboard computer."

Raine's smile returned, brighter than last time. "I like this plan." She looked over her armored body, taking in the details. "How's my ass look in this?"

After a laugh, Charlie grabbed Raine's metal hand, guided her to the closet, and pointed at the mirror. She stepped aside and watched Raine check herself out before she asked, "What you think, Iron Woman?"

"I love it!" Raine turned to her friend and scooped up Charlie in a crushing hug. "This is the best gift ever!"

Charlie winced and gasped. "Ribs. Ribs!" She heard Raine's apology while she rubbed her side where the bones had freshly healed from her crash landing. "And it's not a gift. You're just borrowing it."

"What? Come on, Charlie." Raine held out her arms and argued, "You missed so many of my birthdays. This would totally make up for that."

Rolling her eyes, Charlie ignored Raine's pout and said, "*Joh,* Rae."

Raine huffed and wiggled her eyes, whispering, "*Ja*, Rae." She turned back to the mirror and checked herself out more. "Are there any onboard weapons with this thing?"

"*Joh*." Charlie shifted closer and tapped Raine's outer thigh. "There is a storage compartment on either side for handguns."

Raine mimicked Charlie's motion and beamed when an empty gun holder popped out from her thigh. "Wow! That's totally *Robocop*." She peered up at her friend. "This is the best gift ever."

Charlie shook her head and continued to disregard Raine's attempts to guilt her.

"So why is it called the Galactic Hammer?"

Grabbing her friend's shoulders, Charlie turned her until Raine's shoulder faced the mirror. She pointed at the white emblem stamped into the pauldron. The insignia was of a spiral galaxy with a hammer laid over it.

Touching the symbol, Raine whispered, "Galactic Hammer."

"It's the suit's name, not the model. Like when knights named their swords," Charlie explained. "Usually the name has meaning to the suit, but I'm not sure why this one is called Galactic Hammer. It could be something in its history."

Raine was transfixed on the symbol before she looked at Charlie. "Maybe I'll find out why."

"Maybe," Charlie whispered, then withdrew and smiled at Raine's new toy. "You better get started on learning the suit." In no time, her friend would have the battle suit working like a second skin.

"Aye aye, captain." Raine hurried to the sealed door but flashed a last smile. "Thanks again for the gift, sis."

Charlie sighed and watched her friend leave with her new toy. "I'm never getting that suit back." She shrugged it off and decided to lie down for a nap, forgoing changing into sleepwear. She climbed into bed and used her techbit to check on the ship's status. After taking out her earpiece, she set both pieces onto the nightstand and closed her eyes.

The exhaustion set in within minutes, even if Charlie was headed toward danger. She had no idea when she drifted off, but a familiar and annoying alert begged for attention.

*Beep. Beep. Beep.*

Charlie struggled against her groggy mind. Growling, Charlie looked over and realized it was the comms earpiece rather than her techbit. It was flashing, so she scooped it up and plugged it into her ear. "What?" she barked at whomever was hailing her.

"Charlie, you need to hurry to the shuttle bay," Andren demanded, huffing and growling over the comms.

Charlie scrambled out of bed and searched for her boots while asking, "What's wrong?"

"It's… that…" Andren was out of breath and said, "Just hurry!" She cut off the comms before Charlie could make any more demands.

"*Vuk!*" Charlie had on her socks and jammed her feet into the unlaced boots. She started toward the door but rushed back and snared her belt from the wall hook. Bolting out of the room, she sprinted through the halls and decks while buckling on her utility belt with the holstered gun. In record time, she burst through the bay's open door and heard all the shouts and growls, one more animal-like than the rest.

Off to the left past a long workbench, a handful of Kalmar soldiers had their backs to Charlie and were yelling at someone. Each soldier had a rifle in hand, aimed at the poor bugger who was probably backed into a corner.

"What the fuck is going on here?" Charlie hollered, pushing through the Alphas. "If you shoot those weapons in here, you all are getting strung out on the ship's wings!"

Andren was at the front, sword in hand, and seemed to be holding the line.

"Stand down, now!" Laken's voice boomed through the shuttle bay.

Charlie blew out a breath after the five soldiers back-stepped but kept their weapons trained on the target. Laken came up behind her and shoved two Alphas aside so they had room to get to the center of the problem. Charlie shifted to Andren's side and stiffened at the healthy display of canines, bristling fur, and bright red eyes directed at them.

The locke's snarls were deep and dangerous, then its bark echoed off the walls. It was hunched forward and coiled with raw ferocity, ready to attack all of them. At its feet was a piece of raw meat with bite and claw marks on one end.

"Wow," Charlie whispered after realizing the animal had somehow snuck onto the *Betty May*. She then spotted the familiar ear injury and said, "It's the same locke I saved from the market."

Andren lowered her sword and stared in awe at it. "How is that possible?"

"I don't know, but it has that missing piece on the right ear," Charlie replied. She touched Andren's left arm, pushing against it. "Put away your sword."

"*Joh*, it could attack you."

Charlie gave a pointed look to Andren, then ordered, "Put it away." She looked over her shoulder at the other soldiers. "All of you." After a few grumbles, she further ordered, "Give the locke some space."

"It is dangerous," a soldier argued.

Charlie faced the soldiers, and fire fueled her next words. "The only danger here is all of you with those laser rifles. Someone could get hurt when your shots bounce off something, so put them away." When a few hesitated, she growled and reached for her handgun, gripping it with white knuckles. "Now!"

One by one, the soldiers returned their rifles to their backs and moved back, but remained nearby. Laken was silent and her features dark until the soldiers heeded Charlie's command.

Turning back to the snarling animal, Charlie considered her options and glanced at Andren, who was still leery of the locke. "Can you please put your sword away?"

Andren hesitated, then sheathed it but kept her hand around the hilt. She was prepared to slice the animal in half if it made a wrong move.

Kneeling, Charlie got eye level with the locke and smiled at it. "Hey, remember me?"

The locke's head turned to Charlie, but it continued to bare its teeth. Its eyes were a solid, fiery red, which meant it was angry and prepared to fight.

"So I guess you're an Omega," Charlie whispered, recalling Andren's lesson about lockes with red eyes. She extended her hand, palm up, and hoped the locke would scent her. "And hungry." She tilted her head and asked, "Who found her?"

"I did," an Alpha warrior replied. "I was preparing a meal for us. I left the pantry door open, and she stole the meat."

Charlie smiled to herself and looked back at the locke, who had stopped snarling. She took that as a good sign, but the animal was still agitated, if her flaring eyes were any indication.

"We followed the blood droplets to here," the soldier said.

With her arm outstretched, Charlie noticed the locke was baring her teeth only at the Kalmar soldiers. She lowered her hand and looked over her shoulder at them. "Shield master, please take your soldiers out of the bay."

Laken gave the order and waited for each of the soldiers to file out of the room, but she looked over at Andren.

"You too, Andren," Charlie ordered.

"Charlie—"

"Go." Charlie peered up with hooded eyes at her guard. "I'll be fine." She expected Andren to half listen and stand just outside the bay, keeping an ear open for trouble.

Andren huffed low, then brushed past Laken without another word.

Charlie held Laken's gaze for a moment before she looked at the locke again. She listened to Laken's heavy boot steps fade away; then she was left alone with the animal. Lowering to the metal floor, she sat in front of the locke and smiled sadly at it. "You look better than last time."

The locke went to her left, gaining more space but still close to the meat. She was less hunched and her fur was lowering on her back.

"How did you get on here?" Charlie suspected at some point the animal had sneaked on when they were moving supplies onto the vessel. "Why did you even come on here?" Like the Kalmar people, the animals from the planet weren't fond of technology or unnatural structures like ships.

The locke stretched out her neck and grabbed an end of the meat, pulling it away from Charlie.

Holding up her hands, Charlie said, "It's all yours." She scrubbed her face and watched the locke tear the meat off the bone. "Your winter coat is coming in." Last time, the locke had a raggedy gray coat left over from summer, but now large white tufts were spreading over her body.

The locke ate the raw food and glanced at Charlie a few times. Once she was done, she settled onto her full belly and revealed her white eyes.

Charlie propped up an arm on her knee and leaned into it while she watched the animal. "I guess Kal is right that lockes are pretty mischievous." She admired the locke for sneaking onto the vessel and hiding for about two days before being found by a soldier. "But I'm afraid you're stuck here. We can't go back to Kander right now."

The locke stared back, as if listening to Charlie's rambling. Her tall ears were perky and the line of mohawk-style fur stood up on top of her head, then followed her spine to her tail. She licked her lips and showed off her razor teeth.

"So I think your choice is to stay in here." Charlie scanned the interior of the shuttle bay and felt the cool air settle on her. "Or you can come with me and stay in my quarters." She grinned at the locke and said, "As long as you promise not to bite me when I'm sleeping."

The locke lifted her tail, which had a fluffy ball of fur at the tip.

Charlie was unsure whether the animal trusted her and would follow her from the shuttle bay to her quarters. If the locke left the bay, would it attempt to run freely through the ship? If so, then they would have to hunt it and cage it for the remainder of the mission until she could release the locke back on Kander. After a sigh, she decided to give the animal a chance and stood from the freezing floor.

"Well, I'm going to my quarters." Charlie observed that the locke sat up but rested on her hinds, watching her. She took a few steps away from the animal but kept a close eye. At first, Charlie doubted the locke would join her, then she said, "Come on." She continued toward the sealed bay door and softened when the locke stood, then shadowed her from a distance.

Expecting Andren on the other side of the door, Charlie opened it and propped it open for the skittish locke. She poked her head out and raised an eyebrow at Andren standing on the opposite wall. "I think she'll follow me to my quarters."

"Are you crazy?" Andren asked. "It's a dangerous, mischievous animal."

"I got that part," Charlie replied. "But I think she trusts me, at least enough."

Andren narrowed her eyes and opened her mouth but was cut off by Charlie.

"I just need you to give us some space so she'll keep following me." Charlie offered a bright smile and said, "*Krafka*."

Andren huffed and grumbled, then went farther down the hallway. She waited down by the entrance to the medical bay and rested a hand on her sword hilt.

Charlie glanced over her shoulder at the locke, who was lingering several paces behind her. "Come on, girl." She went to her left, opposite Andren, and walked backward. She continued to encourage the locke to follow her.

The locke crept out of the shuttle bay, sniffed the air, and jerked her head toward Andren. She bared her teeth and flashed her red eyes at her before returning her attention to Charlie.

"It's okay," Charlie promised. She continued through the ship, slowing around corners and ensuring no one else was around to bother them. With each step, clicking nails echoed Charlie's boot steps. Once at the quarters, she voiced the door open, ordered it to stay open, and entered the room. Sitting on the bed, she waited for the locke to come in and hoped they had enough trust. Charlie smiled when the locke crept around the corner and entered the spacious quarters.

"It's a little warmer in here, and nobody will bother us." Charlie remained on the side of the bed and allowed the locke to become familiar with the space.

The locke sniffed the surrounding area and checked every inch of the room before padding across the quarters to a corner. She sat there and stared over at Charlie, as if deciding the tiny area was hers now.

Charlie smiled, shrugged, and said, "That's a good spot." She pushed off the bed and went to the closet, searching the higher shelves for a decent blanket. "Here we go." Going over to the animal, she waited for it to move aside, then she put the blanket on the floor and shaped it like a nest. "How's that?" Backing up, she watched the locke climb onto the blanket and ball up after circling it a few times.

The locke released a heavy sigh and lowered her face into the blanket. Her snow white eyes stayed on Charlie, who was stripping off her boots.

"Lucky for you, there's a garden on this boat." Charlie kicked off her boots and removed her socks. "After a nap, we can check it out." She made a mental note to get a bowl from the galley for water. Going over to the open door, she touched the keypad and reprogrammed the door. "I'm going to close the door but leave a crack in it so you can leave." After the locke had been trapped in a cage for days or even nineths, she wouldn't like being confined to the bedroom.

Charlie allowed the door to slide about two-thirds closed and left enough space for the locke. She went to the bed, crawled under the blankets, and fell asleep just as fast as last time. The locke's presence was reassuring, even if a bit strange. Whatever had brought the animal onto the ship was a mystery. But Charlie always had a soft spot for the beautiful lockes, especially this one.

# Chapter 11

Raine waited for the arriving shuttle to land and anchor itself to the *Betty May*'s hull before pressurizing the bay. Her hand danced across the control panel next to the sealed door, and the shuttle bay started to equalize itself.

Charlie continued to watch the shuttle, making out Starr and Magnar in the front seats and Jerrison in the back. She folded her arms and waited until it was safe to go into the bay. But she noticed Raine's attention flickered behind Charlie's shoulder, checking on the locke's location. "You're paranoid," she teased.

"It's a damn locke," Raine said. "They're like a hybrid *wolf-fox* thing. A wox, I guess." She glanced again at the locke who stood a few paces behind Charlie. "But creepy with the all-white eyes and flashy red-eye thing."

"She didn't bother you back at the cabin."

"Because she was locked in a cage." Raine lowered her hand after the door slid open.

"She won't hurt anyone," Charlie promised, then entered the shuttle bay.

Raine followed next and went over to the shuttle.

Charlie noted that the locke slipped in last and tucked herself under the long workbench against the wall. From the moment she and the locke had forged a bit of trust, the locke shadowed her around the ship and never strayed far—but also didn't come too close. So far, Charlie kept her fed and took her to the garden for walks while Charlie enjoyed her company.

"*Turen*, Charlie," Magnar greeted first, indicating that she was using her Brightbit to communication in Kalmarese.

Charlie smiled and shook arms with Magnar. "*Tah* for coming back to the quadrant." She welcomed Jerrison next, then hugged Starr, who squeezed her too hard. The first thing she noticed was the new tattoo on Starr's left arm, along with the different style of outfit. "What's with the tattoos?"

Starr shrugged and replied, "Gerrison knows how to do them." She then retrieved the rifle from her back and showed it to Charlie. "New toy too."

Charlie snatched the huge double-handed rifle and hefted it. There was no way she would use such a bulky rifle, but it was perfect for Starr. She tossed it back and chuckled at Starr's subtle changes.

"I named it Newt in homage to my human boss." Starr joked, winking at Charlie.

After a snort, Charlie couldn't believe Starr would name the lectra rifle after the character from the *Alien* movies. Years ago she forced Starr to watch the movies about the ugly creatures that had plagued mankind in outer space. Stepping aside, she made room for Raine.

Starr then shook arms with Raine and traded smiles.

"So what's the deal, Charlie?" Magnar asked, folding her four arms. "Starr said you plan to use her as bait to draw out Victor."

"That's the plan." Charlie sighed and hid her hands in her jacket's pockets. "He thinks that I'm giving him Starr to end the bounty."

"But that's not what you're really doing?"

Charlie shook her head at Magnar. "We're going to ambush him, kidnap him, and return him to Kander for questioning."

"So the bounty will stay." Magnar glowered and grumbled a few times.

Charlie grinned at Magnar's displeasure. "After the High Commander questions him, then he's mine." She chuckled when Magnar lifted an eyebrow. "I might be convinced to return him to Serrato Corps if they remove the bounty from our heads."

Magnar placed her lower pair of arms on her hips but kept her upper arms folded against her chest. "I sure hope that's your plan since your rescue mission got this bounty on *my* head."

"Oh please." Charlie rolled her eyes and argued, "It's a bounty for this quadrant only. Mine is for the entire galaxy." She became more serious and said, "I'll return him to get the bounty off us. I appreciate you bringing Starr to me."

Magnar revealed a toothy smile. "Oh, I'm staying to help. I want to make sure you capture this jackass." She then looked about the area and said, "Besides, it looks like you could use the help."

Charlie heard Raine's low snort. "We have lots of help."

"More like a sugar daddy that bought you a ship in a few days," Magnar prodded.

Charlie glared hard at her old friend and said, "The rescue mission for the Omega paid well." She didn't want ideas floating around that the *Betty May* was, in fact, Kal's ship. At least, that seemed to be her agreement with Kal at the moment. Behind her, she heard heavy boot steps approach. "Perfect timing."

Magnar puffed up at the newcomer, and a furrow creased her brow.

"Magnar, this is Shield Master Laken from Kander. She's in charge of a unit of Kalmar soldiers who've joined us for this mission." Charlie tried to be less smug than she felt when Magnar grew wide eyed.

"You're telling me there's Kalmar soldiers on this ship?" Magnar's attention cut from Laken to Charlie. "Right now?"

"Twelve soldiers," Charlie replied.

Magnar whistled and said, "That High Commander must really want Victor if she sent her people to space." She stepped forward and offered an arm to Laken.

After a rumble, Laken hooked arms and held strong before taking Charlie's side again.

"So I think we should get started, which means I need to call Victor to show him I have Starr."

Magnar looked from Charlie to Starr and said, "It needs to be realistic." She turned toward Starr, pulled back a fist, and slugged Starr in the face.

Laken surged forward until Charlie stepped into her path. She growled in Magnar's direction, ready for a fight.

"Fuck!" Starr shoved Magnar back and hunched forward, touching her face.

Jerrison clung to Magnar's arm and attempted to restrain her.

"What the fuck, Magnar?" Charlie snapped.

Magnar held out a hand at Starr's bent form and argued, "She has to look roughed up a bit."

"I do have makeup for that," Raine said and shrugged. "Or a black eye and a split lip looks good too."

Magnar sighed, crossed all her arms, and looked at Starr, who was straightening up. "Don't bother with the ice."

Charlie was relieved when Laken backed up without an order. She went over to Starr and asked, "Are you all right?"

Through clenched teeth, Starr replied, "I'll be fine." She blinked her eyes a few times, then looked at Charlie. She allowed Charlie to inspect her face.

"Anything feel broken? Your nose or cheekbone?"

"It wasn't that hard," Magnar argued.

Charlie shot a bitter look at Magnar, then focused on Starr again. She held down her desire to turn and slug Magnar back. "Let's go to the brig. Get this transmission done." Afterward, she would take Starr to the medical bay.

"I'll join you," Magnar said.

Charlie rolled her eyes. Magnar only want to be involved in the kidnapping mission to ensure the bounty was removed from her head. "Fine." She pointed a finger at Magnar and said, "But if you do that again, I'll put a hole in your gut." She hated Magnar's toothy smile.

"I love a good threat, Charlie."

"It's a promise." Charlie started out of the shuttle bay, leading the way. Laken and Raine left them while Magnar, Starr, Jerrison, and she went to the brig on the lower deck.

"What in the Celestial Fates' tits is that?" Magnar indicated the locke following them from a distance.

"She's a locke from Kander," Charlie replied.

Starr was looking back at the animal, too, and asked, "Why is it on your ship?"

"I'm not really sure." Charlie tried to hide her smile about the locke's constant presence. "She's a stowaway, and I can't exactly take her back right now."

Starr responded with a rumble and continued following Charlie, gazing about the unfamiliar ship.

"So are all female Kalmar big beasts?" Magnar asked from her spot behind Charlie, referring to Laken.

Charlie came to the end of the hall and waited for the door to open. "She's not a female like a human. She's a—"

"She sure looks like one," Magnar argued. "She's got boobs as big as mine. What's between her legs?"

Charlie rolled her eyes and peered over her shoulder at Magnar. "She's a Carnec Alpha. And you can ask her yourself what she's got between her legs."

Magnar laughed and followed Charlie and Starr down the steps to the lower deck. "I'm worried if she's got a cock that she'd tell me to suck it."

Starr barked with laughter but snapped her mouth shut at seeing Charlie's threatening look. She held up her hands in defeat, then continued to the brig. Once inside, Charlie had her kneel with her arms behind her back. Already the black eye was apparent and blood dried in the corner of her lip.

The locke sat on her haunches in one corner, keeping Charlie in viewing range.

"Jerrison, do you remember how long it takes for a transmission to be tracked?" Charlie asked.

Jerrison stood by the sealed door and observed the stage being set up for the transmission. "You have about five to seven minutes before they can lock on you." Like Raakor, he was tech savvy and an excellent pilot under pressure.

"That should be plenty of time to get my point across." Charlie was uneasy about Victor finding out that they were already at Eos Minor and sniffing out the trap. She looked up at Magnar, who had a lectra handgun out as if she was keeping an eye on Starr. After a sigh, she gave Starr a reassuring smile and asked, "Ready?" She mussed up Starr's short, dark hair.

Starr grumbled after Charlie finished and replied, "Ready now."

Charlie grinned, then fished out her techbit. She had messaged Victor once to alert him that she was en route to capture Starr. Victor had replied with a single word: *Waiting.* She had pictured him with his arrogant, smug look and wanted to strangle him.

After a huge, deep breath, Charlie sent out a transmission request to Victor and waited for him to answer it. She wasn't disappointed when his face filled the holo screen.

"*Hello, Charlie*," he greeted in English. "*How is your first bounty mission*?" Victor had a condescending tone and eyes glowing with mirth.

"*Well, actually*." Charlie shifted the techbit's eye to Starr, who had her head hung low. "*I have what you want*."

Starr growled and started to rise. "*You, bitch!*" Magnar slammed her back on her knees and put a gun to her temple. She tried to shove free, but Magnar's lower arm locked her down while another hand wrenched in her hair. She hissed and snarled. "*You both fucking betrayed me!*"

Charlie shrugged and said, "*A bounty on my head is bad business*."

"*And mine*," Magnar snapped, her attention flickering to Victor. She flashed her teeth and demanded, "*I want that bounty gone*."

Charlie wondered if Victor could even understand Jero, but his expression didn't seem lost.

Victor was standing outside with the moon's familiar landscape behind him. "*I'm afraid my arrangement is with—*"

"*And now it's with me too*." Magnar yanked Starr's head to one side and moved her finger to the gun's trigger. "*Or I'll burn a hole in her head right now, which I don't think your client wants*."

Victor held up a hand and said, "*I am sure the Grand Marshal will be agreeable to end the bounty for you too*." He cleared his throat after Magnar withdrew the gun from Starr's head. He focused on Charlie and said, "*I will send a ship to collect our property*."

Charlie curled her hand after he referred to Starr as property. "*I will only release her to you, personally*." She reached for the techbit's screen, wanting to end the transmission before he traced them and discovered they were at Eos Minor already. In a threatening tone, she said, "*We'll meet you at Eos Minor. And don't show up without the signed pardons from the Grand Marshal*."

* * *

The next day, Charlie slung the rifle across her back and walked with the Kalmar warriors to the hiding spot, among trees and brush. Next to her was Raine, who had the Galactic Hammer strapped to her back for the upcoming ambush. The rest of the team waited back in the open field for her return.

Laken ordered the soldiers to get into position, then she turned to Charlie and Raine. "Should we test the comms?"

Raine nodded her agreement and looked at Charlie for confirmation.

"Magnar, Magnar do you read me?" Charlie hailed over the comms and caught Laken's nod that she heard the hail too.

"Read you clear," Magnar replied.

"Out." Charlie then focused on Laken and said, "You hail her next."

For a few minutes, they each hailed one another to ensure that the comms between the earpieces, ships, and shuttles were in working order. Once the ambush was initiated, their comms would stream so they no longer had to waste time hailing each other. Every tick would count while they captured Victor.

Charlie glanced at the time on the techbit, indicating they had about fifteen minutes before Victor arrived on Eos Minor. She tucked the techbit away, focused on Laken, and asked, "Any last minute concerns?"

"*Joh*." Laken peered back at the soldiers, then nodded at Charlie. "We are ready."

Yesterday Charlie had prepared everyone for today's battle, praying everything went according to plan. Their first concern was to apprehend Victor and then squash the Serrato soldiers so that there weren't any loose ends. Charlie didn't want the Serrato ship following them back to Kander.

"Good." Charlie turned to Raine and lifted an eyebrow. "When I give the signal over the comms, you start the attack. Get Victor out of there and—"

"Over to Jerrison in the shuttle. Then come back and kick ass." Raine held up both thumbs and smiled big. "I got it."

Charlie grinned at her sister, who had spent several hours between yesterday and this morning learning how to operate and fly the battle suit. She blew out a breath and nodded at the pair. "All right. Get into position and let's get this bastard." She separated from them and returned to the open grass field where Magnar, Starr, and Andren waited for her. "*Betty May*, start an open comms line between me, Magnar, Andren, Raine, Laken, and the *Four Mag*." With the open comms, everyone would be aware of the conversation between Charlie and Victor.

"Opening the line," the *Betty May* replied.

"Can everyone read me?" Charlie asked, already knowing the answer. As everyone chimed in, she rejoined the team in front of the *Betty May*'s shuttle. "Gerrison, do you see any signs of the Serrato ships?"

"Nothing on the scans," Gerrison replied over the comms from his position on the *Four Mag*. "But they may be using their cloaking system."

Charlie studied Starr's black eye, still irritated that Magnar punched Starr yesterday. It did add to the lie, much like Starr's dirt-covered skin, matted hair, and cuffed hands. She noted that Magnar was pacing and carrying Starr's rifle while Andren stood like a statue, scanning the orange horizon. Sighing, she wished the locke was here, but she had left the animal on the *Betty May* and out of harm. In a short period, the locke's companionship had eased Charlie's current worries.

"I'm seeing a wake disturbance about four leagues from Eos Minor," Gerrison remarked.

Charlie pursed her lips and said, "This is probably them, everyone." She shifted over to Starr's left side and looked over at Magnar, who halted her pacing behind Starr. "Jerrison, warm up the shuttle's engine." About two marches from their current location, Jerrison was in the *Four Mag*'s shuttle prepared to fly their pending captive to the *Betty May*.

"Initiating engine protocols," Jerrison responded.

For several minutes, time passed at a snail's pace until a distant reflective surface caught Charlie's eye. She narrowed her gaze and asked, "Does anyone else have a visual on the approaching shuttle?"

"I see it," Magnar confirmed.

Starr grumbled and whispered, "I see three."

"I can hear them," Andren said, adjusting her grip on the laser rifle. "I think there's four."

"Laken and Raine, we have a visual on the Serrato shuttles. They should land in our field in about three minutes," Charlie said over the comms and received confirmation. "Gerrison, do you have eyes on the Serrato ship?"

"Not yet, but I am searching for it."

Charlie wasn't surprised and expected the Serrato ship to use cloaking technology. It would be up to Gerrison to visually seek out the ship and destroy it once the ambush started. With her attention still on the shuttles, she watched them cut through the air and close in on them. The *Betty May*'s shuttle behind them was giving out a homing signal for the Serrato soldiers to locate them on Eos Minor.

"They're preparing to land," Magnar called out over the comms.

Shielding her face with her hand, Charlie turned her head away while the shuttles started descending in the field about sixty paces in front of them. The tall grasses swirled and danced as the vessels sank down into them. Once the wind died down, she looked over at the four long shuttles that could carry at least six or more bodies. Her hopes were dashed that only six or eight Serrato soldiers were meeting them.

The shuttles' canopy cockpits hissed, then popped and lifted up to allow the passengers to disembark. One by one, the Serrato soldiers unloaded until there were twenty-three soldiers. At the front was Victor, who signaled them to march forward to the meeting spot.

"We have twenty-three soldiers, including Victor," Charlie reported.

"I located the Serrato ships," Gerrison called over the comms.

Charlie frowned and asked, "Did you say ships?"

"*Ja*." Gerrison paused, then said, "There are two Serrato ships."

"*Vuk*," Charlie hissed and clenched her hand around the lectra gun's handle.

"That would explain the extra shuttles," Magnar said. "Don't engage the ships, Gerrison. Not until we can get back to the *Betty May* to assist."

"Standing by," Gerrison confirmed.

Charlie flexed her hand on the gun's grip and prepared for an ugly fight ahead. "Raine, get ready." Over the comms, she heard Raine activate the Galactic Hammer. Charlie walked a few steps ahead of the group and greeted Victor in English. "*I was thinking you may have backed out.*"

Victor wore his typical military fatigues that reminded Charlie of Earth. His olive-colored military beret had the Seal of Serrato on the front of it, and a few pieces of bling were pinned to his chest, including his last name. His blond hair and blue eyes stood out against his darker attire. "*The solar storms delayed us.*" He cut his attention to Starr, who was on her knees in front of Magnar.

Charlie pivoted and studied Starr pretending to be held prisoner. "*I have what you want.*" She looked at Victor and asked, "*Do you have our pardons?*"

Victor reached into a pocket on his pant leg and produced two rolled up papers. "*Yes.*" He withdrew them and said, "*But I want a closer look at my property first.*"

Charlie didn't care about the useless pardons yet pretended to be annoyed about his demands. She held out her hand toward Starr, welcoming him to look more.

After a signal, Victor and two other Serrato soldiers approached Starr along with Charlie. His smiled widened as he approached Starr, then he grabbed her by her hair.

Starr snarled and bared her teeth when her head was twisted up toward Victor. Her razor-sharp canines flashed at him in the morning sunlight.

"*Still as feisty as last time.*" Victor glanced behind her back, most likely confirming that Starr's wrists were lashed together.

"*Satisfied?*" Magnar asked in Jero from her spot behind Starr.

Victor's attention flickered to Magnar, as if noticing her for the first time. He released Starr, backed away, and turned to the two soldiers. "*Get the sedation kit and better cuffs.*" He went over to Charlie, who remained in the middle ground between her team and the Serrato soldiers. He produced the rolled up pardons and held them out. "*In exchange for the slave.*"

Charlie smiled and collected the pardons, then tilted her head as her smile darkened. "*So I have just one question for you. Do you like Whitney Houston?*" In her earpiece, she heard the soft roar, then wind whistled in her ear.

"*What?*" Victor's features tightened and twisted as he stared at Charlie.

"*Whitney Houston*," Charlie repeated. "*She's like the best female singer of all time*." At least in Charlie's opinion. She retrieved her techbit and thumbed through the screens until she located the song on her Badass Mix List.

"*What are you doing*?" Victor asked, signaling the two returning soldiers to halt behind him.

Charlie had a wicked smile and replied, "*My favorite Whitney Houston song is 'I Wanna Dance With Somebody.'*" She tapped the techbit's screen and allowed the song to blast from its speaker. She started to sing alongside Whitney, putting all her heart into it.

Victor reached for his handgun, gripping it and demanded, "*What are you doing?*"

Charlie laughed and pointed up to the orange sky with her free hand. When Victor looked up, she replied, "*I'm distracting you, you dickweed*." Just then, all the roar and rush in Charlie's ear was above her head; she jumped backward.

Suited in the Galactic Hammer, Raine landed between Victor and Charlie, then said, "*Ready to fly, bro*?" She snatched Victor and tossed him onto her right shoulder with ease. "*Better clench up, Legolas!*" Raine launched skyward with a yell from her new prisoner. "*I always wanted to say that line!*"

Charlie chuckled until she focused on the two soldiers in front of her, along with the twenty other behind them. All of the soldiers retrieved their cartridge-filled rifles and swung them toward Charlie and her team. "Shit," she whispered.

But everyone's attention snapped to the side of the field where a chorus of yells erupted from the tree line. The Kalmar warriors thundered across the sea of tall grasses, cheering in Kalmarese and readying their weapons.

Reaching into her pocket, Charlie tore out the Grasshopper, flicked the dial up to full power, and aimed at the Serrato soldiers. "*Let's dance, boys!*" She pulled the trigger and waited for the powerful recoil that rocketed her through the air. With a scream, she sailed for several paces until she collided with a soft but firm body.

"Got you," Starr said in her ear.

Charlie found herself nestled in Starr's bigger body instead of swimming in dirt and grass. She whipped her head up and smirked at the Serrato soldiers scattered across the field. The swarm of Kalmar warriors collided with the enemy, then lasers, bullets, and blades blurred in the sea of screams and war cries. Andren and Magnar sprinted forward and joined the fray.

With Starr's help, Charlie was on her feet, and she put away the Grasshopper. She retrieved the lectra handgun and bowie knife, and as she and Starr hurried to the battle, she ordered, "Nova, play my Fight Playlist starting with 'Centuries' by Fall Out Boy. Volume level fifty!" She hollered again and ducked under a soldier's swing, popped up behind him, spun around, and drove her knife into his back. She finished him with a lectra shot to his lower spine.

"Playing your Fight Workout Playlist," Nova replied from the techbit in Charlie's back pocket.

"Charlie, Captain Asshole is secured and being flown up to the *Betty May*," Raine reported over the comms.

"Great!" Charlie kicked a charging soldier in the chest, sending her backward. "Now get back here and help us!"

"Already on my way!"

"Charlie, Jerrison and I are engaging the two Serrato ships," Gerrison reported over the comms.

Charlie acknowledged Gerrison's call, looked across the battle and asked, "Laken, how are you doing over there?" She fired a shot at a soldier coming up on Magnar's back.

"Two Kalmar soldiers down." Laken huffed and growled, then said, "But we're beating them." Her next roar broadcasted across the fight.

An overhead howl signaled Raine's arrival, and she landed with a soft boom in the center of the battle. In her loudest voice, she said, "Let's get dangerous!" With the battle suit's power, she rolled over the Serrato soldiers without any resistance. She threw two or three of them like a bowling ball into pins. Realizing her threat level, several soldiers attempted to shoot at her, but the bullets bounced off the suit's metal body. Raine's maniacal laughter echoed over the field.

"We got a problem!" Andren said over the comms. "Several soldiers are retreating to the shuttles." She huffed and continued to slice through the soldiers with her sword.

"We have to stop them!" Charlie glanced in the shuttles' direction, spotting the three soldiers escaping to them.

"I got this," Raine said, launching upward with the thrusters. "Oh my god, Charlie. Is that the 'Fight Song' by Rachel Platten?"

"*Ja*, I know it's your—" Charlie yelped after a soldier hit her from behind, taking her down. She rolled to her left before a boot hit her, then fired a lectra shot at him. She blew out a breath and said, "Your song." She flipped onto her feet and looked toward the shuttles.

"I found out why they call this suit the Galactic Hammer," Raine said.

Charlie furrowed her eyebrows and gazed up at Raine, who hovered several hundred paces above the shuttle that the Serrato soldiers were running to. She held her breath when Raine hurled downward like a comet. "Oh gods," she whispered in awe.

A shattering boom erupted through the entire field and tossed everyone onto their backs, ending the battle. After the shockwave faded, the first few people rolled onto their sides and gazed over at the demolished shuttles. Charlie blinked the dirt out of her eyes and gaped at the crushed shuttle in the middle of the other two. Once the dust settled, Raine stood and placed her hands on her metal hips.

"Wow," Charlie murmured, not realizing what the battle suit was capable of when she bought it from Sres. "Galactic Hammer is right." Getting up, she scanned the field and smiled when the last few Serrato soldiers held up their hands in surrender. Kalmar warriors rounded up both the prisoners and their own injured people.

Charlie neared Magnar, who hefted her rifle over her shoulder. "Great fight."

Magnar's toothy smile was bright against her inky skin. "My kind of fight."

"Gerrison and Jerrison, how are you both doing?" Charlie radioed to the twin brothers.

"Good and bad news," Gerrison reported from the *Four Mag.*

"We could only destroy one ship," Jerrison said. "One protected the other so one could escape."

"*Vuk*," Charlie cursed.

"I attempted chasing it." Gerrison paused, frustrating seeping into his next words. "But its trail cools too fast."

Charlie grumbled and said, "They use cryosalt to cool their engines. It's difficult to trace them." She heard Gerrison's soft curse. "It's all right. We were pretty lucky as it was with this fight." She looked at the team and said, "Let's get the prisoners organized and get off this planet."

* * *

Charlie scrubbed her face after a long but exciting night of celebration from their win over Serrato Corps. After a few hours of sleep, it was time to return to Kander, but she first wanted to check on her prize. She entered the brig and peered over her shoulder, when her four-legged shadow slipped in behind her. She closed the door, then went over to the first cage that held her esteemed guest. "*Sucks being on the other side of the bars, huh?*"

Victor paused his pacing and came to the corner closest to Charlie. "*What did you do with my men?*" He gripped the bars and glared at her.

"*We stripped them of their tech and left them on Eos Minor with the natives.*" Charlie smirked and folded her arms. "*I think the dinos will appreciate the extra meat.*" She decided it was appropriate for the Serrato soldiers to contend with Eos Minor's hungry natives, much like when Victor's people first arrived on Serrato.

Victor was breathing harder and his lip curled on one side. "*Serrato Corps will search for me, and they'll start with Kander.*"

"*I know.*" Charlie tilted her head, gauging Victor from a safe distance. She had minor concerns, considering Kander's satellite system that doubled as a defense weapon. "*But I seriously doubt they'll waste too many resources on you.*" She could bathe in Victor's boiling outrage.

"*What do you want with me?*"

Charlie chuckled and replied, "*I was merely hired to kidnap you and deliver you to Kander.*" She shifted closer to the bars. "*You have a date with the High Commander.*" She leaned closer and whispered, "*Then when she's done cutting the answers out of you, you'll be mine.*"

Victor lunged and latched onto Charlie's leather jacket. He jerked her forward, but Charlie grabbed onto the bars, holding her ground. "*You fucking bitch! I'll—*" He was cut off by a hungry snarl to the left, and he looked over with wide eyes.

Gritting her teeth, Charlie tore herself free and glanced at the locke, who had flaming red eyes and huge canines. She shivered at the animal's ferocity and was relieved it wasn't directed at her. She straightened out her jacket and said, "*Losing your cool, Victor?*" She went to the sealed door, opened it, and glanced back at him. "*Until later.*" She blew him a kiss and left with the locke in tow.

On the upper deck, Charlie located Starr, Magnar, and Jerrison preparing to load into the shuttle and return to the *Four Mag*. She felt her shoulders slump and her lips downturn watching them.

Starr tossed her rifle Newt into the shuttle, then approached Charlie. "*Hey,*" she greeted in Jero. "*I have the blockers you asked for earlier.*" She offered the small, metal bottle to Charlie.

Charlie tucked them into her jacket pocket. Last night during the party and libations, she had worked up the nerve to ask Starr about her supply of blockers. Luckily Starr had recently purchased two hundred of the pills and promised a hundred fifty of them to Charlie, after a lot of questions. She had brushed off Starr's attempt to grill her but convinced Starr to let her pay for the pills. If nothing else, Starr had a clue that Charlie was possibly sleeping with a Kalmar.

"*Thanks for this.*" Charlie had paid Starr last night.

"*If you need more—*"

"*I'll contact you,*" Charlie promised. Then her shoulders slumped now that it was time for farewells again. "*I can't convince you to stay?*"

Starr sighed and clasped her old boss's shoulder. "*Not until you leave Kander.*"

Charlie nodded and grabbed Starr's forearm, gripping it hard. "*I have promises to keep.*"

Starr smiled, shifted closer, and whispered, "*I know you do.*" She yanked Charlie into a long hug.

"*Thank you for coming and helping,*" Charlie whispered in her friend's ear.

Starr nodded, then withdrew and climbed into the shuttle.

Magnar approached next and said, "*I plan to go to the twelfth quadrant and lay low. You better let me know what happens with Victor and the bounty.*"

"*I will. There was something else I wanted to ask you.*" When Magnar lifted an eyebrow, Charlie sighed and glanced away before saying, "*About the coalition.*" She grumbled when Magnar bristled in response.

"*Charlie, you know—*"

"*I know,*" Charlie cut off, hissing low and clenching her jaw. "*I get it. I made my choices.*" She took a deep breath to help calm her nerves. "*It's not about me. It's about the Sworne.*"

Magnar tilted her head and folded both sets of arms. "*Starr mentioned that you wanted Victor to find out about the Sworne.*"

"*Did she tell you why?*" Charlie asked and licked her lips after Magnar's head shake. "*I think they're coming back.*" At Magnar's rising tension, she said, "*If that's true, it might take everyone in the galaxy to stop them.*"

"*You think the coalition is going to rally for the Sworne?*"

"*If they won't rally for that, then what are they willing to fight for?*" Charlie asked. "*You might have to be the one to tell them that they're coming back.*"

Magnar closed her eyes for a moment and shook her head before staring at Charlie. "*I don't know if they'll believe it when you're the source.*"

Charlie ground her teeth together and tried to cap her anger, balling her fists in her pockets.

"*You were respected, Charlie.*" Magnar unfolded her lower arms and placed her hands on Charlie's stiff shoulders. "*You were the Galaxy Master and still are to some. But after Ferrafar, you—*"

"*I know!*" Charlie looked away until Magnar's cupped her cheek. "*I'm still the Galaxy Master to many.*"

Magnar had a bittersweet smile and patted Charlie's flushed cheek. "*You're still the Galaxy Master to me.*" She lowered her arms and said, "*I will attempt to talk to the coalition, but I can't promise they'll listen.*"

Charlie nodded and decided it was better than nothing. She exchanged a hug with Magnar and said goodbye to Jerrison. After leaving the bay with the locke, she heard the hissing and hum from the shuttle and knew they were leaving. Looking at the locke, she said, "Come on. We'll go through the garden first, then to the bridge, and finally chill out in our quarters." She could do with a mental break, but she wanted to get the *Betty May* underway and back to Kander.

After letting the locke spend time in the garden, Charlie went to the flight deck and found Raine waiting for her. She took the pilot's seat and helped Raine navigate the ship away from Eos Minor before putting it into leed two when they were clear of the solar system.

"Did you name her yet?" Raine indicated the locke nestled under one of the empty chairs on the upper level.

Charlie rolled her eyes and replied, "She'll be gone once we land on Kander."

Raine smirked and said, "I'm betting the other way."

"She's a wild animal," Charlie argued. "And giving her a name is just attaching myself to her."

"She's wild all right." Raine tapped a few things on the screen and muttered, "Wild about you."

*Are we talking about the locke or Kal?* Charlie asked herself but ignored her friend's remark. "Thanks for coming on this mission. I know I owe you big."

"We'll make it eight noreds instead of six," Raine said, her voice filled with mirth.

Charlie glowered in response and had no intention of staying that long on Kander. At least, that's what she told herself, even though her heart ached at the thought of leaving Kal. Even now, she was antsy to return to Kander and feel her lover's body against hers. Satisfied that they were cruising at a safe speed, she stood up and said, "Don't forget to charge the Galactic Hammer."

Raine twisted her head around and revealed her appalled expression. "I wouldn't forget to take care of *my* battle suit."

Charlie kicked her friend's chair and said, "That's *my* suit." She shook her head at Raine's devious smile and strolled off with the silent, white ghost behind her. The solitude in her quarters was welcoming, and Charlie stripped off much of her attire until she wore only pants and a shirt.

The locke sniffed around the room and settled into her nest of blankets. Her big, white eyes followed Charlie around in the quarters. She released a loud sigh after Charlie sat on the bed.

Charlie wanted to sleep, but she was still too wound up from the fight on Eos Minor. She then decided to attempt the meditation technique that Kal had shown her on their last night together. Once centered in the bed, Charlie crossed her legs and held out her hands, keeping her palms facedown.

At first, she struggled to clear her mind and almost gave up the meditation. But she had promised Kal she would try. She shook her hands a few times, then refocused herself. She took a few deep, steady breaths, which helped ease her taut muscles. Just as her body started to relax, a knock disturbed her concentration. "Come in," she called, which activated the door.

Andren entered and slowed after a few steps into the quarters. She stared at Charlie, opening and closing her mouth a few times.

Charlie dragged her fingers through her hair and looked over at Andren. "What's up?"

Andren cleared her throat and replied, "Just wanted to let you know that the five injured warriors will be fine. One of the Alphas is still in the medical bay after having a bullet removed from his shoulder."

Cringing, Charlie asked, "They were able to get the bullet out?"

Andren nodded and replied, "One of the soldiers has medical experience."

"I imagine that's why Kal sent him," Charlie said, humming at her lover's constant insight and planning skills. "How are the others?"

"Fine." Andren had a slight grin. "I think we are ready to return home."

Charlie thought about whether Kander was home to her. "Space sickness getting to them?"

Andren chuckled and shrugged. "We weren't made for outer space."

Charlie understood after being on a ship with Starr for several years. "It doesn't seem to agree with your people."

Andren tilted her head and neared the bed. "It is difficult for us to be away from our home planet, but it was important to capture Victor."

"*Ja.*" Charlie sighed and whispered, "I hope he has the answers we need." Even if he had any, she had no idea how Kal planned to make him talk. She set aside her thoughts when she noticed Andren's curious look.

"Are you trying *fynil*?"

Charlie stared at Andren and failed to translate the Kalmarese word. "Am I what?"

"*Fynil*," Andren repeated, pointing at Charlie's body. "It's a very old and special Kalmar tradition between mates." She smiled a little and said, "I assume the High Commander showed you."

Charlie bit her lip, then shifted on the bed until she faced Andren. "She didn't tell me it's called *fynil*." Kal also hadn't elaborated on the fact it was a special ritual for bonded mates. Charlie had wrongly assumed it was a meditation technique for Kalmar.

Andren shifted on her feet, then cleared her throat. "It is used for bonding. *Fynil* means 'together' in our old tongue."

Scratching her neck once, Charlie weighed the ancient meaning behind the ritual's name. "Well, it's not easy to do. I have a hard time keeping my mind clear."

Andren canted her head and said, "You are doing it wrong if you are attempting to keep your mind clear." A soft grin spread across her full lips. "You are meant to fill your mind with your mate, then the rest will come." She back stepped twice. "It takes time to master." She went to the door and said goodbye to Charlie.

Alone again, Charlie returned to the center of the bed and decided to take Andren's suggestion. She resumed her earlier position, closed her eyes, and took several big breaths until her body relaxed. This time she concentrated on Kal, beginning with facial features to help center her mind. With each passing tick, she became more immersed in her mental image of Kal until she could hear her.

"Charlie," Kal whispered, her voice twisting in the air. "Charlie," she called again, pulling against Charlie's spirit.

Gasping, Charlie replied, "Sumner." She beckoned her lover to find her, through space and infinite distance. Then she felt the familiar heat under her palms and the pressure against her knees. Her eyes flew open and her mind was jolted by the unformed vision of her lover materializing in front of her.

Kal was crossed legged as well and wearing her normal attire. She was more of a ghost, and the back half of her was fragmented in glowing, floating shards that were trying to merge together. Her distorted presence was becoming more solid with each heartbeat.

"Sumner?" Charlie whispered in awe then jerked her hands away from the large ones under hers.

Kal shattered into millions of flickering grains that faded until there was nothing again other than a broken whisper. "Char…"

Charlie scooted back, crawling on her hands and staring at the spot where she had envisioned her lover. She covered her racing heart and tried to calm it with gulps of air. She then noticed the soft scent of burning wood that was impossible on the *Betty May*. "Th-that wasn't real," she told herself. Looking over at the locke, she asked, "Did you see that?"

The locke was sniffing the air, seeming to scent something. She sneezed before lowering her head to the blankets again.

"Okay. I need sleep," Charlie said, declaring herself deprived of rest. She had plenty of time for a long nap before they were near Kander's solar system. She crawled under the blankets, lowered the lights, and struggled to relax at first. After easing her mind, she whispered, "Don't make something out of nothing."

# Epilogue

Charlie hopped out of the truck bed, stepped aside, and waited for Andren to escort Victor. She smirked when Victor was shoved off the truck and stumbled twice. She grabbed his arms, which were lashed behind his back. "*This way, captain.*"

Andren followed behind Charlie and the prisoner and held her laser rifle at the ready.

Heading up to the Great Tower's massive entrance, a guard started to open the left door for them. Charlie noticed that Victor was taking in the tower's massive stature that reached higher than any building in Tarrak.

Victor turned his head sidelong and asked, "*Is it to compensate for what the High Commander doesn't have between her legs?*"

Charlie snorted, leaned in, and whispered, "*More like a memorial for what she does have between her legs.*" She snickered at his confused expression and pushed him forward into the opening of the Great Tower.

The High Commander waited in the middle of the entrance hall, flanked by several guards. Her eyes were on Victor for a tick before she held Charlie's gaze. She hooked her hands in front of her body and waited for Charlie to present the prisoner to her.

Charlie grabbed Victor's shoulder, halting him several steps from the High Commander. With a brief head bow, she smiled and said, "As requested. This is Captain Victor Petrov from Serrato Corps. The human that had the Omega Fairlee kidnapped and ransomed to you." *And killed me*, she reminded herself and sensed Kal's silent agreement. She looked at him and slammed her boot into his legs.

Victor collapsed to the floor on his knees before the High Commander. He snarled low, then bared his teeth when the High Commander approached him.

Kal neared Victor and held his gaze the entire time. She flashed him a predatory smile, revealing her long canines. "*Welcome to Kander*," she said in English.

Charlie lifted an eyebrow at hearing her native tongue spoken by Kal.

"Take him to a cell and prep him for me to question," Kal ordered the guards, who snared his shoulders and dragged him away. Victor was gone in a few ticks.

Charlie was intrigued by the idea that Kal would question Victor herself. She wanted to know more but held her tongue in front of the audience.

"Andren, you may return to the barracks until Charlie is ready to leave the tower. Also inform Laken that I want a full report by first light."

"*Ja*, Kal." Andren bowed her head, then traded a glance with Charlie.

Kal waited until Andren left them before saying, "I will need your assistance with questioning Victor. Do you have time now?"

Charlie considered her pending plans, which included going back to the *Betty May* to help Raine. They had landed the ship outside the city rather than place it in orbit and use the shuttle. There were too many Kalmar soldiers, including injured ones, and loads of supplies to be removed from the ship's storage holes. Still, she had time for whatever Kal needed help with for the interrogation, which she suspected was translating from English to Kalmarese.

"*Ja*, of course."

Kal nodded. "Then we will go to my office first." She signaled for the two guards to continue their duties. She walked with Charlie up to the elevator lobby, then they slipped into the empty lift.

Charlie tucked her hands into her jacket pockets and rocked on her boots, stealing glances at her lover. "You look good."

Kal canted her head, and a faint smile creased her lips. "You smell good."

Flushing, Charlie sniffed her jacket and joked, "I smell like oil and hyperfuel."

Kal rumbled and said, "*Ja* but that's only on the surface."

Charlie shook her head but faced the lift's gate after a ding. She opened it and went to the office's open door that had two guards on either side. Once they were inside, the doors closed and they were alone.

"Were any of my warriors killed?" Kal asked and steered them over to the sitting area.

"*Joh*." Charlie sat on the sofa with her lover. "A few were hurt, but they'll be fine."

Kal relaxed into the sofa and asked, "What of the Serrato soldiers?"

"We killed a lot of them," Charlie replied. "But there were five that surrendered at the end of the fight. I stripped them of their tech and left them on Eos Minor. They'll get eaten by the animals there, or maybe a ship will come back for them, if they're lucky."

Kal's chest shook with soft thunder, sounding pleased with the results. "And my ship?"

Charlie chuckled at the idea of a High Commander now owning a ship. "The *Betty May* doesn't have a scratch. We landed outside the city, by the old mill."

Kal nodded and released a deep breath.

"I did have one… odd thing happen." Charlie clenched her lower lip between her teeth when Kal raised an eyebrow at her. "So like a day or two before we left for the mission, I bought a locke from a vendor in the market." She shook her head and said, "Actually Andren bought it for me, and I still need to pay her back." She sighed at her ramble and refocused the conversation. "Anyway, it was sick looking, so I fed it and released it the next day."

"You didn't mention this," Kal said.

"It wasn't really important, I guess." Charlie played with her utility belt, staring at it for a moment before looking at Kal again. "So anyway, after we left Kander, several of the warriors found and cornered the locke."

"You took it on the ship?"

"*Joh*." Charlie sighed and touched her lover's thigh. "She snuck onto the *Betty May* and hid there. She just got caught stealing food."

"What happened to it?"

Charlie had a thin smile and replied, "I kind of took her in, fed her, and let her stay in my quarters. She followed me around the ship. After we landed, she followed me out of the *Betty May* and went into the wild again." She studied Kal's downturned lips.

"That is unusual for a locke."

"They are mischievous creatures," Charlie said, hints of amusement in her tone.

Kal remained quiet for a moment, then sighed and said, "You may have imprinted the locke after saving her."

Charlie huffed and argued, "I just let it out of a cage."

"You also fed and sheltered her, repeatedly."

"But she left the ship." Charlie had watched the locke disappear into the field of winter grain despite wanting to call the locke back to her. She frowned at the memory and whispered, "I doubt she'll return after being stuck on that ship for days."

Kal grunted, then leaned down into Charlie's space. "You have a way of alluring wild creatures."

Charlie rolled her eyes and whispered, "Such a sought-after skill." She closed the distance and sealed their lips together, whimpering at feeling them again. The kiss was long and slow until they both struggled for control. Charlie broke first and moaned after Kal bit her neck. *I missed you*, she whispered in her mind. But when Kal pulled away, she grumbled at the loss of contact and hated the restrictions on their relationship. *It's still an affair.*

"Are you hungry?" Kal asked, her voice shaking with an Alpha's desire. Her right hand was curled tight enough that her knuckles were white.

Smirking, Charlie replied, "For food or you?" Her throbbing clit was shocked by Kal's wolfish smile.

"Food. But we can discuss a bonus for your successful mission later."

"I like bonuses." Charlie felt like the cat with the canary at the prospect of getting fucked tonight. "And I am a little hungry." She stretched out her hand and traced her pointed index finger down the length of Kal's coat. When she came to Kal's waist, she trailed her finger to Kal's crotch and whispered, "I could be convinced to eat *something*." She peered up with hooded eyes, noticing that Kal's attention went from staring at her crotch to Charlie's gaze.

"I will have something brought up," Kal said, but she made no effort to handle the request, yet.

Charlie slid her hand to the underside, where she could already feel her lover's hard-on. She smirked at Kal's darkened eyes and whispered, "*Krafka.*" She withdrew her hand and chuckled at the amount of effort it took for Kal to leave the sofa and order something.

*It's good to be… home?*

* * *

"This way," Kal ordered, guiding Charlie to a sealed, heavy wood door tucked in a hidden spot on the ground floor of the Great Tower.

Charlie's skin crawled when the guard unlocked the door and yanked it open for them. Already the damp smells wafted from the opening, and the flickering light put her on edge.

Kal went first and descended the stone steps, one by one.

Charlie almost fingered her handgun, which she'd forgotten to hide in her jacket. She ignored it and instead followed her lover down the windy, narrow steps. Behind her, the door boomed with finality. Once they made it to the bottom, they traveled down a long hallway and passed an occasional guard. On either side were doors one after another; all appeared locked tight.

The dampness was heavier, and the torches' light was bright. After a few steps, she frowned at her boots scraping the dirt floor rather than stone, like the rest of the Great Tower. They had to be a hundred feet or so below the building and perhaps under a street. Perhaps this was the only prison, or there could be more connected to the Great Tower.

They came to the end of the hallway, and a guard stood from a stool. He reached to his side and produced a set of keys.

"Is he prepped?" Kal asked.

"*Ja*, Kal." The guard worked the key in the hole, unlocked it, and pulled on the ring until the door creaked open. "Do you require anything else?"

"*Joh*." Kal entered the cell.

Charlie followed and took in Victor slumped forward on a wooden bench. The six-by-six cell had gray stone walls, a dirt floor, and four lit torches that probably were allowed to burn out and leave the prisoner in total darkness. To the left, a small hole had an ankle tall bucket on it, probably a crude toilet. On the wall behind Victor were two metal rings with chains attached to them, but they weren't hooked to him.

With a furrow etching across her brow, Charlie spotted a metal cup on the bench and clear liquid pooled around it. She shifted a few steps closer and frowned when Victor didn't react to her movements. "Victor?" She placed a hand on her gun and pushed on his shoulder to get his attention.

Victor groaned and slid down the stone wall. He stared upward and moaned.

Charlie jumped back, half expecting him to come at her. She noticed the glassy reflection in his eyes, his features glazed and lost. Glancing over at the cup, she grabbed it and sniffed the contents, which burned against her nose. "*Vuk!*" She tossed the empty cup onto the bench and looked over at her lover. "He's drunk from *mkin.*" The scent of the cup alerted Charlie to the strength of the Kalmar alcohol that hadn't been diluted. Humans weren't capable of drinking much *mkin* and had to weaken it with water, finding it fatal to their liver otherwise.

"*Ja.*" Kal moved to Victor's side and stared at him. "It makes him pliable."

"Pliable? For what?" Charlie stared in worry at her lover, who grabbed Victor's shoulder.

Kal shoved him forward and sent him to the ground. "He is human, but he isn't a Beta." She canted her head and whispered, "The *mkin* will make it easier to control him."

Charlie parted her lips, but her heart pounded against her chest when Kal's eyes glowed bright green. She looked down and stumbled backward, hitting the bench. "Holy fucking shit!" She wanted to hop on the bench when the thick, black mist rose up from the floor.

Every wisp of it seemed hungry, but only for Victor. It consumed him, and he jolted to life with a scream. He attempted to get up, using his hands, but Kal's boot slammed into his back. She drove him into the dirt and held him down while the fog soaked into his skin, eyes, and mouth until it was gone.

Kal released him and ordered, "Get up."

Victor remained motionless for a beat but then he put his hands under his body. He lifted himself, stood, and appeared more alert.

Charlie shifted to her right to stand in front of Victor. She gaped at his black eyes that had once been blue, like hers. She snapped her attention to Kal, whose eyes were still a blazing green. *Fuck! My eyes had been black when I crashed on Kander.* She recalled her reflection in the shuttle that day. Even though she and Kal had discussed Kal's being inside Charlie after the crash, she was at a loss to witness it happening to another.

Kal looked from Victor to Charlie and said, "You must question him and translate it to me."

"You can't understand him even with—" Charlie waved her hand at his stiff form and tried to think of the right question. "—his forced cooperation?"

"*Joh.*" Kal stared at Victor's profile and said, "His thoughts are in a strange language. I can only control his movements."

"It's probably *Russian*," Charlie whispered, then nodded once. "Victor*, can you still understand me*?"

"*Da.*"

Charlie heard the hollowness in his voice and shivered from it. His accent was stronger compared to their previous conversations. She refocused on the task and said, "*We want to know about the Sworne. I heard you discussing with another soldier that they are returning. Is this true?*"

"*Da.*"

Charlie grumbled and asked, "*How do your people know the Sworne are coming back to the galaxy?*"

Victor blinked once, then replied, "*Borba. We began receiving communications from Sworne ship.*"

Charlie combed her hair back after piecing together the information. "*So the Borba's comms connected with a Sworne ship?*"

"*Da. We have been tracking their journey here from their galaxy.*"

"*Do you know when they'll be here?*" Charlie asked.

"*We estimated between six to nine months before arrive in Milky Way.*"

Charlie groaned and checked, "*Earth months?*" After Victor's confirmation, she looked over at her lover and said, "The *Borba*'s comms linked up with a Sworne ship that is coming to the Milky Way." She frowned, stared at Victor's stony features, and whispered, "The systems on the *Borba* must have been activated by the new Sworne ship coming within range."

Kal responded with a rumble, then asked, "How long before they're here?"

"Serrato Corps thinks six to nine Earth months." Charlie estimated the time frame on Kander's calendar and whispered, "That's like twenty to thirty nineths." She narrowed her eyes at Victor and asked, "*Does Serrato know where the Sworne will arrive in the galaxy*?"

"*If continue on course, they arrive in fourth quadrant.*"

Charlie swore and groaned before she turned her worried features to Kal. "They're coming here to the fourth quadrant." She crossed her arms and asked, "*What about Serrato Corps? Why are they gathering so many supplies? For war?*"

"*To flee to Centaurus Galaxy.*"

Charlie went bug eyed at Serrato Corps's crazy plan to travel all the way to the Centaurus Galaxy, which was the second closest major galaxy after Andromeda. "*That's insane. How could they possibly do that? It would take years and years to get there even with the jump technology. And there's no fuel to power the jump drives.*"

A faint smirk appeared on Victor's stony features. "*Nine years, ten months, and sixty-three days.*"

"*You're serious,*" Charlie whispered. "*Does Serrato Corps want the darakar to power the jump drives?*"

"*Da.*" Victor turned his head to Charlie, staring through her. "*We almost had it, until you.*"

Charlie seethed and shifted closer, struggling to keep her fisted hands at her side. "*Oh, I'm going to make sure you and your people are stuck here in the quadrant when the Sworne show up.*"

Victor snorted and argued, "*We will have darakar before then.*"

Growling, Charlie shoved Victor, who toppled onto the bench and sank back against the wall.

"Charlie," Kal warned.

Half ignoring her lover, Charlie advanced on him and asked, "*How the hell does Serrato Corps plan to get the darakar after the kidnapping failed?*" She struggled with her self-control as the buzzing in her ears grew louder.

"*Wheels are already in motion*," Victor replied. "*But I was not put in charge of this mission. I know nothing.*"

Charlie clenched her teeth and grabbed Victor by his collar, unsure whether to slug him in the gut or face. Kal hooked her raised fist, and she hissed at the block.

"He's still my prisoner," Kal said, her voice rumbling with danger.

Jerking her hand free, Charlie released Victor, put space between them, and stared at the locked door. After a deep breath, she said, "Serrato Corps wants to escape to Centaurus Galaxy, which is really far." She turned and looked at her lover. "They need the darakar to power the jump drive that'll get them there." She held out her hand toward Victor. "They're planning something else to get the darakar from us, but he doesn't know what." She frowned when Kal lifted an eyebrow. "What?"

Kal pursed her lips, glanced at Victor, and then stared at Charlie again. Her stoic features softened after a tick, and she seemed prepared to say something. Just as she opened her mouth, a frantic pounding started on the cell door.

Charlie spun around and jumped aside before being hit by the swinging door.

"Kal, there is an emergency!" The guard was distraught and seemed prepared to drag his ruler out of the cell.

Kal's fire green eyes faded, and she hastened after the guard.

Charlie heard Victor collapse to the floor, but she didn't care and rushed out of the cell with her lover.

While the guard relocked the cell, he said, "Three unknown space ships are closing in on Kander."

Kal didn't wait for more details and sprinted through the underground prison. She pulled out the folded tablet just before launching up the spiral steps.

Huffing, Charlie did her best to stay on Kal's heels but struggled when Kal climbed three steps at a time. She lost sight of Kal, but daylight shined on the stone wall above her and encouraged her to go faster. Once at the top, she burst through the opening and was blinded by the sunlight. Blinking her eyes several times, she heard the door seal shut behind her and Kal's voice reverberating throughout the lobby. She was at a loss at how Kal wasn't winded by the run up from the prison.

"Activate both the satellite array and the TDC on the Great Tower," Kal ordered.

"Activating both," Blade Perras radioed back.

Charlie gulped another breath of air and pushed her body to hurry after Kal, who was already moving again. "Wait!" She managed to hold Kal's attention for a moment. "It's probably Serrato Corps." She fished out her techbit and popped out an earplug. "Get Andren to take me to the *Betty May*. We'll go after these bastards."

"*Joh*. Our defense systems will handle—"

"Your defense system is limited to outer space, but they will get by it," Charlie argued. "Their ships are fast!" She started to pull away, heading toward the main entrance. "I got this!" She turned and ran to the entrance.

"Charlie!" Kal's curse echoed off the walls, then she barked out her next order over the comms.

Charlie heard the start of Kal's order for someone to alert Andren. She smiled to herself and activated the comms for the *Betty May*. "Raine, Raine this is Charlie." Ahead of her, a guard stepped aside when she rushed through the open door. "Raine, Raine—"

"Go ahead, Charlie."

"Warm up the *Betty May*'s engines. We got company!" Charlie hurried down the steps to the street and headed toward the barrack to meet Andren.

"What?" Raine snapped. In the background she heard booming as Raine became breathless.

"There's at least three Serrato ships coming in hot. We need to take them down." Charlie neared an intersection and spotted Andren speeding her way, so she hopped into the passenger seat and said, "Get me to the *Betty May*."

Dodging people and horses, Andren slammed the hover truck into gear and sped through the streets.

"Raine, are you on the bridge?"

"*Ja!*" Raine was panting and even more frantic.

"I need you to connect to Kander's comms so I can talk to the High Commander," Charlie ordered. She slammed her palm against the dash when Andren veered around a cart. "Andren and I are on our way."

"What's happening?" Andren asked, frantic worry in her tone.

"Serrato ships are coming. Raine and I are going to get the ones that make it past the satellite defense array." Charlie glanced over at her loyal guard, who was becoming a friend. "Andren, you don't have to go up with us. It's going to get ugly."

Andren huffed and slammed the acceleration pedal once they were past the Great Gate. "There's barf bags left on the bridge."

Charlie smirked and slapped the dash before saying, "That's my girl! I'll make space trash out of you yet."

Andren grunted and focused on speeding down the road to the *Betty May*.

After a quick ride, Charlie spied the ship and radioed, "Raine, how are the engines?"

"Almost ready to go," Raine reported. "Where are you?"

"Be there in thirty ticks." Charlie's muscles were coiled tight, and she launched out of the passenger door when Andren stopped the truck. Her drumming heart fueled her body with wild energy. "Nova, connect to Kander's comms."

"Connecting," Nova responded in her ear. "Connected."

"Kal, Kal this is Charlie." Sprinting up vessel's open cargo door, Charlie's boots boomed against the metal followed by Andren's own. As she raced hallways and decks, she talked to the High Commander. "What's the status on the ships?"

"One is destroyed and one slipped by," Kal replied. "We're attempting to hit the last one."

"We're preparing to take off," Charlie said over the comms. She rushed onto the bridge, jumped down the steps, and hopped into the pilot's seat.

"*Vuk!*" Kal cursed. "There are three more ships approaching Kander."

Charlie swore too and hastened to get the *Betty May* in the air. She glanced at Raine, whose hands were dancing across the screens. Together they started lifting the big boat off the ground. Behind her, she spotted Andren getting into the captain's chair. "Buckle up, buttercup!"

Raine glanced over her shoulder and said, "Flying in the air is different than in space."

"Let's go, let's go." Charlie increased the throttle as the *Betty May* climbed straight up in a few ticks. "Scan for the ships, Raine."

"Roger that." Raine swiped her left hand up and caused a half-holo sphere to form above the dash between her and Charlie. "Got one!"

Charlie glanced at the enemy ship and said, "It's heading for Tarrak." She lifted the ship's nose.

"Charlie, the first ship has entered the planet's atmosphere," Kal reported over the comms. "Two more ships made it past the satellite defense."

"On it!" Charlie boosted the throttle, sending the *Betty May* roaring upward. "Get the weapons ready, Raine." Behind them, she heard Andren groan louder.

The *Betty May* bolted through the sky, heading toward the enemy ships that flashed in the sunlight.

"I got a visual on one," Charlie reported over the comms. "Ready the ion blasters, Raine. I want to take down at least one." She glanced at the holo sphere to confirm their targets. "This calls for a good song. Nova, play the Fight Mix starting with 'Don't Mess with Me,' volume level thirty on the flight deck."

"Brody Dalle *is my jam*!" Raine had both hands on the touch screen. "*Y'all don't wanna mess with our ion guns!*" she called in English to the Serrato ships, ready to shoot them down. But then she tensed and glanced over at Charlie with wide eyes. "We're headed straight for that first ship!"

"I know." Charlie grinned and said, "And I love a good game of chicken." She increased the throttle, knowing that the Serrato ship would bail due to its smaller size compared to the *Betty May*. "Get ready to fire on the two ships behind this one."

"Oh my god, oh my god," Raine prayed louder and louder. "Charlie!"

Charlie laughed as the *Betty May* and the first Serrato ship closed in, then it jerked upward and skimmed past the top of the *Betty May*. "Now, Raine!"

Raine already had the ion blasters locked on the two other ships and hit the trigger on the screen. She cried out as the first round of blasts struck one ship but the second one dodged them.

"Kal, two ships are still coming to Tarrak." Charlie turned the yokes and pulled back on the throttle so that the ship's airframe wasn't torn up by the g-forces. As the ship cut through atmosphere, it slowed and turned until it pointed nosedown toward the planet. Charlie throttled the large ship and chased after the last two ships. For a moment, she prayed that the citizens were prepared for the possible onslaught from the enemy ships.

As they lost altitude, Charlie lifted the nose little by little and stiffened when a huge bolt of energy went roaring past the ship's starboard side. She peered out the cockpit window and noticed Raine was doing the same.

"What the fuck was that?" Raine demanded and started to tap on the screen, pulling up the camera eyes at the front of the *Betty May*. "Oh my god. They have a — shit!" She screamed when Charlie wrenched the ship to the left, just avoiding another massive shot of energy. "It's a fucking ion cannon!"

"What!" Charlie looked over at Raine. "Serrato has cannons on their ships?"

"No, Tarrak does!" Raine pointed at the window as they approached the city. "On top of the Great Tower!"

Charlie stared wide eyed at the massive cannon spinning around on the Great Tower. "Why didn't anybody tell me about a fucking cannon?"

"It's not exactly common knowledge until now," Andren called from her seat.

Flying the *Betty May* around the city, Charlie watched in awe as the ion cannon's next shot struck one of the Serrato ships in the rear of the fuselage. She sucked in a breath after she realized it would crash into the city, near the port area. "Raine—"

"I see it." Raine's hands were already moving across the screen, then she fired two rapid shots striking the downward spiraling ship in the nose. She gasped when the blasts' force was enough to nudge the falling Serrato ship away from the city to crash into the Koblenz River. "Targeting the last ship, but it's moving so damn fast."

Charlie growled at the last Serrato ship shooting at the ion cannon and continuing to hit the buildings behind it. She hissed when Raine attempted to shoot it down but missed due to its evasive maneuvers. Whoever was piloting the ship was a better pilot than the others. "We need to get him away from the city."

"Get on his tail, then we can drive him away."

Charlie nodded and radioed, "Kal, I need you to shut down the cannon so I can get in closer to the Serrato ship."

"Charlie, it's too dangerous for—"

"Just trust me, *krafka*." Charlie bit her lip and exchanged a glance with Raine.

"Defense cannon is on standby," Kal responded.

Charlie took her queue and cut across the city's airspace, coming at the Serrato ship's haul. "Get his attention, Raine."

Raine fired a weak shot in hopes to chase the ship away from the city. "There he goes!"

Charlie made a sharp left and echoed Andren's yell from the g-forces. She refused to lose the Serrato ship and followed its tail. "Keep shooting!"

Raine sent shot after shot at the Serrato ship's tail, scaring it away from the city. "Stay on it, Charlie."

As expected, the Serrato ship flew away from the city and went out over a less populated region. As the ticks passed, it was flying faster and putting space between it and the *Betty May*.

Raine snarled as the ion shots lost reach, exploding behind the distancing enemy vessel. "It's going too far."

"What's going on?" Kal asked over the comms.

"Nova, end music." Charlie waited until it was quiet on the flight deck and replied, "He's trying to outrun us. The *Betty May* is too big and slow compared to a Serrato fighter ship." Charlie nudged the throttle up, but any faster would force the engines to engage light speeds. Her visual on the enemy ship was shrinking each tick. Beyond the cockpit's windows, the autumn landscape brightened to a solid, shiny white. With a glance at the holosphere, the Serrato vessel was almost out of the scanner's range. "We're going to lose him."

"We should fly back to Tarrak," Andren suggested. "He'll probably go back there to attack the city."

"We don't know that for sure," Charlie argued.

"He might hit another city, like Barrik," Raine said.

"There is a defense ion cannon in Barrik," Kal said. "But they are the only two cities with any advanced weaponry."

"Damn," Raine whispered.

"Can you chase the ship back to orbit for the satellite array defense?" Kal asked.

Charlie frowned and shook her head at the likelihood that the Serrato ship would follow them into orbit, knowing that the satellite array was there. "Serrato isn't here to get Victor." She clenched her teeth and whispered, "They came to send us a message."

"We're about to lose him on the scans. I'm completely out of firing range." Raine slapped the panel and cursed under her breath.

"Tighten up your belts!" Charlie's right hand danced across the screen and locked the navigation system on the sleek Serrato ship before it was too late. She refused to allow the Serrato ship to return to Tarrak or another city and kill more innocent people. If the *Betty May* received a burst of powerful thrust from the engines, then they stood a chance of stopping the enemy.

"What are you doing?" Raine asked, seeming to sense Charlie's plan.

"I'm taking that douche bag down." Charlie's hand went to the throttle, which hinged on jumping to light speed.

"Oh my god!" Raine twisted her head toward Andren. "Brace for impact!"

"What is happening?" Kal demanded, a snarl filling the comms.

Charlie's fingertips hovered over the throttle while her sweaty palm slid on the yoke. With a last glimpse of the Serrato ship's location in the holosphere, she made her choice and prayed to Kalatas that it worked, or else their sacrifice was for nothing. "*Betty May,* engage leed one for one tick!"

"Charlie!" Kal's roar echoed through the comms until it was cut off by the greater thunder of the *Betty May*'s engines.

The *Betty May* vanished for a whole tick as it launched into leed one, propelling it toward the Serrato ship like a bullet. With the navigation system locked on the other ship's coordinates, the *Betty May*'s pointed nose was the first site of impact and tore into the upper side of the Serrato ship's fuselage. Once the *Betty May* struck the enemy's dual engine, an explosion erupted and flames engulfed the entangled ships. The Serrato ship broke away and went spiraling downward toward Kander.

Charlie gasped and lifted her head from the cracked dash, as blood trailed down her brow and nose. For a moment, her insides felt like they were outside, and she groaned until the *Betty May*'s systems were screaming at her. She latched onto the yoke, fighting the planet's gravity. Looking higher, she held her breath as the flames swept down the fuselage from the other ship's hyperfuel spraying over the *Betty May*. But it would burn off in a matter of moments.

Raine groaned, lifted herself, and stared out beyond the destroyed nose and cracked windows. Alarms brought her attention down to the screen. "We have a fire in engine bay one!"

"Engine two is losing power. Engine three and four are operating normally in engine bay two." Charlie realized her transmission over the comms was broken after Raine's distorted call. "We have to land." She tightened her grip on the shaking yoke. "Andren, are you all right?" After no response, she peered over her shoulder and found Andren slumped against the captain's chair.

"I should check—"

"There's no time," Charlie cut off. "I need your help to land this beast."

Raine reached under the dash and pulled out the retractable yoke. She engaged it and said, "We're about fifteen marches to the ground."

"Char… Status…What ha—" Kal hailed on the comms.

Charlie swore and said, "*Betty May*, what's the status on the comms and engine bay one?"

"Electrical fires in the communication room and engine bay one. Halon fire suppression systems have been engaged," the *Betty May* reported. "Communications are expected to fail in two minutes and twenty-six ticks. Engine bay one is expected to detonate in thirty-one ticks."

"We're at twelve marches to the ground!"

Charlie checked the digital gauges indicating they were coming down too fast. "*Betty May*, shut down engine one and two." With the engines shut down, she doubted it would blow, at least until they crashed onto the planet.

"Shutting down," the *Betty May* replied.

Once the engines turned off, Charlie felt and heard the quietness. Even with two out of four engines left, they had a good chance to land the ship and limp away.

"We're still coming down too fast," Raine said.

"If we slow our descent, then we give that fire more time to spread down the fuselage to the fuel tanks." Charlie wiped her face and smeared the blood across her cheeks and forehead. "Manually turn on the emergency alert," she ordered Raine, who was already working on it. After the last crash, she wasn't about to rely on the automated systems to do their jobs.

"Six marches." Raine glanced over at Charlie and asked, "What's the plan?"

"At three marches, we'll raise the nose," Charlie replied. "If we can bleed off enough speed, we'll crash safely." She was gripping the vibrating yokes with all her strength. "Find me a good landing spot."

Raine kept one hand on the yoke and used the other to search the ground. "It's all fucking white!" She looked over at Charlie and said, "I can't see anything."

"Are there trees, hills, or other obstacles?"

Raine shook her head and stared at the screen. "I don't see anything. It's pretty barren and flat." She sucked in a breath and hollered, "Three marches!"

Charlie gritted her teeth and pulled back on the yoke, thankful for Raine's help. "*Betty May*, activate the landing system." She gritted her teeth when a new alarm popped up for the landing system.

"Anchors are not responding," the *Betty May* reported.

"Power loss in the landing system," Raine said.

"I guess we'll do this the old-fashion way." Charlie peered out the cracked window after checking the ship's speed. Her heartbeat started to accelerate as the ship's nose lowered for a moment. She gauged the approaching landscape of the area and decided spiraling down the rest of the way was the best method. "Here we go. Give me a count on the distance," she ordered her friend.

"One and half marches," Raine said.

Charlie licked her lips and tasted blood that made her stomach churn. She wiped each hand on her pant leg and prepared for the final descent to the ground with the knowledge she had more lives than her own to worry about this time.

"Char… can you re…." Kal hailed over the distorted comms. But it was useless; the comms would fail any moment and leave them in the dark. The ship's emergency signal would have to be enough to save them now.

"Half a march!"

Charlie raised the nose higher, cut away the rapid speed and also her view of the landscape. Using her peripheral vision, she watched the side windows as whiteness crept up. "Brace for impact, again!"

"Charli… are you…." Kal's broken voice was heavy and raw.

Raine was pulling back on the yoke that was tighter than a guitar string.

"*Betty May*, shut down engine three and four!" Charlie cried out as the first flakes of snow began to fly over the nose and cloud the window. If they were lucky, the pending snow would extinguish the burning engines in the first engine room.

"Engines shutting down."

Without the engines or the anchoring system, Charlie was dependent on the planet's gravity and surface to stop the ship. "Don't drop the nose, Raine!"

She and Raine both yelled as the ship sank into the planet's unforgiving surface.

At first the landing was soft but blinding while snow showered over the windows. The *Betty May* had floated above the surface for a moment, as the swirling air under the airframe gave it a brief cushion. Then it all collapsed under the ship's incredible weight and slowing airspeed and forced the *Betty May* to plow into the snow.

Charlie and Raine's cries were outmatched by the ship's metal screaming against the snow, ice, and ground. The entire window was coated in white that blacked out the cockpit. The ship then slammed into an unmovable object, ending its reckless landing.

With weakened arms, Charlie let her hands slide off the damaged panel where her head rested from impact. She groaned and turned her head to the left and stared over at her friend, who was unconscious or dead and bloody in the face. A brief prayer for Andren and Raine's lives dashed through her mind. As her grip on consciousness was fading, a familiar voice crackled in her ear and tugged at her soul.

"Charl… you… ed me… Char…."

The damaged comms beeped in Charlie's ear, indicating the radio systems were terminating. Even still, Charlie worked her bloody jaw and rasped until one word formed on her lips between her chokes.

"*Sum-n-ner.*"

# Titles available in *The Alpha God* Series:

Dancing in the Darkness
**Book 1**

Come to My Door
**Book 2**

I, Alpha
**Book 2.5**

Born to Be Mine
**Book 3**

I, Finna
**Book 3.5**

Collecting Stars
**Book 4**

I, True Mate
**Book 4.5**

Like a Calling
**Book 5**

I, High Commander
**Book 5.5**

My Everything

**Book 6**

**I, Sumner**

**Book 6.5**

**An Army of One**

**Book 7**

# Other Titles Available:

Titles available in *The Kingdoms Of Gyldren* Series:

Of Iron and Gold
A Prequel

Of Wulf and Wynd, Part 1
*The Vows of Marriage*
Book 1.1

Of Wulf and Wynd, Part 2
*The Bracelets of Ælfwynn*
Book 1.2
Coming 2022!

# About the Author

Lexa Luthor is an avid writer and reader of the Omegaverse trope especially F/F pairings. In her books, each main character(s) is a strong-willed female, who navigates difficult situations but always ends up finding love with their mate. Every tale has a twist and is gripping, sexy, and even a bit adventurous.

When not writing, Lexa enjoys binge watching television shows like Game of Thrones, Gentleman Jack, or The L Word. Her other favorite hobbies are playing cornhole, rooting for the Kansas City Chiefs, and laying around the pool in the summer. At times, Lexa finds time to read romances (both dark and fluffy) and great sci-fi books but nothing else can beat a steamy, downright erotic F/F romance with biting, knotting, and slightly possessive love.

Visit her website at LexaLuthor.com for more information and be sure to sign up for her newsletter for the latest release information, bonus material, and freebies.

Made in United States
North Haven, CT
15 December 2023